ANTHOLOGY

John Murphy

Edited by Gerry Murphy

BRUHENNY PRESS

“

I am but a ghost in the world, bringing ghostly insights to you.

… stay with this author who is so fanatical that, if he didn't have something worthwhile to say, the all too real karma of the world would have locked him away a long time ago.

On most Saturdays for my three years in London I made my lonely way through the carnival thoroughfare of Portobello Road with its antique-sellers and novelty-item-selling hippies. I was following a dream and perhaps I still am.

Songs have so brightened my life at every turn that I am within my rights to celebrate them.

The fact that human beings – all human beings – are only a shadow of themselves contributed perhaps to the formulation of one great religious myth and one great secular myth. The Biblical myth of the Fall of Mankind and Plato's Allegory of the Cave.

I have to confess to being a little impressed by that which is known as Chinese astrology. But other than that I am inclined to agree with Patrick Moore that astrology only proves one thing – there's one born every minute.

”

Bruhenny Press
Booney House, Churchtown,
Mallow, County Cork, Ireland P51 TCC6

books@bruhenny.com

www.bruhenny.com

Paperback ISBN 978-0-9524931-7-4

Design and layout by Martin Keaney

Typeset in Minion Pro

The cover design is based on a photograph of John that appeared in the *Irish Examiner* following a poetry reading and is also shown on the back cover.

The illustration on the inside front cover and on page 105 is of John's family home at Leap, Churchtown. This and all chapter title illustrations are by Martin Keaney.

The illustrations on pages 152, 193, 207, 227 and 239 were created by John Murphy. The drawings in the Yeti section are from the originals by Oliver McCarthy.

Please note, some identities have been changed to protect the privacy of individuals and organisations. All views expressed in this publication are those of the author and not of the publisher or editor.

Printed in Ireland by SPRINT-print Ltd

*D*EDICATION

*This book is dedicated to John's mother, Nora – who loved
him dearly and never gave up on him – his father Jack
and his brothers Pat and Michael who looked after
him as only they could.*

*This Anthology is also dedicated to the people of
Churchtown who had the ability to deal with eccentricity
and to John's two best friends – Mick Culloty and John
Nyhan – who were generous in their time and support
for his creative artistic endeavours.*

$\mathcal{A}$BOUT THE $\mathcal{A}$UTHOR

John Murphy was born in Cardiff in 1951 where his parents Jack and Nora Murphy were residing. They returned to the family farm in Churchtown in North Cork shortly afterwards where John spent his formative years.

John attended Churchtown Primary School, Ring College or Coláiste na Rinne near Dungarvan, St Colman's College in Fermoy and a one-year term at University College Cork in 1968/69. He spent three years in London before returning to Churchtown in 1972 where he remained until his death on 26 February 2014.

John Murphy devoted his life to creative writing. For reasons explained in this anthology a limited amount of his work was published during his lifetime. This anthology fulfills a wish from John that 'some little record' of his time spent writing would survive him.

ABOUT THE EDITOR

Gerry Murphy was born in Churchtown in 1954. Aged 18, he left Churchtown and since then has lived in Carlow, Louth, Cork, Dublin, London and Abu Dhabi. Gerry has maintained a great interest in local community and rural development. He founded the Churchtown Village Renewal Trust in 1997 and the Churchtown Heritage Society in 2015. He is a proud supporter of the Páirc Bhrugh Thuinne / Halla100 development at the GAA grounds in Churchtown. See *www.gerrymurphy.com*

CONTENTS

*E*DITOR'S FOREWORD

My brother John died on Wednesday, 26 February 2014.

John was a writer all his life but only a limited amount of his work was published as he was his own worst critic and no sooner had he written something but he was certain it was not good enough.

Over the years John enlisted my help in bringing his creative works to a wider audience but no sooner had I finished the design and layout but he wanted to either drop the idea of publication or destroy what was written. In reality John destroyed much of what he created. After many years helping on 'publication' projects with John I knew a major publication was unlikely to happen in his lifetime. However, I never followed John's instructions to destroy what he had written but rather saved the material he sent me for a day when it might be possible to publish it. Now is that time.

John wrote poetry, humorous essays, short stories, plays and his poignant autobiography *Like it, or Lump it*. He wrote almost daily for over 40 years and even if he only wrote a page of 250 words every day this would have amounted to 3.6 million words. This anthology contains only what I collected over the years but it is nevertheless a good anthology of John's creative work. Indeed, it probably contains the best of his work.

As you will see if you read *Like it, or Lump it* in its entirety John was obsessed with language and punning and saw hidden meaning in words. Of course, much of what John wrote was defined by his mental illness and its publication will, I hope, offer readers an insight into thought processes which many of us would otherwise never access.

In his autobiography John chose not to name anyone apart from some public figures. In the editing process I have respected his approach even though at times I was tempted to identify those who helped him along the road of life. There are people who will easily identify themselves in the text and I refer especially to the 'Publican', the 'Kerryman' and the 'Musicman' in this regard.

I would also like to thank John's friend, Mick Culloty, for thorough proofreading of the anthology and also acknowledge that he inspired several of the Ballydull yarns.

I added the footnotes in *Like it, or Lump it* as part of the editing process to aid my own understanding and to allow me appreciate exactly what John was referring to in the text. I hope some of the footnotes relating to obscure words are helpful to readers and I apologise if you are already familiar with the words or phrases.

In his autobiography John refers to an event in the 1980s when he thought he was dying and he wrote a letter to his family asking that fragments of his writing be handed over to a relative of the family who was a published writer. As he wrote:

"In my heart of hearts, I knew that these fragments of writing were of no value and that the idea that a writer could turn these fragments into something publishable was merely preposterous. But, thinking that I was to die, I wanted some little record of me and my time spent writing to survive me".

I think John would be more than pleased in his own wry way with this anthology and that far more than 'some little record' of his time spent writing survives him.

Gerry Murphy

Churchtown
June 2017

Tales of Ballydull

BALLYDULL ABÚ

A Sequence of Yarns

LET NO ONE SAY THE BEST HURLERS
BELONG TO THE PAST.
THEY ARE WITH US NOW AND BETTER
YET TO COME.

Christy Ring
1920-1979

*T*OM BEASLEY – THE REAL KING

Doubtless, you've heard of Elvis Presley the Memphis truck driver and entertainer … But did you ever hear of Tom Beasley the Ballydull cattle haulier and cabaret artiste. There are people in Ballydull who maintain that Elvis Presley made his millions by copying every move that Tom Beasley made. They may have a point.

When Tom Beasley recorded 'Bed and Breakfast Hangover', Elvis went straight into the studio and recorded 'Heartbreak Hotel'; when Tom Beasley recorded 'Don't Step On My Brown Hush Puppies' Elvis cunningly went and recorded 'Blue Suede Shoes'.

This shameless plagiarism continued on for years, and I won't bore you with the details, except to say by way of showing what a lying, cheating, thieving, liardly impostor Elvis Presley was that when Tom Beasley had his first hit and built a luxury bungalow on a half-acre site outside Ballydull and called his new homestead 'Grasslands', Elvis couldn't contain his jealousy and bought a little mansion in Memphis, which, as you all know, he called 'Gracelands'. 'Grasslands' – 'Gracelands' ! – That's how far Elvis Presley's twisted mind went in his attempts to imitate Tom Beasley.

And it is a curious thing, a thing that would make you more superstitious than suspicious that, after Tom Beasley died, people in Ballydull refused to accept that Tom Beasley was actually dead. About a year after Tom Beasley was buried, reports began to appear in the *Ballydull News & Star* of sightings of Tom Beasley. One farmer said he saw Tom Beasley carrying a lorry load of TB reactors to the factory under licence from the Department; but that couldn't be the case, because Tom Beasley was banned for years by the Department from transporting reactors, after a famous incident when Tom sold the carcasses of an entire herd from a depopulated farm – 150 cattle in all – for the home deepfreeze market in Ballydull.

Another party – a Ballydull housewife – said she saw Tom Beasley a month after his Anniversary Mass driving by in his lorry with the window down and he singing 'You Ain't Nothing But a Sheepdog', with the cattle in the back bellowing for accompaniment. But I don't believe that either – Tom Beasley never sang for pleasure, but for money and money only. And personally I think Tom Beasley is as dead as Elvis and that's dead enough for me.

THE MOST DRAMATIC DAY IN BALLYDULL

Opinion differs as to what was the most dramatic day in Ballydull. Some say 'twas the day a woman first appeared in Ballydull wearing slacks. The woman in question Mrs Binchy of Binchy's public house – now O'Mahony's bar and lounge – had been reading "them foreign magazines" and nothing would stop her one sunny day but to appear ever so briefly at the open door of her public house in a pair of black and grey striped slacks. Consternation spread throughout the village, and everybody was asking everybody else, "Did you see Mrs Binchy and she wearing a man's trousers?"

Others say the most dramatic day in Ballydull was the day they installed a condom machine in the toilet of O'Mahony's public bar … and the old parish priest, Father Cuddy, went mad with a Kango hammer, causing £2,000 worth of structural damage to O'Mahony's and the neighbouring dwelling, while shouting all the while, "As long as I am parish priest, the only rubbers in Ballydull will be – wellingtons!"

But for my money the most dramatic day or rather most dramatic night in Ballydull was the night the new schoolmaster, Ted Hanlon, brought a new computer to Ballydull and put it on display in the Community Hall. The new computer was actually an old computer – a first generation model in fact – and a very cumbersome, heavy piece of machinery it was; and it took an awful lot of pushing and shoving and sweating to get the computer in the door of the hall and up on stage. But, eventually, Ted Hanlon was able to stand proudly between Fr Tomás Healy, the parish priest, and the latest oracle, the new computer; and Ted was able to tell the people with the superior air of all schoolteachers that the computer was able to answer any question under the sun.

And so the crowd in attendance began to throw questions at the computer. In what country is Addis Ababa? What year was Muhammad Ali born? Who won the 1957 Grand National? And the computer answered authoritatively and correctly every time. But, then, a bunch of lads at the back of the hall got fed up of the constant airing of questions followed by a predictably correct answer from the computer, and one of the lads decided to ask the computer, "Who put Mary Coakley in the family way?"

The schoolmaster got very angry indeed, as he shouted over the uproar: "That is not a scientific question! The computer only answers scientific questions. Another question, please!"

But, just then, Father Tomás the PP put out his hand and waved it downwards to indicate that he wanted silence, and a great silence came over the crowd. In the otherwise perfect silence the PP spoke: "Our schoolmaster has assured us that this technological marvel before us can answer any question under the sun; and I think it right and proper that this same technological marvel be afforded the opportunity of answering the difficult, if salacious question of the young gentleman in the audience."

Ted Hanlon the schoolmaster was left with no choice but to feed the question to the computer, namely the question 'Who put Mary Coakley in the family way?' The tension was deadly as the old-fashioned computer whirred and buzzed and clicked in an effort to come with an answer to this most difficult of questions. Finally, the ticker tape with the answer came out of the old machine; and the schoolmaster, who was quite flustered by this stage, unthinkingly read out the answer: "Fr Tomás Healy."

Needless to say, there was bedlam with this announcement. And the schoolmaster maintains to this day that it was all the rough handling his computer received on the way into the Community Hall which so upset the machine; but, no matter, this was the first and last computer to appear in Ballydull. And the whole event has gone down in folklore, so much so that if you ever say anything to a Ballydull man which strikes him as particularly odd, he will say to you: "You're as wrong as Ted Hanlon's computer!"

$\mathcal{L}$OCAL PATRIOTISM

Rome – the Eternal City. Venice – the jewel of the sea. Paris – the city of romance. New York – the city that never sleeps. They mean next to nothing to the denizens of Ballydull. As far as Ballydull people are concerned Ballydull is the centre of the universe. In short, Ballydull people are proud of Ballydull.

Ballydull patriots – that is a man or woman who puts Ballydull first – are many. One Ballydull patriot was walking down the street one day and he saw two men talking by the post office and he shouted to them: "You're talking about Ballydull!"

"No, we're not!" replied one of the two, surprised to have their conversation so rudely interrupted.

"Is it how Ballydull isn't good enough for ye?" responded the Ballydull patriot, as he walked away with a disgusted look on his face.

HYGIENE

I want to speak about the hygiene in Ballydull. By this I don't mean anything as close to the bone as personal hygiene. 'Personal hygiene in Ballydull' is a subject that one should only address when one has in the security of one's hand a boarding card for a trans-Atlantic jet. By which I would wish to imply that Ballydull people are touchy about the racially-charged subject of personal hygiene.

Ballydull people are not so sensitive about personal hygiene as to actually wash themselves or even hose the slurry off their wellingtons before they go and enter a supermarket; but they are sufficiently sensitive about the subject that anyone casting aspersions about the body hygiene of Ballydull folk is likely to become the particular victim of 'a little argy-bargy' or even a bit of a 'schemozle' and end up in a hospital bed with one leg pointing at the ceiling and more bandages on the head than an Egyptian royal mummy.

But my subject is not personal hygiene, but hygiene in the production of milk on a Ballydull dairy farm. Now, fair is fair and one must allow that in these latter years milk production in Ballydull is a squeaky-clean business. The deadly science of chemistry has entered the equation, and with the likes of somatic cell-count analysis and milking parlours that are parlours, there is no longer any opportunity for dirty milk as such to enter the food chain. It wasn't always so.

One time, not that long ago, it was a regular occurrence for the creamery manager or one of the creamery workers in Ballydull to have to pull a dead (that is to say drowned) cat out from a just-delivered supply of milk, before the milk and, but for the just-mentioned intervention of the creamery staff, the cat entered the creamery tanks themselves.

Even in the old days a cat in a farmer's milk was a minor calamity (there was always the regrettable probability that the cat had consumed his fill before he expired); but no farmer had much misgivings about a leaf or two – or even a heap of leaves – getting into his milk supply. And as for flies, well nobody even cast such insignificant creatures a thought.

All that changed in the sixties, with the introduction of the much-hated 'gun'. By today's standards this so-called 'gun' was a very crude instrument. Effectively a suction pump, this 'gun' sucked up a body of milk and any of the more coarse dirt was trapped on a paper pad; and, if this dirt was of sufficient volume and seriousness, the manager (going purely on the judgement of his naked eye) condemned that particular farmer's supply for that day; and, ignominy of ignominies, the same milk had to be taken back to the farm to be otherwise disposed.

All in all, it is fair to say that the sixties in Ballydull were typified not by LSD and love-ins but by the 'gun'. And they weren't summers of love!

In this new order of the 'gun' there were two innocents who suffered greatly. One was the Ballydull creamery manager himself, a pleasant, diffident man who, against his own outdated instincts, often had to condemn a supply of milk as unworthy. And then he would have to placate the great anger of the owner of the condemned milk. And sometimes the great embarrassment of the manager in this situation would lead him into spoonerism of sort, as he would say to the near-violent farmer: "Clam yourself, Peter; clam yourself!"

Another innocent in this business was the working man whose duty it was to deliver milk to the creamery on behalf of his farmer-master. If such a working man had to return to his master's farm with churns full of rejected milk, well then you can guess that no great welcome awaited him. And, worse, there might be no boiled egg awaiting such an unfortunate man for breakfast the following morning.

On one famous occasion it was not the 'gun' which was instrumental in milk being turned away at the creamery, but that other sophisticated instrument at the disposal of the manager – a spoon which he brought to his own tongue to determine whether or not the milk was sour. On this famous occasion the milk in question did indeed prove sour to the manager's taste; and, mustering up quite uncharacteristic anger, the manager said to the hapless working man who delivered this foul supply of milk – "This milk is sour!"

"You're sour yourself," retorted the working man more out of grievance than wit.

THE ARGUMENT

Ballydull is a village and parish somewhere. A parish so preternaturally slow that for a local to bother to get up and to appear in the open doorway of their house in the course of a morning is for any onlooking Ballydull person a remarkable life-affirming event …

WEATHER IN BALLYDULL

When it's not raining in Ballydull,
it's drizzling;
when it's not
drizzling in Ballydull,
it's misting;
when it's not misting in Ballydull,
there's drops in the air;
when there are no drops in the air in Ballydull,
there's a black cloud overhead;
when there is no black cloud overhead in Ballydull,
there's rain again in the forecast.

When it's neither raining, nor drizzling, nor misting, with no drops in the air and no black cloud overhead, with no rain in the forecast in Ballydull, you're not in Ballydull at all, but on an agricultural Co-op holiday to Tenerife.

A BALLYDULL THEORY

Ballydull has the highest level of rainfall of any parish in Ireland. Ballydull also has the highest number of alcoholics per capita of any parish in Ireland. I'm convinced that the two problems are related.

Picture this: a man is at home of a night, nursing a headache from the night before. The children are fighting; the wife is watching a cop show on television – with each gunshot ringing out like thunder. In such circumstances what can a man do only look out the window in despair. And what does he see – as the nodules of thirst begin to itch in his larynx? But raindrops, raindrops glistening like jewels on the black window pane. And of course he's off to O'Mahony's for a pint and a short for starters.

I'm convinced that the parish priest of Ballydull shares my particular theory about the causes of alcoholism in Ballydull. Because each time he dispenses the pledge to yet another recovering alcoholic, he always says, "Now don't as much as look at a wet glass, my good man!"

LORD TAFT THE TAILOR OF OLD BALLYDULL

Yes, Jim Wilson the tailor that lived and worked in the village had grandiose ways. Once, after returning from a losing Cheltenham, he was undaunted and declared in O'Mahony's public house: "Its metropolitan and overseas from here on." This was Jim's way of saying that he was a cut above the servant boys and wouldn't be seen at point-to-point and local 'inside the rails' race meetings. The target of his insult, the servant boys only laughed at this and many another boast from the tailor, as they shouted to the tailor's own pleasure: "Good man, Lord Taft!"

Once there was a fashion for red shirts in Ballydull and district. There was a fashion for other types of shirts too at the time but, I'm not making this up, there was also at this very time a fashion craze for red shirts. To be hip at the time you had to have a red shirt and possibly a blue one as well. Alas, the only way most young men of the parish could afford a red shirt was to dye their existing white shirts. So, there was quite a trade in six-penny packets of red dye. Mrs Brady's, the huckster's shop next door to Jim Wilson's tailor shop, covered this market.

But then, Jim was offered 'a line' in real red shirts by a travelling salesman. Needless to say, Jim couldn't resist this offer and he purchased a large consignment of real red shirts and he put a sign in his window that read:

GENUINE RED SHIRTS
No Dying

Ballydull people considered this episode to be another instance of 'Lord Taft's' bravado.

Eventually the tailoring business lost its capacity to generate income for Jim Wilson and, for a sort of swan song, Jim innocently engaged in some pyramid selling. Jim would go around to the houses with a big cardboard box of entirely useless products, and as he would enter a house he would declare, in line with the instructions he received from his new American masters, "I used to be working with men but now I'm working with women!" And as he was saying this Jim would take a cloth from the box and begin to clean the floor.

But it was perhaps for another pyramid product that Jim became most famous, his shampoo. Jim would take out this bottle of expensively priced shampoo and proudly declare: "There's a lemon in it." Unfortunately there was no shampoo in it. And to this day the phrase "There's a lemon in it," is always uttered to laughter in Ballydull whenever anybody speaks of the contents or ingredients of a product. Innocent people.

Not all Jim Wilson's jokes reflect badly on him. Once in his tailor's shop, the matter of Gideon bibles was up for discussion. And somebody explained that these Gideon bibles were bibles placed for free in hotel bedrooms.

"Those bibles would never do in Ballydull," commented Jim. "They'd be stolen."

BALLYDULL FOR THE 'ESSENTIALS'

A Ballydull man would never dream of using place mats. If he wants to protect his plastic tablecloth from the effect of hot plates or hot saucepans, he can always use a piece of a cornflakes box or, better still, one of those large brown envelopes in which the local Co-op dispatch their bills. A Co-op brown envelope does the job dandy!

Ballydull is a place that has never lost faith with the power of the basic, with the potential of ordinary things. And three of the most trusted 'essentials' in Ballydull are Bread soda, Three-in-one Oil and urine.

Bread soda cures just about everything – a loose tooth, rashes on the skin, fungus in the feet, just about everything.

No less famous are the rehabilitative powers of Three-in-one Oil. On one occasion, one of these modern young farmers was baling hay in a cottager's half-acre and, alas, the high tech baler broke down. Consternation! For if you know anything about the countryside, you will know that there is more pride invested in the saving of the hay than in any other enterprise in the world. Remember that a cottager who loses his hay will have to endure the derision of his neighbours for a full year, that is until the next harvest time when he has the chance to recoup his reputation.

So, when our angelically bright (that is to say clean) young farmer stepped down from his tractor to inspect the malfunctioning baler, the elderly man who owned the half-acre rushed up to him in a state of some anxiety and asked: "Would a bit of oil help?"

At this intervention the young farmer could only laugh, he being more accustomed to the esoteric science of machine parts nomenclature.

On another occasion an eminent heart surgeon from Dublin paid a visit to Ballydull. And wishing to do as the Romans do as it were, he joined a group of Ballydull men in a drinking session; but, as the night wore on and the ninth and tenth round went by with no hint from the Ballydull men of a 'cessation', the eminent heart surgeon began to regret his gallantry in deciding to mix with the locals.

And then these same drunken locals began to inform the heart surgeon of the curative powers of drinking your own urine. And when the heart surgeon expressed doubts as to urine consumption having any beneficial or regenerative effect on the heart, the locals rounded on him and called him a thick ignoramus.

The eminent heart surgeon left Ballydull next morning in a hurry, protesting: "Let me out of this place fast; the indigenous population do nothing else but produce urine – and take it!"

GALA NIGHT IN BALLYDULL

The big night out of the year in Ballydull is the GAA Club and Invalids' Society annual dinner dance. The menu and venue are always the same; chicken and chips in O'Mahony's lounge bar, restaurant and funeral home. The photographer from the *Ballydull News & Star* likes to get there early, and snap the people on their way into the dinner dance before trouble begins and the pool cues and hurley sticks are produced. After all, the headline 'Another Glorious Year For Ballydull' would look very odd above a photograph of broken teeth, broken chairs, fractured limbs and blood-strewn faces, clothes, table linen and carpet.

If the Ballydull GAA club hasn't had a good year – no matches won, half the matches not played, a long list of injuries and sendings off, massive fines and litigation, with talk of larceny, impersonation, forgery, embezzlement, grievous bodily harm, kidnap, gun warfare and poor attendance at meetings by officials – the night is sure to end in recrimination, with the police and ambulances called; and also the fire brigade to extricate the chairman from his unbecoming predicament halfway up the chimney, this the result of a foolhardy attempt to escape.

But, make no mistake, people do enjoy themselves at this the highlight of the Ballydull social calendar. Couples dance to the tunes of the Three Musketeers, a two-piece band famous for their big local hit 'I've Got Ballydull On The Brain'. And people do look forward to the big raffle, third prize a bottle of whiskey, second prize two bottles of whiskey and the grand first prize of a case of whiskey and the committee's sincere best wishes with the hospital, the court case and the jail term. And, of course, the highlight of the evening is the pint drinking contest, the winner declared to be all right provided he remains standing ten seconds after all other contestants have collapsed and have been removed from the premises in the wheelbarrows at the ready.

Win or lose, Ballydull people know how to enjoy themselves!

SHOPPING FOR THE GROCERIES

Do you like buying the groceries? Nobody seems to like buying the groceries. But buying the groceries in Ballydull is a doddle or, as we say, a cinch. You pop into Smith's Food Store and throw a few white slice pans, a few packets of plastic-wrapped rashers, a big bottle of Chef Sauce and a tub of margarine in the basket – and that's it. In and out the door in five minutes. Couldn't be simpler!

But, as you come out the door of Smith's Food Store, your eyes are drawn to the building directly across the road – O'Mahony's Bar & Lounge. Now, 'twould be unlucky, unsociable and uncivilised not to cross the road and call for a pint. And so doing, you have another and another and another, until you stumble out the door of O'Mahony's at one o' clock in the morning, not knowing where you are. But then the familiar aroma of TONI'S FAST FOOD takeaway strikes your nostrils and of course you slip in for a chicken supper. Which consists of the leg of a chicken, a big portion of chips and some peas, all coated in so much grease that, after you've consumed the lot, you've got to be very careful not to strike a match too close to your stomach, lest you burst into a fireball the likes of which hasn't been seen since the Gulf War. In any event, full to your tonsils with Guinness, Whiskey, Crisps, KP Nuts and the recent chicken supper, you can go home completely satisfied with your trip to town for the groceries.

TRUE INNOCENCE

At a certain time of year some of the fuel for the kitchen fire was provided by the twigs hopeful crows dropped down the chimney overnight. The persistence of the crows in fruitlessly bringing twigs to the chimney-top puzzled one Ballydull man; and he would keep saying to himself as he milked the cows of a morning: "You'd think they'd cop themselves on!"

TIMMY BRADY – DISC JOCKEY

The most famous man in Ballydull these days is Timmy Brady, disc jockey and farmer. Timmy Brady has his own show five nights a week on local FM radio. As far as Timmy Brady is concerned it's money for jam. Every week night Timmy bids farewell to his bullocks grazing contentedly on his fifty acre farm, gets into his old Cortina and drives the fifteen miles to the radio station, humming to himself all the way.

Timmy Brady's radio programme is a phone-in request show. That suits Timmy fine. Timmy is quite happy that there are enough fools out there prepared to run up phone bills and ask for songs that sound so mournful that they sound like a man whose doctor has ordered him off the fags and booze purchasing two flagons of 7 Up and a packet of Ritchie's After Dinner Mints. Not that Timmy Brady is worried. He plays the songs the people want to hear and every night he conducts a phone-in quiz. Nothing too difficult, mind you. In what country is New York? On what date is Christmas Day? And what do you call a male cow? And so on.

Occasionally people phone up Timmy with requests for strange songs. One party rang in asking for 'White Rabbit' by Jefferson Airplane. But Timmy had never seen a white rabbit and he had never been in an aeroplane and he had definitely never seen a white rabbit in an aeroplane; so Timmy didn't play the request. Another guy rang in asking for 'Waiting For The Sun' by The Doors. Timmy thought this request most strange. You'd wait for a bus or a train, or wait for the cattle report to come on the radio; but Timmy Brady never in his life ever heard of a set of doors waiting for anything. So 'Waiting For The Sun' was a non-starter; instead Timmy resourcefully gave 'The Moon Behind The Hill' a spin, expressing the hope that this would help the listener.

The Monument

At a recent meeting of the Ballydull Community Council it was decided to erect a monument on the village green. You might ask what prompted the Ballydull Community Council in this direction. And the answer is simple: The rival parish of Kilnadreary recently erected a monument right smack in the middle of Kilnadreary village, this monument to the memory of Kilnadreary's most famous son – a greyhound by the name of Gentleman Jim who won the Cork Laurels in 1963 and would have won the English Derby in White City if the English dogs hadn't decided to gang up on him and squeeze him out of the race at the first bend.

Now, you must understand the great and bitter rivalry between the Ballydull and Kilnadreary parishes, and perhaps the best way I can explain this rivalry is to say in football matches between Ballydull and Kilnadreary the ball can be missing for up to ten or fifteen minutes before anyone notices the fact. That's how intense the rivalry is.

So, naturally, when Kilnadreary erected a monument to Gentleman Jim, there were those in Ballydull who felt that Ballydull shouldn't let Kilnadreary away with it and that there should be one – if not two – monuments erected in Ballydull to preserve 'parity of esteem'. But who or what could Ballydull erect a monument to?

The only famous man to come out of Ballydull was John Maloney, a quack doctor who was arrested and hanged in Arizona in the 1840s for claiming his special elixir MALONEY'S WAKE-'EM-UP MIXTURE could bring people back from the dead. Clearly, it wouldn't do to erect a monument in Ballydull to the infamous 'Wake-'em-up' Maloney.

Then somebody at the Community Council meeting suggested that they erect a monument to the famous Ballydull piebald donkey known as Tinker Joe who won a lot of donkey derbys at the carnivals in Ballydull and neighbouring parishes in the sixties. But then somebody at the meeting pointed out in all innocence that it wouldn't look good if Kilnadreary had a monument to a Gentleman as it were and all Ballydull could manage in reply was a monument to a Donkey. And with that the meeting broke up in uproar, with the man who was only trying to be helpful in pointing out the potential *faux pas* being removed to hospital and spending ten days in intensive care.

I can tell you that at the next meeting of Ballydull Community Council the pressure was on to come up with a suitable theme for a monument in Ballydull. And then somebody at the meeting made the suggestion that they erect a life-size monument to Joe Cashman, a Ballydull man, of course, and a legend and a leader of fashion in his own lifetime as the first man in Ireland to draw the dole.

Really the Community Council had no choice but to go along with this idea, and that is why every Friday when the unemployed come out of Ballydull Post Office with a wad of notes in their hands, before they head to O'Mahony's lounge bar and secret casino, they always tip their caps in the direction of the imposing monument to the first man in Ireland to draw the dole. Joe Cashman – Patriot.

TACITURNITY IN BALLYDULL

Some people blame the English, other people blame the Famine; but, one way or the other, the fact is Ballydull people are either very guarded or else very restricted in what they have to say. In other words, Ballydull people are as tight with words as they are with their money. They don't give much away.

Once, a plain clothes detective from Dublin Castle was in Ballydull investigating a big robbery; and he stood on Main Street, Ballydull and he asked a passer-by: "Is this the Post Office?" "Are you looking for a stamp?" asked the passer-by, by way of reply. Needless to say the plainclothes detective didn't make much progress in his investigations, and he went back to Dublin a sorry man, with a very low opinion of Ballydull people as being the most ignorant, most clannish people on earth.

There was another Ballydull man – a farmer – who responded to every situation in life with one of two statements: either "That's right!" or else "I suppose so." For instance, if you ever said anything to this farmer and there was the slightest possibility that he could agree with you, he was more than happy to say: "That's right!" But, if you said something to this farmer which he couldn't under any circumstances agree with, he still couldn't bring himself to contradict you, and he would say to you: "I suppose so."

On one occasion this farmer met another Ballydull farmer, a famous hypochondriac, and the hypochondriac farmer said: "I'm dying!" Clearly our hero, the first farmer who ever only spoke two sentences couldn't say to the hypochondriac "That's right!" so he had no choice but to reply: "I suppose so." There was a moment's silence and then they both laughed.

THE TALK IN BALLYDULL

I ask a very simple question: How do you know you are in Ballydull? Is it from the fact that everybody is talking about the rain? Or is it because all the men wear green anoraks, smoke Major and love eating Chocolate Goldgrain Biscuits – as a treat? No; everybody in Ireland talks about the rain, wears a green anorak, smokes Major and loves eating Chocolate Goldgrain Biscuits as a treat. But Ballydull has one distinguishing characteristic …

Ballydull is the only parish in Ireland where people are out on the roads flagging down cars in the hope of hearing a bit of news, in other words gossip. Now, what Ballydull people find interesting in the way of gossip might surprise you. For instance, any news about the parish priest – however trivial – is sensational stuff in Ballydull. That the parish priest went to the doctor, or that the parish priest went to the supermarket, or that – God forbid – the parish priest is going to retire is all big news in Ballydull.

And why wouldn't it be? Isn't the parish priest, Father Tomás, the man responsible for getting us all into Heaven. And if you've ever been to a Munster Final, I needn't tell you getting into Heaven is no joke. Mark my words, there will be a lot of people turned away at the gate, and they won't be able to watch the proceedings on TV in a nearby pub either!

But I was talking about gossip in Ballydull. And as you'd expect not all gossip in Ballydull is about the parish priest. You might in fact expect the hottest gossip in Ballydull to be of a scandalous nature; but there you would be quite wrong. To grab the attention of a Ballydull man or woman leaning over the garden gate, out for a walk or having a drink in the pub, it's no use talking about sex, politics or the latest film.

This is Ballydull, after all! And what Ballydull people most like to hear is news of illness, disease and death. Start talking about back pain, rheumatoid arthritis, shingles, TB, pleurisy, pneumonia, cancer of the colon, strokes and heart attacks and a Ballydull man will listen to you for hours and go away thinking you're a most intelligent, most interesting man.

What a Ballydull man most wants to hear is that somebody is actually dying. That's really hot news! And phrases with an air of finality about them such as "That's the way!", "It's only a matter of time!" and "I suppose they'll be flying in from England?" are eating and drinking to a Ballydull man. In truth, there are only three questions which perplex Ballydull people: Who is going to win the Junior B Championship? Who is going to buy O'Mahony's public house? And who is next for removal?

THE ESSENTIAL FASHION ITEM

The essential fashion item in Ballydull is Farah pants. You might remember those Farah pants: they were jeans of a sort that a person with notions of respectability and standing might wear without being seen to wear jeans as such. The fundamental appeal of a Farah pants to someone caught between the demands of fashion and the demands of respectability still holds good in Ballydull.

A Ballydull man likes his Farah pants. No Ballydull man in a Farah pants is likely to be mistaken for a drug dealer or a TV producer. In its own way a pair of Farah pants is the stuff of the soil: unpretentious. And these Farah pants are versatile. You can just about feed your bull calf while you are wearing your Farah pants and then proceed, without change of costume, to an interview with your bank manager. Like I say, versatile, handy.

You might be familiar with that TV commercial that goes: "I have a headache, I'm late for work and where's the Paracetamol?" In Ballydull things are a little different, and the morning utterances of a Ballydull man are more likely to be: "I have a hangover, I'm late for signing on and where's my Farah pants?"

BALLYDULL THRIFT

People say that the big farmers in Ballydull are a bit mean, a bit tight, a bit miserly. But I don't know. Suppose you were after a bad harvest, with two fields of hay washed away, and on top of that you lost two cows to grass tetany. And then suppose you were in the city of a day and you had to go to the toilet? Wouldn't you be inclined to wait a few paces back from the toilet cubicles, in a state of complete watchfulness, until that precise moment some man began to emerge from one of the cubicles …Whereupon you would make one good charge at the toilet door, before it clicked shut in your face.

All to save a penny! And why not?

THE SECOND SMARTEST MAN IN BALLYDULL

The smartest man in Ballydull is the parish priest. He even writes books … big books … with big rockers of words in them. But the second smartest man in Ballydull can only be the schoolmaster.

His general knowledge is amazing …

Not alone does the school master know the name of the pharaoh at the time of the building of the Great Pyramid of Cheops, he also knows the name of the man who served as head foreman on the site … before and after they opened the canteen.

One day the school master was talking to a past pupil of his, and the past pupil had just returned from working in the Middle East, and the same past pupil in his shiny white suit was inclined to boast quite a bit. Funny thing, the schoolmaster remembered the past pupil in question as one of his less promising subjects, and it was very painful now for the schoolmaster to hear him go on about what a fabulous time he had in Kuwait and Amman and Cairo. Eventually the schoolmaster had heard enough, and he asked his boastful companion:

"Were you ever in Algebra?"

"No," replied the past pupil, "but I passed within ten miles of it!"

ANOTHER BALLYDULL PROBLEM

Ballydull people will know what I am on about here. A visitor from England or America calls to the house, and in the middle of the festivities he asks, "Where is the loo?" or "Where is the water closet?" And, of course, there is always somebody a little bit smart, a little bit coarse, and they take the visitor outside the front door and they point proudly to the open countryside and say: "There you are!"

Once, a Ballydull man who had made good in America came home to visit his parents and, seeing the situation, he instantly called in the builders to install a luxury bathroom in the old home place. Then nothing would stop him but to hold a barbecue in his old home place before he returned to the States. And as the barbecue was in full swing, he said to his father: "Ain't it grand to be eating out under the stars!" But the father wasn't so impressed, and he simply said to his son: "Ye have a funny way of doing things in America: ye eat outside the house, and ye crap inside!"

ALCOHOLISM

I ask a very serious question, a very serious question indeed. What is an alcoholic? Certainly, in Ballydull we have our own ideas as to what constitutes an alcoholic.

A psychiatrist may say that a man who needs five pints and two shorts every night is an alcoholic. In Ballydull we say nothing of the sort. A man who drinks five pints and two shorts nightly is what we in Ballydull call a lemonade drinker, that is a fellow only one step removed from a complete pioneer, in other words a complete killjoy who you would be ashamed to be seen talking to.

A man who takes nine pints a night is what we in Ballydull call "a man who likes a drop". Not a serious drinker by any means; but a decent sort of bloke who'd probably dip his hand in his pocket to support the Ballydull Hurling Club and give 50p to a child while he was at it.

You might be inclined to say that a man on fifteen pints per night was overdoing it a bit. But we in Ballydull wouldn't agree. In Ballydull the fifteen pints per night man is a man. The sort of man who would have died for Ireland, if he hadn't spent so long in the toilet.

Surely, surely, you will say that even a Ballydull man would agree that a fellow who drinks eighteen pints a night is nothing short of an alcoholic. But there again you would be wrong. A man who drinks eighteen pints a night is not, is not an alcoholic. No. He's a man with a problem. Not a drink problem, mind you; but a problem. It could be a problem with his wife, a problem with his health, a financial problem, a problem with his neighbour, or a problem doing the easy crossword. But never a drink problem as such.

Of course a man who drinks twenty pints a night is a man with a big problem. There are even those in Ballydull who would describe a man who swallows twenty pints a night as a semi-alcoholic, no offence to anybody reading this.

Finally, finally, you might say that a man who drinks twenty-four pints a day is surely an alcoholic. But once again you'd be wrong. A man who drinks twenty-four pints a day in Ballydull is a man with a throat. There are a few men with throats in Ballydull – but NO alcoholics as such.

BALLYDULL FOR EXCITEMENT

Young people from foreign parts sometimes ask: What do people do for excitement in Ballydull? There is an implication with this question that people want for excitement in Ballydull; but, as I always say, New York – London – Paris are only cities, but Ballydull is a place where you are accepted in your own right, accepted as long as you can open your mouth to take a slug of Guinness, accepted as long as you can proceed to utter some sort of guttural noise, which Ballydull people will understand perfectly and take to mean:

You're not feeling too bad,
The weather is terrible,
Ballydull still have a chance in the championship,
The country is finished,
And would you get me a pint.

And quite apart from being a place that is tolerant of it's own kind, be they of modest IQ, little IQ, no IQ or sub zero IQ, downtown Ballydull is a hot, happening place with a night life second to none. Consider an average week in Ballydull …

On Monday night there's bingo and tombola in the Parochial Hall, with tea and Marietta biscuits served at the interval. On Tuesday night Sister Anthony shows slides of her trip to the Holy Land in the Parochial Hall. Apart from her obvious religious interests, Sister Anthony is a keen amateur botanist and in between shots of the thatched cottage where Jesus was born, the Christian Brother Synagogue where he went to school and the garden where he was arrested during Easter week, you are bound to see some thrilling slides of the wild flowers of Palestine. Tea and Marietta biscuits served on the night.

Wednesday night is the traditional night 'inside' in Ballydull. Watch a bit of telly, have tea and Marietta biscuits before you retire and thank God you were born in Ballydull where your right to remain as ignorant as a donkey looking out over a ditch on a damp day is respected in custom and law. Thursday night there's a Karate class in the Old Parochial Hall, conducted by the new curate, the energetic Father Kiely, who remembers injured, hospitalised and violently deceased members of the club at end of evening prayer – just before the tea and Marietta biscuits are served.

You might consider all these events just a little old-fashioned and as interesting as a Marietta biscuit dunked in a cup of cold tea; but please remember you have the opportunity every night in Ballydull of getting paralytic drunk. And most do just that on Friday night – dole night – when the four Ballydull pubs are every bit a hectic as a Tokyo subway in the grip of a nerve gas attack.

And there's nothing at all old-fashioned about the blue movies they show in O'Mahony's on a Saturday night, when open-mouthed locals cheer and throw their caps in the air at the pornographic equivalent of Ballydull Novice scoring the winning goal in injury time against their arch-rivals Kilnadreary. Sunday is, admittedly, a rather quiet day in Ballydull; and, if it's raining, as it's very likely to be, you might as well spend the whole day in bed, getting up in the evening to fry a few spuds and shave (if you feel like it) before heading out for another night – and another week – on the 'tare' in dear old Ballydull, where, long before the experts, they appreciated the virtues of a liquid diet.

THE OLD VALUES

Jim Smith, the proprietor of Smith's Food Store, is a good businessman. But there are some things Jim finds very hard to understand, like why would anybody want to eat yoghurt. Jim always gets a good laugh when somebody comes into his store and purchases a carton or cartons of yoghurt; and Jim gets very serious and very talkative when anybody is in the actual process of purchasing yoghurt. "Ah, Mrs Byrne, strawberry yoghurt for yourself, six petits filous for the young monsters, and hazelnut yoghurt for himself! Very Healthy!" And as soon as Mrs Byrne has her back turned, Jim Smith is laughing heartily at the foolishness of people. That's Jim Smith for you, an unpretentious Ballydull man, one of whose jobs as a young fella' was feeding separated milk to calves and who can't understand that people are now eating it.

And as for bottled mineral water, Jim often lies back in his bed at night laughing out loud at the idea.

$\mathcal{J}$HE PRIEST AND THE BISHOP

Father Tomás Healy, the PP in Ballydull, is a fair man. But he is known to take offence at certain manner of behaviour and certain manner of talk. And God help the man or woman who offends Father Tomás Healy.

Strange to say, one of the people who has a talent for offending Father Tomás is the Bishop. Recently Father Tim was celebrating his Golden Jubilee amid a gathering of lay people and clergy including the Bishop; and the Bishop decided to tell a joke. The Bishop's joke went as follows:

'A rabbi and a priest used to meet every year on a train, and invariably the rabbi would enquire after the priest's nephew. The rabbi was very impressed one year when the priest was able to tell him that his nephew had just got ordained. The next year the rabbi enquired after the priest's nephew again, and did he get a surprise when he heard the nephew had become a parish priest. The following year the rabbi made the same enquiry, and was he astounded to hear that the priest's nephew had become a bishop. The next year the rabbi enquired after the priest's nephew again; and the priest proudly told him that his nephew had become a cardinal. And the year after that the rabbi made the same enquiry only to learn that the priest's ambitious nephew had been made Pope ...

The year after the rabbi heard the news that the priest's nephew had been made Pope the rabbi and the priest met once again on the train. And in the time-honoured fashion the rabbi enquired after the priest's nephew.

"He's still Pope," replied the priest in a very self-satisfied way.

"Is that all?" asked the suddenly testy rabbi.

"Well you can't expect him to become God," remonstrated the priest.

"Well, one of our boys made it!" said the rabbi triumphantly.'

I have to say that the lay people of Ballydull and assorted clergy greeted the Bishop's joke with only polite laughter. And not laughing at all was Father Tomás Healy, who took double offence at the Bishop's joke ... Firstly, he considered the joke to be irreligious; and secondly, rightly or wrongly, he couldn't but be reminded of his own nephew who left Ireland under a cloud as they say and was now wanted in America for selling the Golden Gate Bridge.

Very annoyed with his own bishop was Father Tomás Healy, and when Father Tom's turn came to do a party piece, he didn't do his usual number and sing 'The Old Lady Who Swallowed A Fly' but purposely decided to tell a joke.

Father Tomás' joke went as follows: 'Once upon a time in a diocese far, far away there was this bishop who was constantly hearing that the priests of the diocese gave very boring sermons. The bishop decided to remedy this situation and began to advise the clergy of his diocese about the composition of their sermons. The bishop called on one old priest who was notorious for the boring sermons he gave, mostly about his own aches and pains.

"You know, Joe," the bishop said to the old priest, "if you want people to be interested in your sermons, you ought to say something startling. Something startling like 'Last night I was in the arms of a beautiful woman' … And then towards the end of the sermon you can reveal that the beautiful woman was your mother; and the congregation will go away happy thinking that you gave a most interesting sermon."

The old parish priest decided to try out the bishop's advice, and the following Sunday he commenced his sermon with the immortal line, 'Last night I was in the arms of a beautiful woman.' And needless to say the congregation was astounded to hear this and were all agog as to what the priest would say next. Unfortunately, when the time came to give the entirely innocent explanation for the startling statement with which he begun his sermon, the old parish priest forgot himself and he couldn't remember the exact advice the bishop had given. The old parish priest then became very flustered, making his congregation suspicious that there was another revelation on the way.

"I've got it, I've got it," exclaimed the priest at last – "last night I was in the arms of the bishop's mother."

Hearing this joke, the lay people of Ballydull broke into loud laughter and someone shouted, "You know how to tell 'em, Father Tomás!" And I can tell you that later in the night it was a very sour faced bishop who on behalf of Ballydull Community Council presented Father Tomás Healy with a colour TV.

THE PHLEGMATIC BALLYDULL MAN

What does a Ballydull man say when the foreman hands him his cards?

I was coming for them anyway.

What does a Ballydull man say to the waiter who only serves one potato for dinner?

Take them up – they're boiled.

What does a Ballydull man say after selling land / cattle / sheep / pigs?

Well, I didn't get as much as I expected but then I never thought I would.

And what does a Ballydull man say to the drunk who maintains there's cows beneath the sea?

There's probably silage pits there as well.

THE POPE IN BALLYDULL

It's a little known fact but in the course of his visit to Ireland in '79 the Pope put in an appearance – an undignified appearance – in Ballydull. He had just made his appeal to the IRA to lay down their arms and was leaving Drogheda, when he suddenly decided he wanted to go to the Limerick races. He was in receipt of information from a *Cork Examiner* journalist about a 'dead cert.' running in the 4.30 and he was convinced that if the chauffeur put the foot on the pedal they might just about make it.

"Faster, faster" or "Yaster, yaster" the Pope kept telling the chauffeur as they tore through the towns of Ashbourne and Lucan. But, by the time they got to Naas, the Pope's impatience with his chauffeur had reached boiling point. So, in the middle of a traffic jam in Naas he ordered the chauffeur out of the driving seat and took the wheel himself. The towns of Monasteravin, Abbeyleix and Urlingford were but a blur to the terrified ex-chauffeur as the Pope steered the car at speeds of 120 mph plus. The Pope looked like fulfilling his ambition of making the 4.30 at Limerick when the Thurles white-squad spotted this limousine doing a hundred and fifty and naturally they decided to give chase. Suddenly the Pope's whimsical ambition of making the 4.30 in limerick was no more, as he became altogether obsessed with evading arrest.

His new obsession was to dictate both the speed at which he drove and the now random itinerary he took, careering through Tipperary, Cahir, Ballymadra, Kilbeggar and Kilnadreary at speeds of 160 mph … until, eventually, he was forced to bring the car to a full stop behind a massive combine harvester taking up most of the Ballydull by-road. The white-squad had him at last!

But when the white-squad Gardai went about making the arrest, the white-squad garda suddenly looked more worried than forbidding and there and then he made the political decision of radioing the local Marshville guards about the delicate situation in hand.

"We have a very important customer here", he explained to the Marshville Sergeant.

"Is he a TD?" asked the sergeant nervously.

"More important than that", replied the white-squad Garda.

"Is he the Taoiseach?" asked the sergeant more nervously.

"More important than that," replied the white-squad garda almost superiorly.

"Is he the head of the UN?" asked the sergeant letting impatience get the better of his nervousness.

"No, he's more important than that," answered the white-squad garda on the radio line. "Indeed he must be really important because the Pope is driving him!"

THE BALLYDULL PSYCHIATRIST

Whatever you say about John Joe Twomey, you have to admit he's well got. Isn't he a nephew of Old Joe Twomey the famous Ballydull inventor? They said Shakespeare was mad; they said Beethoven was mad; and they said Old Joe Twomey was mad. Old Joe Twomey was mad! But his nephew John Joe Twomey is as sound as the Rock of Gibraltar. And a clever young man if ever there was one.

Doctor John Joe Twomey we call him in Ballydull. Now, it should be understood that we don't use the word 'Doctor' in this context by way of nickname; for as far as we are concerned Doctor John Joe is every bit as good as a real doctor. And what about his qualifications, I hear you say … And indeed before you said it I knew you were going to say it! And if I might be allowed to reply, I can say that Doctor John Joe Twomey has qualifications to beat the band.

When the Professor came out from the city and conducted a Social Science course in Ballydull GAA Hall, didn't our John Joe come first in the class! And by way of general compliment to the standard of learning in Ballydull, didn't the Professor say that it proved a Herculean task to teach the citizens of Ballydull anything. High praise indeed! Ah yes, I hear you say, but where did John Joe Twomey get the qualifications to practise medicine?

And I say John Joe Twomey got his qualifications by watching. Watching the cows come home in the evening to be milked, watching the clouds darken before rain, watching the web weaving of the spider and watching the workings of the beehive – a third-level education in itself. I'm saying in other words that John Joe was a 'natural'. A natural doctor.

Of course, it wasn't long before John Joe became quite bored with general medicine. As he said himself, "Any five-eight can fix a dodgy radiator, any five-eight can repair a banjaxed TV, and any five-eight can perform open-heart surgery; but it takes a particular class of lunatic to become a psychiatrist!" This was good ol' John Joe's typically self-deprecating way of telling the world that he was leaving the world of general medicine behind him, and that from now on he would become the first of his family to take on at a professional level the care and cure of diseases of the mind.

This was no rash decision of the good doctor. As he explained himself at the time: "You can go into a pub in Ballydull any night of the week and you can plainly see that the population of Ballydull are clearly a physically healthy bunch of people; but you won't be long into your second pint before the thought strikes you that the regular clientele of this typical Ballydull pub are bonkers. And seeing this for myself, seeing that those who frequented the Ballydull pubs were raving mad, and knowing that those in Ballydull who didn't frequent the pubs but went to Bingo instead were Bonkers with a capital B, I said to myself there is clearly no demand in Ballydull for GPs, health nurses and blood-pressure clinics, but Ballydull is crying out for psychiatrists."

And who would argue with that? Certainly not the people of Ballydull who began to flock to Doctor John Joe Twomey as soon as he began to practise as a psychiatrist. And what was it that brought people in such numbers to the door of Doctor John Joe Twomey, psychiatrist? Some say that what marked Doctor John Joe out from other practitioners was that John Joe was a great listener. You could tell your average psychiatrist that you were worried sick over a bullock of yours that was down with pneumonia and this psychiatrist would hastily write you out a prescription for a big jar of Tolvon tablets for yourself and completely ignore the real problem – the bullock. But as measure of John Joe's expertise as a psychiatrist he will completely ignore your history and proceed to compel you into the disclosure of a most detailed and intimate history of the bullock!

Of course, Doctor John Joe is no slouch either when it comes to the prescribing of medicine. And there are people in Ballydull and Kilnadreary and beyond who maintain that Doctor John Joe is the most gifted pharmacologist the world has ever seen. And Doctor John Joe himself makes no secret of his great contempt for the pharmacological talents of his rivals, the general practitioners in Ballydull and neighbouring parishes. Incomprehension is the word that best defines Doctor John Joe's attitude to the prescriptive habits of other general practitioners in the area …

"These doctors are mad," he's often known to say. "Tell them you're unhappy with the weather and before you can say Jack Robinson they are writing out a prescription for little white rocks of tablets that you couldn't break with a sledgehammer. And the craziest part of all is that, once swallowed, these little white rocks are notorious for creating an unquenchable thirst – as if anybody in Ballydull had a need for a savage thirst induced by artificial means … when they happen to be born with it!"

Time and time again a patient of one of these sad doctors decides enough is enough and seeks out the help of Doctor John Joe, and even though such a patient is barely able to speak with the thirst and is, besides, dog-sick from drinking TK lemonade, Doctor John Joe Twomey is able to make an instant diagnosis and speedily write out a prescription for twenty Benson & Hedges, six pints of Heineken and a double vodka, nocte. And Doctor John Joe always warns such a patient to come back to his clinic within the fortnight, in order that he – the physician – might decide whether it is a case of 'first time lucky' and the existing dose is the optimum dose or, if it is not, proceed to increase 'the medication'.

PRIORITIES

In the telephone box in the village of Ballydull there is a sign that reads: In case of emergency, ring 61796, for priest, doctor or hurler.

Only people from the city could have a problem with this notice. And indeed it would take a very staunch atheist from the city to object to the importance, the precedence given the figure of the priest in this notice. A man or woman who is in danger of dying in Ballydull knows full well that a doctor only stands at best an even money chance of saving their life; but the same grievously ill man or woman knows that, if the doctor is given precedence and he fails (and he's bound to fail eventually), it's a very poor lookout for this man's or woman's immortal soul. And everybody in Ballydull has a tactual appreciation of immortality, of Eternity.

Everybody knows from their schooldays that Eternity is like a huge rock-mountain visited once every thousand years by a bird of the air; and every time this bird touches down ever so briefly on this rock-mountain, the friction between the bird's feet and the rock surface has the effect of wearing away a tiny, tiny portion of the rock surface of the mountain; and the duration of Eternity is therefore the length of time it takes this migratory bird to wear away this vast mountain to nothing.

In the light of this awesome imagery the question who should take precedence at the sickbed of a Ballydull man or woman; the question should it be a priest or a doctor is really no question at all. The doctor, at best, can keep you going for another few miserable, rain-sodden years in Ballydull, and in each of these years it's a certainty that Ballydull will go out in the first round of the championship, and neither will there be any joy in the autumn when once again the harvest in the family farm is washed away with the flood, prompting further lamentation … It's enough to make one wish for Eternity! And this is where the priest comes in. This is where the priest triumphs over the temporal remedy maker; for the priest dispenses or doesn't dispense (as he sees fit) the Privilege to witness the long awaited, joyful return of the above described Bird-of-Eternity's return to the mountain again and again each millennial Spring.

In fairness, the doctors in Ballydull and district know their place. They may still be greeted in the street by old-timers doffing their caps in their direction, an act of respect which even old-timers no longer afford the clergy. But the doctors know from experience that, when it comes to the sick and the dying, their services are secondary to the services of the same clergy. And lackeys of real-politick that they are, the doctors go out of their way to acknowledge the real status quo.

The first question a doctor attending a sick person is likely to ask is: "Have you sent for a priest?" And like every question the doctors ask, this question is many pronged. For one thing, the doctor knows that should the ailing patient answer yes, they have sent for the priest, chances are that the patient is not a malingerer. And malingering is a big problem in Ballydull … What with people feigning the symptoms of concurring typhoid pneumonia, bubonic plague and rabies, in a gallant effort to set themselves up for life with a disability pension. I could tell you stories!

It is, moreover, quite a comfort to a doctor on a sick call to know that the priest has been to the patient or it is on his way. In this way, the doctor can be confident that the most he or she can be accused of is causing the premature death of the patient, and by the same token he or she will be absolved of the far more serious charge of depriving the patient of eternal life.

So far there is no problem. Ballydull people in their sick bed like to be visited by the priest and a doctor, in that order. But even the city dweller most sympathetic to rustic culture will be inclined to ask: "Where is the logic in the requirement of a hurler at the bedside of a Ballydull man or woman whose life hangs in the balance?"

The use of hurlers at the bedside of a seriously ill patient is an innovation unique to Ballydull, an innovation of which we are justly proud – it being our local contribution to the science of alternative medicine. For we have found that the presence of a hurler at the bedside of a dying patient – a hurler telling glorious stories of his poleaxing opponents on the playing field – can have a remarkably invigorating effect on the patient. Indeed, many such a dying patient on hearing graphic tales of Kilnadreary men and Dromduller men being stretchered off the hurling field and leaving such a trail of blood in their wake that the referee has great subsequent difficulty in discerning any of the white lines so carefully whitewashed into the grass the previous day. Isndeed many a dying patient on hearing these tales of gore and glory from a hurler's own lips 'decides' he won't bother dying after all and will stick it out for the first round of the championship. Ballydull has justly come to value the services of a hurler at the bedsides of the sick.

But I have to make one small criticism here. Some of the new breed of hurlers are a disgrace to the game. And a disgrace to Ballydull! Instead of learning how to flake the ball and flake the opposition, they are more conscious of what they call their 'image'. These fellows prance around with fake Rolex watches on their wrists – and they're good for nothing! And these fancy men that call themselves hurlers are particularly obnoxious when called to the bedside of a sick patient. Instead of waiting for their moment, as it were, and allow the priest and doctor to conclude their ministrations to the sick, they push the priest and the doctor aside as they exclaim the likes of: "Let me at the patient, I want to tell him about the goal I scored against Drumduller in the '93 Coca Cola Tournament" or "The patient has got to hear about the time I knocked six Kilnadreary men and the referee unconscious."

_A_ TOUGH CUSTOMER

Before the coming of that great leveller and great spoiler, the television set, wit and verbal dexterity of all kinds from the learned to the unlettered was highly valued in Ballydull and throughout Ireland. One such unlettered wit, a famous man to this day in Ballydull, was Bill Drinan. Once, Bill was working in the local hospital and his job was to make the dead presentable for burial. Bill was, in other words, an embalmer of sorts in the days before the art of embalming had become a degree course.

On this particular day Bill was to encounter a very tough customer with a big black beard on him. And of course, it was Bill's job to shave this. But Bill, the worse for drink, did a very indifferent job, only managing to scrape off bits of this intractable beard here and there. When the matron came to inspect the work and saw the 'performance' she gave out stink.

"I'll tell you what," said Bill, responding to the criticism, "bring me down a few candles, Matron."

"What's the idea, Drinan?" said the matron, unimpressed. "We don't wake the dead in the mortuary anymore."

"Won't you be said by me?" replied Bill. "Bring me down a few candles and we'll singe it off him. And, anyway, 'twill get him used to where he's going."

ᒍHE BALLYDULL NUTTY POETS' SOCIETY

"Anybody who describes his vocation as a poet, purveying the modern style of formless verse, is invariably among the meanest and most despicable in the land: vain, empty, conceited, dishonest and dirty, often flea-ridden and infected by venereal disease, greedy, parasitical, drunken, untruthful, arrogant … all these repulsive qualities, and also irresistibly attractive to women", Auberon Waugh, *Literary Review*; quoted in *As The Poet Said*, edited by Tony Curtis from Dennis O'Driscoll's *Poetry Ireland Review* column.

As their name suggests – a name they chose themselves – the members of Ballydull Nutty Poets' Society are different. Why they even count a cleric – Father Milo Shaughnessy – among their number. The dominant figure in the group is however the feisty yet feminine, Mrs Maeve Kennedy. She's been all over the world thanks to her day job as a McDonald's PR consultant.

A certain arch wit typifies this particular group of poets. For instance, frequently and perhaps with a measure of sincerity, Father Milo declares:

"I am a celibate."

"And I am not a celibate," Mrs Kennedy interjects at this point, to the kindly yet great amusement of the foot soldiers in this particular casualty prone battalion. (More aspiring poets have been dismissed from this society than workers are likely to be sacked from a hotel owned by a Fine Gael councillor with Fianna Fáil connections.)

Even if nobody else does, the members of Ballydull Nutty Poets' Society value themselves. And so they can't but entertain some grievances. For one thing, they were not one bit pleased when they appeared on local radio and the disc jockey asked why their poems didn't rhyme. (Some of their poems do.) And to make matters worse, off-air, the disc jockey asked Mrs Kennedy would she compose a ballad about the miraculous cure of a heifer calf of his from yellow scour.

But the Ballydull Nutty Poets' Society's biggest grievance is rather inevitably with the local branch of the Gaelic Athletic Association. Recently this talented group of poets set about hiring the GAA hall for a poetry reading of theirs. But they didn't stop at that. Instead of being of a mind to simply pay the GAA for the use of the hall and leave well alone, they seriously set about having the social committee of Ballydull GAA club sponsor the meal and refreshments for the evening. And believe you me, this talented bunch of poets weren't thinking of tea and Marietta biscuits. No, they wanted the GAA catering woman, Mrs Assumpta 'Thatcher' Daly to serve up a truly exotic meal consisting of delicacies from four continents, including freshly shot grouse to be flown in from Scotland.

I can tell you the secretary of the social committee of the Ballydull GAA didn't as much as convey this request to Mrs Daly; but instead, more in abject terror than anger, he told this bunch of poets to take their business elsewhere. I would like to report that negotiations are on-going and there is hope of a peaceful settlement; but the truth of the matter is that this request and subsequent refusal has caused more bad feelings in the area than when some mischief-maker told Dick Colley, the impecunious horse trainer, that he wasn't paying various cottagers for the use of their grass, and the very high and mighty Dick Colley fell for this and accused Jim Kelly, cottager, as the former was entering O'Mahony's and the latter was leaving same, of spreading untruths about him.

Plato had the right idea: poets are no better than spies and informers and anyone caught reading poetry – not to mind writing it – should be tied to an ESB pole and shot.

VISIONS OF BALLYBRIGHT

P.J. Burke is a dreamer. But dreamers are acceptable in Ballydull. As long as they take their Guinness and draw their dole and live more or less within their means, dreamers are mystics and are acceptable in Ballydull. And, after he has a few pints taken, P.J. Burke's favourite dream, P.J. Burke's favourite topic is of a fantastic place to which he gives the name of Ballybright.

Ballybright is everything that Ballydull isn't.

In Ballybright nobody has to labour, nobody has to work. Nobody has to endure the indignity of signing-on. Nobody in Ballybright has ever heard of FÁS schemes (or BÁS schemes as P.J. bitterly terms them). Ballybright is the land of the minimum wage (or maximum wage as P.J. misconstrues the phrase). And nobody has to as much as go and collect this minimum wage.

No. The minimum wage which is index-linked to the cost of beer and tobacco and betting tax is hand-delivered to the Ballybright man's split-level bungalow twice a week. This twice a week delivery of the minimum wage serving to eliminate that dreadful condition that strikes present-day Ballydull men every Thursday when the dole money has long run out, and there's hunger in the belly and such a thirst in the throat that some Ballydull men even contemplate drinking water.

And in Ballybright, of course, the twice-weekly delivery of this minimum wage to your doorstep is not executed by some mangy postman. Nor is this handsome cheque handed over to you by some Social Welfare Officer with a face so ugly and so sour that his mother must have turned her face away every time she was nursing him. None of that!

In Ballybright this minimum wage is handed to you in a gold-crested white envelope by a 'facilitator' dressed in tiger-striped tights and cashmere jumper, who smiles disarmingly as she asks whether you want the complimentary bottle of champagne or the six-pack which is still the preferred tipple in outlying areas of the Ballybright.

You might think that this complimentary bottle of champagne or six-pack is mere prelude to an almighty booze-up down in your local in Ballybright and in this you would not be greatly mistaken. Except that no Ballybright man would be so coarse as to describe his twice-weekly 'marathon session' as a booze-up. No. Ballybright men are a cultured lot and they refer to their twice-weekly big drinking session as their habitual Little Feasts of Bacchus.

A similar delicacy of expression, indeed a corresponding elevation in the choice of subject matter befalls the conversation of farmers in Ballybright. No Ballybright farmer will spend all night in the pub talking about his cows and expecting you to listen enthralled. Instead of talking about frisky cows, cross cows and downright vicious cows, cows with mastitis, cows with no mastitis and cows that might have mastitis, our typical Ballybright farmer is an expert on French cinema and fine wines. And if you are lucky, he will take the time to give you a guided tour of his wine cellar; and afterwards he will uncork a decent vintage and ask you straight out not, "Is Leo Yellow still the best cure for mastitis?" but, "Is the contemporary engagement with the novel a mere *idée fixe* of a boorish intelligentsia in symbiotical degeneration?" (Yes, it is!)

So far so good! But you might be of the suspicion that the one solid fixture of Ballydull would be a no less solid fixture in Ballybright. I speak of the parish priest. Surely the parish priest in Ballybright would be your same typical Irish parish priest with an interest in keeping parish funds and necklines up and parish debts and hemlines down? Alas, my friend, they do everything different in Ballybright.

In Ballybright the priest of the parish is not referred to as the parish priest, this being considered too particular a term. The preferred alternative is to address the priest by the more folksy, not to say classy title of 'Pater', as in Pater Adrian. And as you would expect from a priest who drives a Saab turbo, takes two foreign holidays annually and has no interest in promoting bingo, Pater Adrian is a self-consistent atheist. And the people of Ballybright are quite untroubled by this. As long as the good wine flows, all is well.

And at night Ballybright truly comes alive. As Romanian gypsy musicians entertain, assorted nationalities and Ballybright folk themselves drink and dine on the sidewalks of Ballybright beneath a seemingly perpetually full June moon. And, amid the chatter and clatter, you can just about hear the somewhat coercive tones of a worried Ballybright GAA official – some things never change – you can just about overhear a worried GAA official say: "We're a bit short for Sunday; we're putting you centre-forward. Bring your shin guards, Gunter."

*M*ODERN TIMES

'Modern Times' have come to Ballydull! In the old days it was the pilgrimage of a lifetime for a Ballydull man to go to the All-Ireland Final in Croke Park and see the sights of Dublin. But now, if you listen attentively to conversation of the fashionably dressed folk in the Ballydull pubs, you will realise that Ballydull people no longer set their sights on going to the All-Ireland. No. They hope to go to Dublin and take in the All-Ireland.

I think I can pinpoint the precise moment the modern age began to impinge on Ballydull. It was August 1979 and stories of the anti-Nuclear Power festival in Carnsore Point were all over the newspapers. Not of much concern to a Ballydullman you might think. But Billy Joe Keogh the Ballydull carpenter was always a bit different, in that – like nearly all tradesmen – he was a bit Bolshie, a bit lefty. And about this time Billy Joe happened to be constructing a 'draw drum', this being a multi-angled container for raffle tickets for Ballydull GAA club. And the construction of this 'draw drum' was not going according to Billy Joe's wishes, and beside him on the bench there just happened to be a two-day-old copy of the *Evening Herald* full of news of the impending festival in Carnsore. Now, Billy Joe had read this copy of the *Herald* earlier in the day and left it at that, but now in his frustration didn't he give a sideways glance at the newspaper and quite suddenly decide he wanted to go to Carnsore Point. Billy Joe mentioned this strange idea to his mate, and his mate agreed that it was a capital idea. So there and then Billy Joe and his mate decided to down tools and head off for Carnsore. But first Billy Joe had to tell the wife!

When Billy got back to his house, he was a little disappointed to discover that the wife was out, the door was locked and he had no key; so he hastily wrote out a note and stuck it to the door; and the note read 'Gone to Carnsore – back Tuesday'. That was tempting fate, to say the least of it. But worse was to follow.

I should mention here that Billy Joe Keogh had a big moustache – I said he was a bit Bolshie – and as you know from a certain distance all men with moustaches look alike. Now, when Billy Joe and his mate returned from Carnsore Point completely enthused by their adventures, Billy Joe was met with an angry silence from his wife and Billy Joe and his mate were both the object of stunned amazement by everybody in Ballydull. Eventually the awful truth dawned on Billy Joe.

The sad fact was that, on the very day the two adventurers returned from Carnsore, *The Cork Examiner* published a big photograph on the front page of a group of people of both sexes bathing in the nude at Carnsore Point and, worse, one of the men in the photograph had a moustache. The man with the moustache in the photograph wasn't Billy Joe Keogh of course! But Ballydull people were convinced it was; and it was lean rations for Billy Joe for a month afterwards.

BALLYDULL NIHILSM 1

Never ask for directions in Ballydull. For a Ballydull man will earnestly say to you: "You see that turning on the left beyond the old waterpump. It's not that road at all!"

BALLYDULL NIHILSM 2

I repeat never ask for directions in Ballydull. For the Ballydull man or woman will say to you: "You see that road further on the left, beyond the farmhouse with the blue galvanised iron on the haybarn. It's not that road either!"

THE GAA AND THE MEDIA

The newspapers are only interested in soccer, Royalty and sex! And that goes for the Dublin newspapers and *The Cork Examiner*. And now the local newspapers are going the same slimy way, with their madly exaggerated anti-GAA stories. Just recently the *Ballydull News & Star* reported under a banner headline that a Ballydull player had been seriously and maliciously injured in training. And, of course, the national media picked up on the story, with Marian Finucane asking how many stitches the player in question got and when were they coming out?

But I can say emphatically that this story about a Ballydull player maliciously injured in training was a pack of lies. I am not denying, of course, that the Ballydull full-forward Joe 'Elbows' Fleming received severe lacerations to the left shoulder, a fractured nose and a serious knee injury. I am not denying that, at all! But, like the fellow in those English Murder-Mysteries who knows 'twas the butler did it, I know who did it, I know who did it to Joe Fleming.

"Twas the cow that did it!'

BALLYDULL REPRISE 1

Recognised and unrecognised 'delusions of grandeur' are the norm in Ballydull. Consider the case of John Sullivan (also known as Reics Carlo) who believed that he was not alone a writer but also head of his own intelligence gathering organisation. Sadly, John Sullivan's intelligence gathering had very unhappy consequences for one Ballydull man. This particular Ballydull man who shall remain nameless was in the habit of receiving his daily newspaper a day after its publication, these day-old copies of the newspaper coming into the Ballydull man's possession thanks to the generosity of John Sullivan's father. (I needn't tell you the nature of the problem that prevented the subject of John Sullivan's father's generosity from buying his own newspaper.) Tragedy ensued when John Sullivan began to take clippings from the one newspaper on the day it arrived in the Sullivan household. John of course was only innocently adding to his data file. But the result of all this intelligence gathering was that John Sullivan's father's friend began to receive copies of a day-old newspaper with an increasing number of holes in it. I don't know if you've ever tried to read copies of a newspaper that is in the process of vanishing before your eyes as it were; but you will understand that this exercise can only be deleterious and you won't be surprised to hear that John Sullivan's father's friend lost his sanity entirely. So be warned! Never read a newspaper with holes in it.

BALLYDULL REPRISE 2

A Ballydull man was buying half a head of cabbage in Kilnadreary. (The Ballydull countryside is fine agricultural land, and you'd think you'd be able to buy half a head of cabbage in Ballydull village, but you can't)

While the purchase of the cabbage was in progress the Ballydull man and the proprietor chatted amicably. The Ballydull man brought up the subject of a village some distance from Ballydull, this being none other than the scenic village of Ballycrabit.

"I'd have nothing to do with that parish," said the shopkeeper abruptly and most vehemently … "All the women there are either camogie players or whores."

"Well actually my daughter has moved to Ballycrabit," said the Ballydull man testily.

"What position does she play in?" asked the shopkeeper helpfully.

BALLYDULL REPRISE 3

A schoolteacher's working day in Ballydull or anywhere offers insight into the community that a GP or a Garda Siochana might envy. A case in point. On one occasion in Ballydull National School Miss Ford asked her class of infants to each paint a picture depicting panic. A quarter of an hour having been allotted to the completion of the exercise, Miss Ford went around the classroom to inspect the artwork of her pupils. First she came to a pupil who had painted a picture reminiscent of the sinking of the Titanic. There was a big ship in the water and people frantically scrambling for lifeboats … and Miss Ford couldn't deny that this painting captured the spirit of the condition that is panic. Another pupil had painted a picture of a skyscraper on fire with people jumping out of windows. Again Miss Ford couldn't but recognise this as good work. But then she came to a pupil who, instead of painting a descriptive scene on his sheet of paper, had merely drawn a big X. "What's the idea, Diarmuid?" asked the schoolteacher more in puzzlement than anything else. "Well you see Miss," Diarmuid replied, "I have three sisters at home … and every month they have to put an X on the wall … and last week there was one X missing … AND THAT'S PANIC."

BALLYDULL REPRISE 4

It's a damp night in Ballydull, and it's probably drizzling in Kilnadreary town park and in the playing fields and other outdoor amenities of Dromduller; likewise, it's probably lashing on the pieta in Ballycrabit and the headstones in Kilradlit graveyard; and the night is probably just as dirty in Marshville, Headerstown, Ballymadra, Kilbeggar and Millbridge. It's probably raining in Dublin, London and Chicago as well. Thank God we will never die of drought.

The Extra Magnificent Yeti

for all the twopercenters

John Murphy 1994

Illustrations to the poems by
Oliver McCarthy

The Stratagem of the Yeti

Yeti like publicity
but he diffident

Yeti diffident
but he like publicity

Yeti walk on snow
Yeti leave big footprints
Yeti like that

Upon Mousing Project Hill it's either fortune or fame ...

THE YETI AND THE DINOSAURS

Yeti speculate on what exact happen to his
Dinosaur brothers
Did a giant meteorite
or a number of giant meteorites
strike the planet
ushering in millennia of darkness and cold
making life literally impossible for Dinosaur?
Or did – as some think – a rare blight
strike a small but important plant species?
Important because it help keep Dinosaur regular

Such speculation make Yeti sad
as he resolve to watch out for falling objects
and eat plenty of roughage

I have one thing in common with Jehovah:
I don't like referees either. Of course with Jehovah
it's a case of pure selfishness; while my belief in the moral
correctness of the hatchet man has helped sustain me through
fourteen million long years in the wilderness.

The Empirical Yeti

Yeti don't know whether
or not there is a Loch Ness Monster
Yeti never been to Scotland
and he keep an open mind

This I know: In forbidding the use of the eye and in outlawing
the ear entirely the law is an illusion with no future.

ᴛʜᴇ Yᴇᴛɪ ᴀꜱ Aʀᴛɪꜱᴛ

Yeti send movie script to big Hollywood producer
Yeti script have yetis take over the world
Big Hollywood producer write back
saying Yeti script unrealistic
Yeti know that big Hollywood producer only pretend
he think Yeti script unrealistic
Because (Yeti know) big Hollywood producer afraid
to say Yeti script badly written
Yeti know Yeti script good
Yeti think Hollywood producer no nice man

To Carthage I came looking for a recording contract ...

The Yeti and the Alien

Turquoise spaceship land near Yeti
Out pop pink alien
Alien invite Yeti to distant planet
With blue snow
Lovely blue snow
Friendly blue snow

Yeti tell alien:
Alien come a bad time
Work scarce
And Yeti got job helping mountaineers

When alien don't take no for an answer
Yeti kick extraterrestrial in the zesones

You must listen to B.B. King's 'Don't Look Down'.

THE PREFERENCES OF THE YETI

Journalist ask local how to ward off Yeti
Local tell journalist way is to throw excrement at him
Journalist enquire what to do if there is no excrement about
Local explain that there is always plenty of excrement
When the Yeti is about

Yeti don't like journalist report
Yeti like liberty, equality and fraternity

Because they realised that this joke was aimed at them.

The Yeti as Stoic

Yeti have philosophy that things work out for the best
Yeti don't really believe things work out for the best
But Yeti believe it necessary to believe they do
When his mate die in avalanche
Yeti cry
But Yeti say:
"And *yeti* it would be worse if she pregnant"
When his son die in another avalanche
Yeti cry
But Yeti say:
"And *yeti* it would be worse if he had family"
When his daughter die in yet another avalanche
Yeti cry
But Yeti say:
"and *yeti* it would be worse if she abducted
and lead into a life of sin by blue movie producers"

They say Death can hide behind a full stop.
But that has no relevance for me.
What has is another matter.

THE HALLUCINATING YETI

Yeti look in mirror
and see John Travolta

Brooklyn Bridge is falling down.

The Yeti in a Holistic Universe

When his favourite tobacco go off market
Yeti lose job teaching French classics

It ain't no rock 'n' roll show ...

*T*HE *T*RUE *A*RT OF THE *Y*ETI

Yeti music
Yeti tone-deaf
Yeti write the songs
Good, indifferent and bad

Yeti don't like what happened to his sister
Yeti take the Bronx
And Staten Island too

For our contention is not with blood and flesh,
but with dominion, with authority, with the blind
world rulers of this life, with the spirit of guzzling
in things heavenly ...

THE YETI AS GNOSTIC

Yeti entertain outlandish ideas
The Earth might be flat after all
And the supreme being is a Dog
And Yeti himself control both light and darkness
– a big responsibility

I myself was among the Firstborn to give
the orders to search and to destroy ...

*Y*ETI THE *P*OLITICALLY *C*ORRECT

Yeti no racist
Yeti used to have big Bud send him Bob tapes
and the Watchers smile in post office
and say Yeti get happy hour

Yeti confuse
Yeti offer Yeti explanation
Yeti has seen the future
and it's Yeti

To not be or be that will be the question.

The End of Yeti

Yeti is torn between Durga the fiery and Aphrodite with the dramatic cough and by consequence gets into trouble both with Lord Mara and Lord Shiva's widow – not to mention the fire-eating dragon; then Jupiter, Thor and the Eskimo's doppleganger and a cast of thousands exact revenge (as they see it) for they know not what they do and choose to forget that the Sheila is waiting for them …

The Observation Ward

Selected Poems of Sam Pharoah

and

Selected reflections of Simon Smith Jnr.

"Rome wasn't built overnight"

John Murphy © 2001

Editor: John Murphy

The man with the computer: Gerry Murphy

Another man with a computer: Gerry Corbett

Back up Organiser: Pat Murphy

Back up Adviser: Michael Murphy

CONTENTS

$\mathscr{I}$NTRODUCTION

I hope this little book of poems – first published on the web – sheds some light on a vast and normally hidden feature of human endeavour. The endeavour in question involves that populous army of people who take to composing literature of the kind never likely to be published. If not for the web then in the normal course of events the poems and reflections to follow would never be published in any format whatsoever, and so published here they may help prove that that sad vast book of life – the 'book' of all unpublished material – is not quite as bad as you might have previously assumed.

John Murphy 2001

THE WIND

[According to Carlos Castaneda death presents itself as a wind – no metaphor.]

The wind comes
A changing swill
Where it blows
No one knows
The wind like a shadow
Stalks the shape shifter
Unseen by eye
It knows all
Sees all

The bravest
Cannot kill it
The sword is to no avail
The sharpest lance will fail
The wind wanders
The world at will
And strikes
Mere men
For good or ill.

– Sam Pharoah

How large are the cumulative errors of the medical.

– Simon Smith Jnr.

Freedom Cry

Butterfly,
free butterfly,
how I envy you
dear creature.
No longer earth-bound,
you fly on silver wings,
rejoicing in your
new-found freedom.
Hear my spirit
cry for freedom
from within this cage
of flesh and bone.
How I long to cast
aside
this earthly robe,
to free my inner self,
and rise like you
on silver wings
and fly away.

– *Sam Pharoah*

The dawn arrived as it always promised it would …
As the darkness faded, a strange sort of happiness filled
the air: the sound of a thousand crows waking from
their drowsiness and taking to the air.

– *Simon Smith Jnr.*

ℒove ℬurns

Love is not my friend.
it comes and lights
a fire within my soul,
then strips me of my wings
while I am still in flight.

"No more shall love
invade my heart,"
so many times I swore;
but how, in truth,
was I to know
what fate held in store.

For there you stood
before me,
and the flame
was lit no more.

I'd give the world
both sea and land,
if I was sure
to hold your hand.

Or even just for a blip
in time
to feel your lips
pressed close to mine.

But well I know
I'll be alone
until I reach
life's end.
For mine, I know,
you'll never be;
for love is not.

– Sam Pharoah

The slowest and most foolish will evolve in
their own time.

– Simon Smith Jnr.

UNTITLED

List to the story of a knight of old
as fresh today as when first told
about the Viscount Barry high
and a little drummer boy.
The Norman offered bags of gold
the drummer took it, so I'm told
a secret passage soon he found
hidden safe from all around.
Donegan's Fort was taken fast
for the drummer the die was cast
Lord Viscount Barry got his way
showed that treachery did pay.
The Barry men got slow and lazy
that drove his Lordship Barry crazy
he said this drummer has to go
I decree that this be so.
His trial was fast
the die was cast
head hobbled on the green
but up he got
and took the lot.
And has long since been seen.

– *Sam Pharoah*

Man is the peninsula of evolution.
– *Simon Smith Jnr.*

REMEMBER ME

When your day is at an end
and you feel you need a friend.

When your dream was not so good
and nothing is as it should.

Remember me, I'm very near
think of me, and I'll be here.

– Sam Pharoah

Dreams are the dipsticks of the DNA.
– Simon Smith Jnr.

The Pessimist's Philosophy

Why am I afraid to love?
I guess I'll never know.
Why am I afraid to live?
It's just not worth the trouble.
What's the point?
It all will end
when the big man bursts the bubble …

– *Sam Pharoah*

Trees know nothing that they shouldn't know.
– *Simon Smith Jnr.*

UNTITLED

Forever blow
the winds of change.
They twist and rend,
and rearrange.
All life's a play
of changing scenes.

– Sam Pharoah

Branches reaching for the stars never collect their
fallen fruit.

– Simon Smith Jnr.

Snow melts in order of shape.

- Simon Smith Jnr.

The stars are there to lead the way; the wind will
fill our sails.

- Simon Smith Jnr.

THE TRAGEDY OF

DIARMUID AND GRÁINNE

DEDICATION BY JOHN MURPHY

*I was prompted to write this play by a
suggestion of Mick Culloty and
I respectfully dedicate it to him.*

CHARACTERS

FIONN MAC COOL

DERING

OISÍN

OSCAR

CONÁN MAOL

CORMAC MAC ART, the High-King

DONAL, a servant

GRÁINNE

THE QUEEN, wife of Cormac Mac Art

ORLA, a maidservant

TWO MALE SERVANTS

DIARMUID

A STRANGER

ANGUS-OF-THE-BIRDS

TWO TRACKERS

SHAVRAN THE SURLY

A MUSICIAN

TWO CHILDREN

Note: Perhaps because stories of the Fianna have tormented Irish school children of various generations, the spelling of names in this play is an odd mixture of the phonetic and the original Irish.

ACT ONE – SCENE ONE

Main fort of the Fianna, Hill of Allen. Hill circled with bothys on backdrop. Enter Fionn, Dering, Oisín, Oscar and Conán Maol. They speak in unison:

> The brave Fenian band are we,
> From the Earth we take freely –
> It feeds and heals us gladly
> And we praise it constantly
>
> Our traits they number three:
> Our hearts are set on liberty,
> Our limbs as strong as oak tree
> And our word we honour truly
>
> We roam the hill and valley
> And take joy in all we see:
> The wolf, the boar and the deer,
> Lakes and rivers and the sea
>
> Our traits they number three:
> Our hearts are set on liberty
> Our limbs as strong as oak tree
> And our word we honour truly

FIONN: My heart is longer in those lines. I care not for poem, nor music. I don't even care for hunting.

DERING: Fionn, that is not like you. How many mornings were you the first to rise and look down from a hill or mountain, look down on the river Boyne or the river Shannon or the river Maigue and say, 'This is going to make a lovely day and a lucky day for hunting'.

FIONN: You speak of old times, Dering. I haven't felt in the mood for hunting this long while, not since my wife died six months ago.

CONÁN MAOL (*approaching Fionn and slapping him on the shoulder*):
Nonsense, Fionn! There's plenty of wolves in the mountain, plenty of deer in the lowlands, plenty of birds in the sky and plenty of fish in the sea; and there's many a woman who would only be delighted to throw her lot and more in with the famous Fionn Mac Cool, a man whose fame has reached the shores of Scotland, a man whose fame has reached the shores of Greece, a man whose fame has even reached the shores of –

OISÍN: Whist, Conán Maol, have you no respect for a man so recently bereaved?

FIONN: Don't upset yourself, Oisín; don't take offence, Conán Maol. I know you all mean well. It's just that since my wife, the daughter of Glenduv, died and left me on my own every day has been worse than the one before. *(Off, the sound of beagles barking.)* Observe how the sound of beagles barking interrupts my flow of speech. There was a time when that sound was music to my ears: now it just serves to fill me with feelings of great sadness.

> What good to me is the beagles' call?
> What good to me are my warriors tall?
> What good to me is the wine cup small?
> What good to me is the banquet hall?
> My wife has gone to the silent clay
> I take no joy in this lonesome day

> What use the tune, what use heroic rhyme?
> For the hunter is but prey to Time
> And the hunter dead but prey to rhyme
> And rhyme itself be but prey to Time

> What good to me is the game of chess?
> What good to me is all this contest?
> What good to me is all female dress?
> What good to me is all mortal flesh?
> My wife has gone to the silent clay
> I take no joy in this lonesome day

> What use the tune, what use heroic rhyme?
> For the hunter is but prey to Time
> And the hunter dead but prey to rhyme
> And rhyme itself be but prey to Time

DERING: I have to say that's a very sad poem.

OISÍN: I am of one mind with Dering. That poem you just recited is so sad it's not one bit like you. It's sad and even improper to hear such mournful and defeatist words come from the leader of the Fianna's own lips.

FIONN: I know there's truth in what you're saying, Oisín. But a man can find neither rest, nor contentment when he doesn't have the support of a woman.

OISÍN: How can you talk like that, when there isn't the daughter of a king or chieftain throughout the big world that, if you were to as much cast your eyes at her, wouldn't there and then take up with you?

DERING: I know where you could find a woman and a wife for yourself, Fionn, if that's what you want?

FIONN: Who is she?

DERING: Gráinne the daughter of Cormac Mac Art, the High-King. Gráinne is the most shapely and well-spoken woman of all the women in the whole wide world.

FIONN: You never failed to come up with good advice, Dering! But for many a long day I have had a quarrel with Cormac Mac Art the High-King and it wouldn't be wise for me to go courting his daughter; it would be far better if you, Dering and Oisín, were to go to Cormac Mac Art and try and arrange a match on my behalf.

OSCAR: That's a good idea! Will I go along with Dering and Oisin to talk to the High-King?

CONÁN MAOL: And I can go too! I have a lot of experience in match-making.

FIONN: No! This is a task that calls for diplomacy, and the more subtle skills of diplomacy only come with age. Let Oisín my own son and Dering the wise travel to Tara to meet the High-King. This new plan of ours has come as rather a surprise to me and, begging your pardon, I'd like to go down to the woods to reflect a while.

(Fionn's exit prompts a pause.)

OISÍN: Through no fault of his own my father Fionn has allowed his mourning for his wife and my mother to demoralise the Fianna present here.

DERING: That is so, Oisín. And it's not proper for warriors to be despondent, rather they should be ever joyful and watchful. So might I suggest that, as a means of dispelling our sense of gloom, we repeat the motto of the Fianna.

(They all recite:)

Our traits they number three:
Our hearts are set on liberty
Our limbs as strong as oak tree
And our word we honour truly

ACT ONE – SCENE TWO

In the outdoors at Tara. A grove of bushes on backdrop. Off, the somewhat distant sounds of a gathering of people.

Enter servant Donal and Cormac Mac Art. Donal obsequiously makes way for Cormac the King as the latter goes forestage.

CORMAC MAC ART: There's nothing I like more than a gathering of people at a fair. People seem to be at their happiest when they are in assembly. *(Removing crown from his head)* But just for a few moments in the course of a long day I like to get away from it all to reflect a while, so that a few minutes later I can return to the happy assembly and relish all the more the smiles and the laughter of people meeting old friends and making new acquaintances, and enjoy all the more the chattering and shouting of people making deals and forging alliances; and, needless to say, every second man at gatherings of this sort comes to me their King to ask some favour or other. Which reminds me, did I not a few minutes ago happen to see two warriors of the Fianna at the edge of the crowd ? Dering and Oisín, no less. Dering the wise and Oisín who is quite an astute fellow in his own right. I needn't be in any doubt that these two gentlemen didn't come to this fair at Tara just to pass the time; nor did they come to Tara in the hope of seeing a man with two heads. No, these two brave fellows came on business, important – important business with me no doubt. Any minute now I can expect these two warriors to seek me out. What did I say? *(Cormac Mac Art returns the crown to his head as Dering and Oisín enter.)* Here comes two of the Fianna, the same virtuous Fianna that allow no crime go unpunished in my kingdom and that preserve the mystic land of Ireland from foreign invader.

DERING & OISIN: Greetings, your noble Majesty.

CORMAC: And greetings to you, Dering and Oisín, I'm happy to meet you both.

DERING: Great weather today, and great weather for a fair day I might add. I was just saying to Oisín where on earth would so many people come together in good humour; where on earth would you meet so many people of diverse trade and costume; where on earth, for that matter, would you see so many horses and strange creatures of the world? Where on earth but on a fair day at Tara in the reign of Cormac Mac Art!

CORMAC: In your wanderings about this assembly of people on this lovely day you didn't happen to catch glimpse of a man with two heads, did you, Dering?

DERING: I assume you jest, your Majesty.

CORMAC: I do indeed. For I know full well that it is not the custom of two warriors of the Fianna such as yourselves to spend half the day loitering around on a fair day like thieves or vagabonds intent on roguery. I know you've come on important business and it would please me if it would please you to say what it is.

DERING: You judge matters correctly, your Majesty. We come on important business. Indeed, there are many people who would say that our business here today is the most important business there is; and even a warrior like me wouldn't be inclined to say that people with such an opinion have got it wrong.

OISÍN: Dering is a little shy, your Majesty, Dering is a little shy about saying that Fionn Mac Cool, the leader of the Fianna, has sent us two to ask for the hand of your renowned and beautiful daughter Gráinne in marriage.

CORMAC: I might have guessed, for most of the time is there not a very simple explanation for what brings men to Tara. Isn't every second visitor to Tara either seeking to marry my daughter or else trying to arrange a match with her on behalf of someone or other? Now the great Fionn Mac Cool is added to the long list of men who wish to marry Gráinne; and, of course, I can't but remark that the same Fionn Mac Cool and myself have had our differences and have our differences. But, that said, I would never allow my own feelings of anger with Fionn ruin a chance of happiness for my own dear daughter, Gráinne. I would allow nothing of the sort; for it is my wish that everybody be happy and it is my great wish that Gráinne be happy in marriage. But, then, there isn't a king or a prince in his own right in the green island of Ireland who hasn't come to me asking for the hand of Gráinne in marriage; and then, of course every man that Gráinne has refused puts the blame on her innocent father. So, for the sake of a quiet life, I intend telling my servant here to bring Gráinne here this very minute, so that I can ask her to her face will she marry Fionn. Donal!

(Exit Donal.)

DERING: You were speaking there just jokingly, your Majesty, of a man with two heads. But, in all seriousness, I would point out that, if you were to meet those who have travelled to the faraway Eastern world, they would tell you tales of more fabulous things than a man with two heads. Indeed, a very experienced traveller once told me that he saw a –

(Enter Gráinne.)

GRÁINNE: O Father dearest, I hope you didn't summon me here for folly. Pardon me, I spy two warriors of the Fianna here and somehow I suspect important business is afoot.

CORMAC: Yes, daughter, your suspicions are most apt. Fionn Mac Cool, the warrior-chieftain of the Fianna, has sent these two emissaries to ask on his behalf for your hand in marriage; and you have but to say the word 'Yes' and my agreement is with and my blessing is upon the marriage of Fionn and Gráinne.

GRÁINNE: If Fionn is good enough to be your son-in-law, he's good enough to be my husband.

CORMAC: My daughter has consented to marriage; my daughter is to be wed at last. All that remains is for the happy couple to meet and a day and place of the wedding to be decided.

DERING: Might I suggest that a party of the Fianna including Fionn Mac Cool pay a visit to the royal palace of Tara a fortnight from today, so that the lovers may meet.

CORMAC: Yes, that is a most sensible plan. No one could imagine how happy I am that my daughter Gráinne's future has been decided.

How happy I am today
As father and a king;
My child I give away
To warrior bold and strong.
She will know no poor day
Nor will she suffer wrong;
From love she will not stray
As summer's day is long.

O Gráinne faithful child
To Fionn be faithful wife
That your weathers be mild
And happy be your life

How happy I am today
As father and a man;
My daughter well did say
Fionn is to be her man.
Happy this union I say
All as happy as I am;
Faithful couple always
As each minute is ran

O Gráinne faithful child
To Fionn be faithful wife
That your weathers be mild
And happy be your life

OISIN: Noble sentiments, your Majesty, on this most auspicious day.

(Enter Donal and the Queen. Donal briefly shows displeasure as the Queen pushes past him. She brings her hands to tear-filled eyes as she speaks.)

THE QUEEN: Gráinne, Gráinne! My child, my child! I couldn't but overhear that my child is to be married to the brave and illustrious Fionn Mac Cool. O what happiness! As happy as we are today, it is but a foretaste of the happiness that is come, as the union of Fionn and Gráinne bestows peace and good fortune to everyone throughout the land. We're all going to be so happy!

ACT TWO – SCENE ONE

Banquet hall at Tara. A table at right and a table at left. Seating.
Two male servants are roasting a pig on open fire at back. Maidservant Orla is
busy completing table setting. Enter the queen.

THE QUEEN: Is everything in complete and absolute readiness for our little
    feast, good servant?

ORLA: I can safely say, your ladyship, that everything is in perfect order and as
    good as ready for our guests.

THE QUEEN: I don't mind telling you even if you're only a servant to the
    household and a servant to Gráinne in particular, I don't mind telling you
    that I'm very excited.

(Enter Cormac Mac Art.)

CORMAC: I take it all is at the ready for our guests who I observed just this
    minute in the half-light make their way to the palace gates. Nothing that I
    will say to these warriors of the Fianna will allude to the fact that Fionn Mac
    Cool and myself are in some disagreement. Do I not this very minute hear
    this brave party in happy mood ?

(Off, the warrior party are heard in song and banter. Fionn, Diarmuid, Oisín,
Oscar and Conán Maol fall silent as they enter.)

FIONN MAC COOL: I sincerely hope that the exuberance of the Fianna here
    caused no offence to this royal household, nor to your royal self, Cormac.

CORMAC: No offence at all, no offence but great joy. It is good to see you Fionn
    and good to see your fellow warriors here. But let us not wait on ceremony,
    but let you all take your seats and let the maidservant Orla fetch Gráinne
    here this instant and also instruct servant Donal to be in quick attendance.

(Exit Orla. The company take their seats, Fionn and royal couple at one table
Diarmuid, Oisin, Oscar and Conán Maol at the other table. All engage in
animated conversation as loud music plays. During which music Orla and Donal
enter and assist in the pouring of the wine. Gráinne also enters and is found
chatting with a standing Conán Maol as music fades.)

CONÁN MAOL: And just then the monster with three eyes in his head appeared
    at the top of the hill, and Fionn Mac Cool was very frightened and Oisín
    was very frightened and Oscar was very frightened; and they were all about

to make quick retreat, when I with great courage walked up the hill against the coming monster; and I didn't stop walking until I could see the whites of the monster's six eyes and I could see the sweat dripping from his huge nostrils and cool as a breeze I sunk my sword into the monster's heart and the monster fell over and died!

GRÁINNE: I thought you said earlier that the monster had three eyes. But tell me, Conán Maol, what cause or occasion brought Fionn Mac Cool to the town of Tara tonight ?

CONAN MAOL: If you don't know what brought Fionn Mac Cool here tonight, it should be no surprise that I don't know!

GRÁINNE: I want to know from you what brought Fionn Mac Cool here tonight.

CONAN MAOL: If that's the case, I should say that Fionn came here to claim you as his woman and his wife.

(A pause.)

GRÁINNE: It would be no wonder if Fionn wanted me as a wife for his son Oisín, or even as a wife for his grandson Oscar; but it's a great wonder to me that he wants me for himself, since he's every bit as old as my father.

CONAN MAOL: If Fionn was to hear you say that, he'd have nothing to do with you and Oisín would have nothing to do with your either.

GRÁINNE; Tell me, Conan Maol, who is that sweet-tongued, handsome man to the right of Oisín the son of Fionn?

CONAN MAOL: That's Diarmuid of the shining face, the man most loved by all the women throughout Ireland. Of course, I myself as one of the bravest of the Fianna am much loved by women.

(Gráinne drifts away from Conán Maol. Conán Maol returns disappointed to table.)

GRÁINNE *(beckoning to Orla)*:The plan and scheme that is afoot tonight does not agree with me. It is time I performed some mischief.

ORLA: You summoned me, Mistress Gráinne.

GRÁINNE: Bring me the large jewel-studded drinking cup. The jewel-studded cup can hold enough wine for nine times nine men and on this night I shall fill it with a special enchanted wine that does send all who drink it into a deep sleep. *(Exit Orla.)* It is peculiar, is it not, how all things seek out their very opposite. For men drink wine of all kinds so as to forget and, often as not, so as to sleep. Surely, there can be no more perfect imitation of death than sleep. Perhaps all the joys and glories of the world possess one quality in common: they all grant a little of the freedom of death.

The peace of death is life's goal
Some seek it in the noise of war
The peace of death is life's goal
Some seek it in the heat of bed
The peace of death is life's goal
Some seek it in song or a star
The peace of death is life's goal
Some seek it in the wine so red

(Enter Orla and she places the jewel-studded drinking cup on the table. Gráinne then fills the drinking cup from a special wine jar.)

The wine I pour is the stuff of death
It grants death's peace for small sojourn
The wine of life is more potent yet
It grants death's peace without return

Orla, take this jewel-studded cup to Fionn and tell him it is Gráinne who sends it to him.

(Orla does as instructed. Fionn takes a long draught from the cup and passes it to the king who, in turn, passes it to the queen. The three who drink from the cup fall asleep. Gráinne then grabs Diarmuid by the arm and drags him forestage.)

GRÁINNE: Will you be my love, Diarmuid, and take me from this house tonight?

DIARMUID: I will not take you from this house, for you have promised yourself to Fionn, and I will have nothing to do with a woman who is promised to Fionn.

GRÁINNE: I put you under bonds, Diarmuid, bonds that no true hero is known to break, to take me out of Tara tonight and rescue me from a marriage to an old man.

DIARMUID: These are evil bonds, Gráinne, and nothing but trouble and strife can come from them. Please Gráinne, give your love to Fionn as you promised; for Fionn is more noble and courageous than any man of the Fianna and there is no man more deserving of a woman's love.

GRÁINNE: You are under bonds, Diarmuid, and should you break these bonds you will be forever known as a traitor and a coward.

DIARMUID: Don't you know that when Fionn sleeps at Tara he enjoys the right and privilege of keeping the keys of great gates on his person, so even if we wished we could not leave Tara.

GRÁINNE: I have the answer to that difficulty: there is a secret door leading from my bower and we could go through that door before Fionn and my royal parents wake up.

DIARMUID: It is not fitting for a honourable warrior to escape through a secret door like a thief.

GRÁINNE: It is well within the ability of any member of the Fianna to jump over the palisades using his spear as a jumping pole. Or could it be, Diarmuid, that you are only trying to raise petty objections in order not to help me?

DIARMUID: Let us not be rash. Let us ask the advice of Oisín and Oscar. My faithful friends, Oisín and Oscar, Gráinne here has put me under bonds to rescue her from an unsuitable marriage to Fionn and take her from Tara tonight. Am I not in all fairness entitled to break such cruel bonds?

(Enter Oisín and Oscar.)

OISÍN: It is a sad predicament you are in, Diarmuid, but no honourable member of the Fianna would refuse to come to the help of a woman in distress.

OSCAR: Sad as I am to say so, I am of one mind with Oisín. You cannot break the bonds Gráinne has placed on you.

(A weeping Diarmuid puts on his weapons.)

DIARMUID *(clasping the hands of Oisín and Oscar)*: Never again will I know the joy of your comradeship either at the chase or, after a long day's hunting, at the ale-feast.

(To Gráinne) It's a sad journey you are bringing on yourself and upon me, Gráinne; for there is no corner of Ireland that Fionn Mac Cool will not search for us.

GRÁINNE: I am resolved to go with you, Diarmuid, and I will never part with you until death itself comes between us.

(Exit Diarmuid and Gráinne. Conán Maol accidentally topples wine cup from table. Fionn stirs and wakes up.)

FIONN: What treachery is this? *(Fionn sounds hunting horn. King and queen wake up.)* Tell me Oisín and tell me Oscar that my eyes do not deceive me and that the woman I intended to be my wife and the warrior I trusted so have fled together from Tara? Have Diarmuid and Gráinne fled?

OISÍN: Your eyes do not deceive you.

OSCAR: Diarmuid and Gráinne are gone.

CORMAC: What?

FIONN: This treachery I will punish. No matter where in Ireland Diarmuid and Gráinne make home, no matter where they hide I will find them.

THE QUEEN: What calamity is this?

CORMAC: Fionn says that he will hunt down the man who has stolen my daughter from her palace home and from Fionn who was to be her husband. I must believe Fionn.

THE QUEEN: You believe too much, husband Cormac. I could have known something would happen to spoil our happiness. Why did you not foresee and prevent Diarmuid's treachery? You brought all this unhappiness upon us, Cormac.

CORMAC: I brought all this unhappiness about, I brought all this unhappiness about, I have never been more outraged! But Fionn has vowed to hunt down Diarmuid and my daughter Gráinne who he has tricked into going along with him; and Fionn Mac Cool I must believe.

FIONN: You can believe me, Cormac. I shall search every glen and every mountain, every forest and every cave until I find Diarmuid and Gráinne.

ACT TWO – SCENE TWO

A year later. Backdrop, a moonlit wood. A fire smoulders forestage. Diarmuid has almost completed the construction of a small bothy.

GRÁINNE: We have been walking through glen and up and down mountain this past year. And every time we see a hare rise from its sleep and run away in fright and every time we see a bird rise from its nest and fly away in distress, our own two hearts beat faster and we wonder was it ourselves alone that caused such creatures to flee in terror, or have such creatures fled in terror because Fionn Mac Cool happens to be in the vicinity.

DIARMUID: We are fugitives now and our lives are every bit as uncertain as the life of any creature of the wild.

GRÁINNE: I wouldn't wish for any other kind of life than the life of a fugitive: I wouldn't wish for any other kind of life if it meant that I could not have you, Diarmuid. But, ever so often, when I grow tired of walking on wet land and walking up hill, I think how sweet it would be if you could command two horses and a chariot and we could drive through the fair land of Ireland.

DIARMUID: Those are idle dreams, Gráinne. When we fled from Tara we had to abandon our horses, for had we kept our horses Fionn would have tracked us down instantly.

GRÁINNE: Sometimes I think the world is designed to increase our difficulties. Fionn is the most capable of huntsmen; is a man who has dedicated his life to the chase, and now Fionn Mac Cool intends to hunt us down.

DIARMUID: That is so, and that we must accept. We are fugitives now. And all of those who would once have shown us hospitality will no longer do so lest they incur the wrath of Fionn.

GRÁINNE: As I was walking over a bog today I stepped in a bog-hole and a splash of water wet my leg. It seems to me, Diarmuid, that for all your bravery in war and battle, the splash of water had more courage than you!

DIARMUID: That's true, for up to now I kept away from you for fear of bringing the anger of Fionn down on top of me; but no man can get the better of a woman and I'm not prepared to put up with your insulting talk any more.

(Diarmuid kisses Gráinne.)

GRÁINNE (startled): Did you hear the east wind blow the sound of footsteps in our direction?

DIARMUID: Tell me true, who goes there.

(Enter a stranger, colourfully dressed and carrying a blackthorn stick.)

STRANGER: Take it easy, you have nothing to fear from me. Be you outlaws or men with a history of murder playing on your minds, you have nothing to fear from me. Nothing to fear from good ol' Solfred. I mix with all sorts of people, and no one as yet has as much as disturbed a lock of my hair. I have the confidence of one who knows this world, and in a manner of speaking I own this world.

DIARMUID: Are you some hireling sent by Fionn Mac Cool to find out where we are hiding and return to him with the news?

STRANGER: Worry not, I am no hireling of this Fionn Mac Cool nor of any other man. I am that happiest of things and that rarest of things: a poet and a man of wealth. I am also a traveller to these parts, and in these parts I hear much talk of Fionn Mac Cool and the Fianna. Why only today I happened to hear that the woman this Fionn Mac Cool hoped to take for a wife had fled with her lover into the wild countryside. And by this and by that I gather you are the very two that Fionn has vowed to search every corner of Ireland for. But I understand love as I understand all human afflictions and not a word of your presence here in this wood will I breathe to Fionn Mac Cool nor to any of his associates should I happen to meet them.

GRÁINNE: I am thankful for your promise of secrecy about our presence here in this wood. But, as thankful as I am and aware as I am that you are a stranger in this country, I can't but be impressed by your detachment and independence from all the great and little troubles that bother people of great and little standing in Ireland. Are all the people in your native country as free of life's tribulations as yourself?

STRANGER: Not at all, good lady. I have been in many a strange land and all these lands are as familiar to me as my native land; and everywhere I go I find people are forever engaged in little conspiracies and little disputes and they never take time to stand back and observe. But I observe! I observe great and little creatures defend their territories and establish little kingdoms for themselves, until they grow old and not as fast as before and they themselves fall to some new challenger and their territory, their kingdom is lost and gone forever. I have observed all this, and I have resolved not to fall into this way of life. I have decided instead to go my own way as a wanderer and observer.

DIARMUID: It must be a lonely life for you, to wander this rich world and never say to yourself 'There is something here of beauty that I would claim for my own.'

STRANGER: It is not for you to say that my life is lonely, you that are not master of your own fate but live in fear of every noise on the wind, lest it be a sign that the people that are searching for you have caught up with you. As for me, I am happy to see all things as but a shadow and go my way just comparing shadow with shadow. And speaking of going my way, I'm on my way this minute. I am the guest of some local chieftain. I find that chieftains and kings throughout this world never tire of hearing of my philosophy. It is, I suspect, a pleasant diversion from the troubled lives they lead. Good night and may you find some respite on own your troubled journey.

(Exit Stranger)

GRÁINNE: What an interesting stranger that was!

DIARMUID: We are two people on a journey that has no foreseeable end, and we can expect to be beset by many terrors and trials and for these reasons alone we would be well advised to pay no heed to the boastful talk of strangers.

GRÁINNE: You speak with a brave sort of pessimism, Diarmuid. It is true that I have abandoned my palace home and you have left behind your warrior-companions; but these are not the greatest of evils. Have we not our love to share all the long day as we wander the trackless wastes of Ireland, and as we feed on the berries of the forests and salmon from the rivers can we not also take delight in the many strangers we will meet and the fabulous stories they have to tell?

DIARMUID: I would dearly love to sleep, but I fear this wood is alive with people who are searching for us.

GRÁINNE *(embracing Diarmuid)*: Sleep my love !

Sleep my love sleep tonight
Ancient lovers knew our plight –
To fear to walk in the sun,
To fear to rest in the night

The stag eastward does not sleep
The hornless doe does not rest
The grouse sleeps not in the heath
The lively linnet shuns her nest
Fionn's men are on our trail

Diarmuid, I will watch the while
That Fionn's search will fail
And I will have you all the while

Sleep Diarmuid, my love, and I will keep watch.

(Diarmuid begins to enter the bothy, only to suddenly spring to his feet and prepare for combat.)

DIARMUID: Our pursuers are all around us.

(Enter Angus-of-the-Birds.)

ANGUS-OF-THE-BIRDS: You have no cause to fear me, Diarmuid. For I am none other than Angus-of-the-Birds your foster father, and I have long ago pledged myself to your protection. This very moment is a moment of great danger for you; for Fionn Mac Cool is nearby and ready to avenge himself on you for the stealing of his bride. But fear not Diarmuid and Gráinne, for this cloak that I wear has magic properties; and if you two fugitives hide within the folds of this same cloak you will both be able to make your escape unseen by Fionn and his people.

DIARMUID: My heart rejoices at your coming to our assistance, my dear foster father. I will be greatly pleased if you spirit Gráinne away to some safe hiding-place. But I fear I myself cannot avail of the offer to steal away under the protection of your cloak; for I am a warrior and a warrior is duty-bound to stand his ground and fight his way out of trouble.

ANGUS: Very well, my foster son. I will spirit Gráinne away to the Headland of the Two Swallows, and if you Diarmuid happen to survive this encounter with Fionn Mac Cool, you may join us there and Gráinne and I will be more than happy to see you.

(*Exit Angus-of-the-Birds and Gráinne.*)

DIARMUID: Fionn and his people have found me. (*Diarmuid goes to the right as music plays. Music stops.*) Who goes there?

THE VOICE OF OISÍN: Not an enemy of yours, Diarmuid, but your friend Oisín and if you come this way no harm will befall you.

DIARMUID: I won't go that of yours until I know where Fionn is waiting. (*Off, music resumes. Diarmuid goes to the left. Music stops.*) Who goes there?

VOICE OF OSCAR: Your friend Oscar. Come this way and I will fight to preserve your life even at the cost of my own.

DIARMUID: I won't go that way of yours until I know where Fionn is waiting. (*Off, music resumes. Diarmuid goes to the left. Music stops.*) Who goes there?

VOICE OF CONÁN MAOL: This is the brave Conán Maol. Come this way and you will have nothing to fear. Fionn Mac Cool lives in great fear of me.

DIARMUID: I am determined to make my escape past Fionn Mac Cool, so that Fionn Mac Cool cannot blame any of my one-time comrades for my escape. (*Diarmuid goes to the left and shouts:*) I will pass this way, Fionn, I will pass the way you are guarding yourself.

(*Diarmuid jumps in exit. Moments later Fionn enters.*)

FIONN: The young and athletic Diarmuid has eluded me one more time. But, if he did elude me, he did not do so without the help and assistance of the Fianna, the same Fianna I brought along with me to search for Diarmuid and Gráinne. Very well, if the Fianna bear more loyalty to Diarmuid than they do to me, I will hire other men to find Diarmuid and Gráinne and hand them over to me.

ACT TWO – SCENE THREE

'Headland of the Two Swallows'. Mountain on backdrop.

As Gráinne and Angus-of-the-Birds wait, they walk about to give expression to their anxiety.

GRÁINNE: Hours have passed since we bid farewell to Diarmuid and all the while I am left wondering did he survive his encounter with Fionn or is his young body lying in wet clay as I speak.

ANGUS: Do not let your mind be overtaken with morbid imaginings. Diarmuid is young and brave and all times we must be of the belief that Diarmuid will survive. Only when you see with your own eyes the body of Diarmuid with the breath of life no longer in it must you ever begin to think of Diarmuid as dead.

GRÁINNE: Your words should inspire me with hope, but they only fill me with foreboding.

ANGUS: The ways of a warrior are different, the ways of a warrior are –

(Enter Diarmuid.)

GRÁINNE *(running to Diarmuid)*: Oh how great is my delight to see you, Diarmuid.

DIARMUID: There is no time to take delight in my survival. Fionn does not rest in his desire for vengeance, and we have to make our way from this spot at once.

GRÁINNE: This is a weary and a troubled life we lead. Wherever we cook our food we cannot eat there; wherever we eat our food we cannot sleep there; and wherever we sleep one night we cannot eat or sleep there the following night. Surely we deserve some rest from this life of constant journeying?

DIARMUID: These thoughts of yours, Gráinne, are unworthy. We must make haste.

ANGUS: Let us pause briefly and allow me to make a suggestion. There is one spot in this island of Ireland where Fionn is unlikely to search for you. I speak of the Wood of Duvros. In that wood there is a special tree, and this tree is guarded by an ugly one-eyed giant by the name of Shavran the Surly. How that magic tree came to be in the Wood of Duvros and how Shavran the Surly came to guard that tree is a story in itself.

GRÁINNE: Everybody knows that story. The story of how many years ago two women of the Fairy people by the names of Aoife and Aine fell into jealous dispute as to which of their husbands was the better hurler. Aoife was married to a captain in the Fianna and Aine was married to one of her own people, that is to say the people of the Fairy. So, as a means of settling the dispute, 'twas agreed that the men of the Fianna should play a hurling match against the men of the Fairy in order to determine who were the better hurlers. The match was to be played near Loch Lene. The Fairy people came from their own land and they brought with them food for the journey and the food they brought consisted of crimson nuts, the sweetest of apples and juicy rowan berries. But, as the Fairy people were passing by the Wood of Duvros, one rowan berry of the berries they were carrying accidentally fell to the ground and it took seed and a tree grew on the spot.

DIARMUID: And the remainder of the story is predictable. The fruit of this rowan tree was intoxicating as fine wine and all who ate of it lived beyond their natural life span. But the Fairy folk were of no mind to share the fruit of this magic tree with mortals; and that is why the Fairy folk employed Shavran the Surly to guard the tree. And no weapon is capable of killing Shavran the Surly, no weapon except three strokes from his own iron club which he never leaves out of his hands be he awake or asleep. Is it any wonder that not even the Fianna dare to hunt in the same wood?

ANGUS: And that is my point. A wood where even the Fianna dare not hunt is surely a place where you both will be safe from the vengeful Fionn.

DIARMUID: It does seem as if the Wood of Duvros is the only place in Ireland where Gráinne and I can rest awhile. So to the Wood of Duvros Gráinne and I must go. But walk with us a little while, Angus-of-the-Birds, before we say goodbye and you return to the solitary ways of your magic and I attempt to come to some arrangement with this terrible giant Shavran the Surly.

GRÁINNE: We can delay no longer. Fionn and his people are here.

(Diarmuid, Gráinne and Angus-of-the-Birds make hurried exit. Enter Fionn.)

FIONN: I believe Diarmuid and Gráinne have fled from this place this instant. Indeed, I should be thankful in some ways that so far I have failed to catch up with them. For it is true that since I began this pursuit of Diarmuid and Gráinne I have completely shaken off the dark feelings of mourning. Yes, while I will never rest until I make my capture of the two fugitives, I am happy to say that my old mood has returned where I am pleased to delight in the prospect of each new day and the chance of enjoying the thrill of the hunt.

The blood in me rises again
For the music of the chase:
The stags belling in the glen
And my hounds hot in the race

I want to hear the sound again
Of my hounds in great uproar,
As the stag-flesh they do rend
And make the grass red with gore

But it's not the stag I now chase
But Diarmuid thief of my wife:
Diarmuid, cause of my disgrace,
Diarmuid will pay with his life

(Enter Oisín and Oscar.)

OISÍN: We are happy to overhear that the dark days of mourning are over for you, Fionn and that once more your chief delight is to partake in the chase.

OSCAR: We also realise that the elopement of Diarmuid and Gráinne weighs heavily upon your mind and we intend to assist you in every way possible in capturing the unfaithful two.

FIONN: Do you mistake me for a fool? And a fool I would be if I had not realised long ago that those who have resorted to every trick and device in helping Diarmuid and Gráinne stay at large were the same members of the Fianna that I innocently enlisted with a view to they helping me find them.

OISÍN: Jealousy must have poisoned your mind, Fionn; for only a poisonous jealousy would have you cast doubts on the loyalty of the Fianna to you as their leader.

FIONN: I have learnt the hard way that the Fianna are more loyal to the traitor Diarmuid than to me their rightful leader. And that is why I have arranged to enlist the help of men who soldier for money to hunt down the unfaithful two.

OISÍN: I am saddened by the drift of your talk, Fionn. For it is an evil day that portends even more evil days when Fionn Mac Cool places more trust in mercenaries than in the Fianna.

FIONN: Evil or not, Oisín, I have arranged to employ professional trackers to find Diarmuid and Gráinne. And, as luck would have it, two such trackers make their way to me this minute.

(Enter two trackers. They are dressed in neat animal skins but bear a greater assortment of knives on their persons than any of the Fianna.)

FIONN: I take it you are the two trackers who I sent for and who I heard are so adept at chasing a man or a beast that as you walk along the earth no man or animal that has passed the same way within a fortnight escapes your notice.

FIRST TRACKER: We are the same two you speak of, and we have come to do business.

SECOND TRACKER: Provided you make it worth our while, of course.

FIONN: I suspect you two fellows are not much given to sentiment; but let me remind you that when Diarmuid Ó Duivne stole my bride, Gráinne the king's daughter, Diarmuid broke his pledge of honour to the Fianna and so more than deserves to be hunted down like animal quarry.

SECOND TRACKER: You can save yourself the trouble of making excuses for your own actions, Fionn. All we want is rich payment and we will deliver Diarmuid and Gráinne to you.

FIRST TRACKER: We will hunt down Diarmuid like you would hunt a stag.

> We will hunt down Diarmuid
> Like you would hunt a stag;
> It's not glory we want
> But gold, gold in the bag
>
> Give us the gold, Fionn
> We care not for poetry
> Nor for tales of old
> Give us the gold, Fionn
>
> Men die in the field
> Men die like wild dogs
> But gold don't lose value
> While flesh rots in the bog
>
> We will hunt down Diarmuid
> Like you would hunt a stag
> It's not glory we want
> But gold, gold in the bag

FIONN: Do not fear, gentlemen, I will pay you handsomely if you fulfill the task I set you. And in the task I set you I give you a choice: either bring me the head of a particular warrior or else bring me a fistful of berries.

OISÍN: The head of Diarmuid is what he is asking of you. And, if you were a force of two hundred fighting men, Diarmuid would still get the better of you.

FIRST TRACKER: And what about the fistful of berries he is looking for?

OISÍN: It is an even harder task to get those berries. For the berries Fionn speaks of are Fairy berries growing on a magic tree in the Duvros wood, and that tree is guarded night and day by a terrible giant by the name of Shavran the Surly.

FIRST TRACKER *(To second tracker)*: Fionn has given us a choice of task and the second task is as bad as the first.

SECOND TRACKER *(to first tracker)*: We've come a long way to do business and it would be a shame to go back empty-handed.

FIRST TRACKER *(To Fionn)*: We will get you the berries, because we're not of a mind to let anybody accuse us of being afraid of Shavran the Surly.

FIONN: Well promised! The lure of gold may be all that motivates you two; but the words you utter have more sincerity than the false promises coming from my fellow-warriors in the Fianna. One way or another, I will have my revenge.

ACT TWO – SCENE FOUR

A sunlit Wood of Duvros. Trees on backdrop and a particular magic tree at back. Shavran the Surly is asleep at base of tree.

SHAVRAN THE SURLY: Shavran the Surly wakes up. Shavran not very smart, but Shavran smart enough to let nobody come near this magic tree. Shavran the Surly kill anybody that try to eat berries from this tree.

> A big big giant am I
> I have but one big eye
> I am slow in the walk
> And I am slow to talk
> But I can grab your neck
> And give a mighty kick
> And you die like a rat
> If you dare cross my path

> I know no one loves me
> I know they all fear me
> That's how it is with me
> And that's how it should be

Shavran the Surly go get nuts for breakfast. *(Shavran the Surly goes to exit; but as soon as he turns to do so Diarmuid tosses a stone on the stage. Shavran the Surly turns in direction of the sound.)* Shavran the Surly hear sound he don't like.

VOICE OF DIARMUID: Shavran, Shavran, this is the warrior Diarmuid Ó Duivne and not alone do I promise that I won't take any berries from the magic tree, I also promise that I will kill any man who would attempt to eat the fruit of the same tree

SHAVRAN THE SURLY: Shavran the Surly like what Diarmuid say, because now Shavran and Diarmuid protect the magic tree. Shavran no longer alone.

DIARMUID: That is right, Shavran. I will be your friend, and together we will stop any stranger from eating the berries of the magic tree.

SHAVRAN: I was hungry before you came along, Diarmuid, and I am still hungry now that you are here and so I go for breakfast.

(Exit Shavran the Surly.)

DIARMUID: At last I found a place where Gráinne and I won't be bothered by Fionn. But I speak too soon, for do I not hear the sound of two sets of footsteps.

(Enter the two trackers.)

FIRST TRACKER: Are you Diarmuid Ó Duivne who has fled with the king's daughter?

DIARMUID: What is it to you that I am Diarmuid Ó Duivne, for I am Diarmuid Ó Duivne!

SECOND TRACKER: Well, Diarmuid, let me tell you that Fionn Mac Cool has hired us two either to return with your head or else return to him with a fistful of berries from the magic tree yonder.

DIARMUID: The choice in task that Fionn has offered you is not much in the way of a choice. But choose what task it is to be, ye miserable hirelings: chose between combat with me or taking the magic berries and incurring the wrath of the terrible giant Shavran the Surly.

FIRST TRACKER: We're more of a mind to engage you in combat.

(Diarmuid wrestles with both trackers, quickly overcoming both and binding them both hand and foot with their own belts. Enter Gráinne.)

GRÁINNE: More trouble, and not a day has lapsed since I fled from Tara with you, Diarmuid, without its share of trouble. But I was just thinking there as I overheard the trackers speak of Fionn's interest in acquiring a fistful of berries from the magic tree; I was thinking how wonderful it must be to taste those berries and how wonderful again it must be to experience the intoxication and invigoration of those berries.

DIARMUID: Has it not occurred to you that if we go against Shavran the Surly and chose to eat those berries we will lose whatever chance we have of finding peace and contentment here in the Wood of Duvros! Do you not realise that it is only his fear of Shavran the Surly that stops Fionn from hunting us down this minute?

GRÁINNE: Life is for enjoyment, and I will never eat again until I taste those magic berries.

DIARMUID: That being so, I have no choice but to go and challenge Shavran for the right to eat those berries.

FIRST TRACKER: Will you free our hands and feet and we will go and challenge Shavran for the right to pluck those berries and we will bring them to Gráinne.

DIARMUID: I can't agree to set you free to go and challenge Shavran the Surly. For I have just stopped short of taking your lives, and I don't want you to die at the sight of a giant so horrible as Shavran the Surly.

SECOND TRACKER: We are not so delicate that we would die at the sight of a giant. Will you at least set us free, so that we can at least watch you in combat with Shavran?

DIARMUID: I suppose no harm can come of you watching me in combat with Shavran.

(Diarmuid frees the two trackers and exits to face Shavran. The two trackers go to Diarmuid's exit point to watch.)

GRÁINNE: How helpless is a woman in this world! Not a day goes by without my man Diarmuid coming under threat of his life, and all I can do while Diarmuid fights for his life is wait and worry.

FIRST TRACKER: The giant has refused Diarmuid permission to pluck the magic berries.

SECOND TRACKER: The giant is attacking Diarmuid with his spiked iron club. Diarmuid has ducked the blow from the iron club, Diarmuid has jumped on top of the giant, Diarmuid has torn the iron club from the giant's own hands; and now Diarmuid prepares to attack the giant with the giant's own club. One! *(off, sound of first impact of club on giant)* two! *(sound of second impact of club on giant)* three! *(sound of third impact of club on giant).* Shavran is dead!

(Enter Diarmuid.)

DIARMUID: Shavran is no more. *(Taking fistfuls of berries from the tree and sharing them with Gráinne and the two trackers.)* Now we call can eat the berries from the magic tree, not that I imagine there is much luck in eating those berries.

SECOND TRACKER: Business is business, and we must return to Fionn Mac Cool with these berries he has asked for.

(Exit the two trackers.)

DIARMUID: How wonderfully invigorating these berries are! I've completely forgotten that just a few moments ago I was in a life-and-death struggle with a giant.

GRÁINNE: These berries are the most delightful food I have ever tasted. How sweet it must be to be one of the immortal little folk. The food they eat is sweeter than the food we mortals eat, and the clothes they wear are finer than the clothes we mortals wear; and, as is quite different from the lot of us mortals, the little folk have all eternity in which to dance and love.

DIARMUID: Never were the workings of your imagination, Gráinne, more at odds with the danger of the moment in which we find ourselves. Fionn and his people are sure to be upon us any second. Come, let us hide behind the tree.

(Diarmuid and Gráinne hide behind the tree. Enter Fionn, Oisín, Oscar and Dering.)

FIONN *(with berry or two in hand)*: I sense the smell of Diarmuid's skin upon these berries, and, unless I am greatly mistaken and I don't think I am, the fugitives Diarmuid and Gráinne are hiding behind the magic tree over there.

OISÍN: What great jealousy has gripped your mind Fionn for you to think that Diarmuid and Gráinne would hide where you are most likely to find them.

FIONN *(brusquely)*: Place the chessboard on the ground, Oisín, and we can while away the midday hour in a game of chess.

(Oisín sets up the chessboard on the ground and he and Fionn begin to play. Fionn hums to himself as the game proceeds.)

OSCAR *(excitedly)*: You have the beating of Oisín once again, Fionn!

FIONN: There is but one move left that would allow you win the game, Oisín, and I defy you and your advisers to recognize what move that is.

DERING: You have set us all a puzzle, Fionn, and I can't say that I know the answer.

(Diarmuid, who is watching the game from behind the tree, throws a berry down on the piece that has the winning of the game.)

OISÍN *(moving the piece)*: In all my games of chess with you, Fionn, it's the first time I have defeated you.

FIONN: It's no wonder that you have defeated me, Oisín, when you happen to have Diarmuid prompting you from behind yonder tree.

OISÍN: Jealously, Jealousy, Fionn! Diarmuid would never linger behind the magic tree and he knowing you want to kill him.

FIONN *(shouting)*: Which of us is telling the truth, Diarmuid?

DIARMUID: Your judgement is as sound as it always was, Fionn. For it is quite true that Gráinne and I have been here all the while.

(Diarmuid gives three kisses to Gráinne in full sight of Fionn.)

FIONN: I promise that you will pay with your life for those three kisses, Diarmuid.

DIARMUID: I will face you in combat now, Fionn. For I can find no refuge from your hatred, and this great hatred of yours I don't deserve. In all my time as a warrior I defended you and the Fianna in all manner of war and strife.

OSCAR: Diarmuid is telling the truth, Fionn. No warrior has given you greater service. Grant him the pardon he deserves.

FIONN: I will not do that.

OSCAR: I promise solemnly as a warrior that I will let no man harm Diarmuid. Diarmuid is now under my protection.

(Diarmuid and Oscar challenge Fionn in swordplay and make their way past Fionn and make their exit. Meanwhile Gráinne makes hurried exit.)

DERING: Look now even loyal warriors of the Fianna are facing each other at swordpoint. Fionn, can't you see it time you softened your heart and made peace with Diarmuid.

FIONN: The day Diarmuid stole my bride Gráinne a poison entered my heart and that poison will fester for as long as Diarmuid and Gráinne are together.

(Enter Angus-of-the-Birds.)

ANGUS: What unhappy scene is this! People running in terror of their lives and swords drawn among the Fianna themselves. I beseech you, Fionn, to bring to an end this sad quarrel with Diarmuid.

OISÍN: You would be well advised to listen to Angus-of-the-Birds and all your comrades in the Fianna. Otherwise, the Fianna will turn on each other and lawlessness break out in Ireland.

ANGUS-OF-THE-BIRDS: Oisín speaks the truth, Fionn. The king himself is unhappy that your quarrel with Diarmuid threatens the peace of his entire kingdom. And as for the queen, she has known no peace since this unhappy business began. End this quarrel now before greater tragedy afflicts us all.

FIONN: The fear of great tragedy enters all human hearts from time to time. Even the heart of a warrior knows fear of this kind. And, for my part, I would never wish to be responsible for division entering the ranks of the Fianna. So, yes, I will say that I no longer intend to slay Diarmuid. No doubt you will wish to arrange peace terms on behalf of your foster son, Angus-of-the-Birds?

ANGUS: Peace terms can be arranged later. Now I must haste to the High-King with the good news that Fionn Mac Cool no longer desires to kill Diarmuid Ó Duivne.

ACT THREE – SCENE ONE

Banquet hall at Tara. The party music of Act Two, Scene One is reprised. The festivities here have reached a stage that they are not seen to reach on that previous occasion.

Diarmuid and Gráinne, King and Queen, Fionn, Oisín, Oscar, Dering, Conán Maol, Angus-of-the-Birds and musician and the servants are all on stage.

CORMAC: For many a long day I doubted that things would ever come to such a happy ending. But let me not recall the bad times now that Diarmuid and Gráinne are wed. Diarmuid and Gráinne are wed and all is settled for a bright and untroubled future for all here present.

ANGUS: You must take credit, your Majesty, for finding it in your heart to accept Diarmuid as son-in-law and Fionn Mac Cool deserves credit for making peace with Diarmuid.

CORMAC: I said it before on previous occasion, I said it before on previous occasion only for subsequent events to mock my words; but I say it again, I say it again in different context, I say it again without fear of misfortune – How happy I am today !

How happy I am today
As father and a king;
My child I give away
To warrior bold and strong.
She will know no poor day,
Nor will she suffer wrong;
From love she will not stray
As summer's day is long –

(Gráinne taps her father on the shoulder, bringing his speaking to a sudden stop.)

GRÁINNE: Those words I heard before in circumstances I would rather forget. Besides, Father, have you never heard of the superstition that it is unlucky to tinker with the words of a poem to suit a new occasion?

CORMAC: Have you never heard, dear daughter, of the more venerable superstition that it is unlucky to interrupt a poet or singer in performance?

GRÁINNE: You promised, Father, to announce the details of the peace settlement with Diarmuid.

CORMAC: I promise so, and what I promised I will do, Gráinne. Attention, everybody! As king and father, I am more than happy that my daughter Gráinne is wed to Diarmuid Ó Duivne and that their days of wandering throughout Ireland are at an end. I welcome this marriage, and I welcome the peace it brings with it, and I will be as generous in the terms with which I greet these events as these events require. To my daughter, Gráinne, I give back her cantred of land in Kesh-Corran, and to Diarmuid I grant full pardon and to Diarmuid also I return the land that was his. Indeed, I don't doubt that in Diarmuid's own time there won't be a man in Ireland with more gold and money and more cows and cattle than him.

FIONN: For my part, I promise that neither I, nor the Fianna will hunt in Diarmuid's lands without his permission.

DIARMUID: These are generous terms indeed. And, as measure, of our gratitude and respect, Gráinne and I will make our home a good distance from the places freqeuented by your Majesty and by the Fianna.

CORMAC: Gracious terms have been offered and they have been kindly accepted. Let the feasting continue!

(A drunken Conán Maol approaches Gráinne.)

CONÁN: This is as good a do as I've ever been at. *(Indicating wine in drinking cup)* This is the best yet. *(Gleefully)* My head is wrecked. *(Conán Maol spills wine on Gráinne's dress)* I'm so sorry, but I reckon that Diarmuid has done worse in his time.

GRÁINNE *(moving away)*: I suppose he has.

(The space forestage that was occupied by Gráinne and Conán Maol is taken up by the Queen and Fionn Mac Cool.)

THE QUEEN: It's the first time in years that I have been able to smile. But now all is settled as well as it could be. Now the names Gráinne and Diarmuid will be forever linked in the minds of people, and people will say that from troubled beginnings Gráinne and Diarmuid went on to lead lives of peace and contentment. I am so glad.

FIONN MAC COOL: I'm pleased to hear that your days of worry have come to an end, your ladyship; but I myself had hoped this long while that the name that would be forever linked with the name of Gráinne would have been my own.

THE QUEEN: You must cast aside all thoughts of what-might-have-been, Fionn. *(The King shouts: Let everybody dance!)* Surely, Fionn, you will join in the dance by way of token that all has caused division and strife is no longer of concern among us.

FIONN: For me to dance at the wedding of Diarmuid and Gráinne is more than I am prepared to do.

(Fionn exits, as all but the servants begin spirited dance. Troubled as she is by Fionn's attitude, the queen is last to join the dance.)

ACT THREE – SCENE TWO

The home of Diarmuid and Gráinne, in the west of the country.

Diarmuid and Gráinne are seated either side of a fire. A male and female child are at play with a ball.

GRÁINNE: As evening draws in, how sweet it is to sit by the fire and contemplate past times.

DIARMUID: Most of our past times were of the troubled sort and you were most inclined to complain at the time.

GRÁINNE: That is more or less my point. As it can be sweet to contemplate a storm from the safety of one's own home, it is sweet to contemplate the trouble and adversity of other days when you are safe in the knowledge that all is well.

> The danger we once knew
> Our love it does renew;
> The fears of other days
> Are gone like a bad dream.
> The danger of other days
> Our love it does renew;
> The fears of other days
> Are gone like a bad dream.

DIARMUID *(calling to children)*: Come here, Donncha and Druinneach Dhil, and I will tell you of truly happy times. *(Children gather at Diarmuid's feet.)* Only those who are free know what it is to be happy. And those who best know how to be free and happy are the men of the Fianna. When I was but a young man I was happy to be a warrior in the Fianna, a warrior and bodyguard to Fionn Mac Cool the leader of the Fianna. To give you both an idea of how much Fionn Mac Cool and the Fianna valued freedom, I need only tell you what was the favourite music of Fionn Mac Cool. You might think that Fionn's favourite music would be sweet music played on the harp while everybody sat around eating and drinking. But it was not as you think. For Fionn's favourite music was the noise of the hunt itself and all the other sounds of the wild countryside. But these thoughts only serve to make me sad. It's time you were asleep my good children.

(Exit children.)

GRÁINNE: A sadness has crept over your normally shining face, Diarmuid.

DIARMUID: It's just that my head is filled with thoughts of times when I was a champion in the Fianna.

> Happy I should be
> Happy I am not
> The joy of family
> Is less than my loss.

> Oh to be on a hill
> With the Fianna strong,
> The hounds about to kill
> And the day not long
> And the day not long
> And the day not long

GRÁINNE: I regret I changed your mood to one of sadness.

(Off, sound of hounds barking.)

DIARMUID: I know what causes those hounds to bark in the distance. They bark at a wild boar, not an ordinary wild boar but a special creature, that is to say a creature of the people of the other world.

(Off, barking again.)

GRÁINNE: I know also that those hounds bark at no ordinary animal, but at a magic boar that has taken the life of many a warrior. But neither the affairs of the Fianna, nor the affairs of the other world bother us anymore. We have our children and we have each other and that is all that matters.

DIARMUID: I am still a warrior and I intend to go out and slay that evil boar that has taken the life of many a champion.

(Diarmuid rises to go.)

GRÁINNE *(running to Diarmuid)*: Diarmuid, please don't go out. The night is not of the best and no good can come from your pursuing that magic beast.

DIARMUID: I am resolved to slay that boar.

(Exit Diarmuid.)

GRÁINNE: I was too quick to boast that the dangers of other days were gone for good. Now Diarmuid's life is threatened anew.

(Curtain closes and opens to signify the passing of the night and the beginning of a new day.)

GRÁINNE: Morning has come, and still Diarmuid hasn't returned. I fear evil. I fear it with all my mind and body. *(Enter a changed Diarmuid.)* Tell me Diarmuid no harm has come of you, tell me!

DIARMUID: I can only tell you what is true. I slew the magic boar; but in the course of the struggle the boar managed to poison me with one of its bristles, and the poison from a bristle of that otherworldly boar is fatal. My strength is ebbing away. I must lie down.

(Diarmuid lies down on bed.)

GRÁINNE: What am I to do?

DIARMUID: Bring the children to me. I want to speak to them one last time.

GRÁINNE: No, the children must not witness a tragedy such as this.

(Enter Fionn, Oisín, Oscar, Dering and Conán Maol.)

FIONN: We were hunting in these parts, and we heard that the magic boar that had taken the life of many a noble warrior had been slaughtered. I instantly assumed that the man who dealt the death-blow to this evil boar was none other than the famous Diarmuid Ó Duivne, and looking around me here I don't believe I was mistaken. I am pleased to see you like this, Diarmuid, and 'tis a pity the women of Ireland can't see you now with all the vigour and beauty that once was yours departed from your body.

DIARMUID: It lies within your ability, Fionn, to restore me to full health.

FIONN *(sardonically)*: How could I do that?

DIARMUID: Ever since you ate the Salmon of Knowledge at the Boyne you have the power to cure any disease with a drink of water from the palm of your hand.

FIONN: It wouldn't please me to give you a drink of that sort.

DIARMUID: You gave me drink from your palm once upon a time when I saved your life and you have no right to refuse me the same drink now.

FIONN: You don't deserve such a drink from me. You don't deserve any favour from me ever since you stole Gráinne, my bride-to-be from Tara.

DIARMUID: It was not as you make out. I was never guilty of stealing Gráinne from you, for it was Gráinne herself that put me under bonds to help her escape. And I well deserve a drink from you considering all the times that I saved your life.

(Fionn pours water from a flask on to his palm, but before he gives the water to Diarmuid he lets it slip through his fingers.)

OSCAR: I swear by my weapons, Fionn, that, if you don't give water from your palm to Diarmuid quickly, the only one of us two to make it out of here alive will be the strongest.

(Fionn pours water from the flask on to his palm once again, but once again lets the water slips through his fingers. Diarmuid dies.)

OSCAR: Diarmuid is dead, and I swear I will have your life, Fionn.

OISÍN: My son, it is true that you would be within your rights to take the life of Fionn, as would any member of the Fianna, but let us not bring another sorrow upon us.

GRÁINNE *(embracing the dead Diarmuid)*: The threat of vengeance that has followed us all our time together has finally visited you, Diarmuid my love. The life has gone from you and I am left alone.

(Curtain closes and opens to signifgy the passing of few hours. Diarmuid's body has been removed and buried and only Gráinne is onstage.)

GRÁINNE: His comrades have buried Diarmuid Ó Duivne in a manner befitting a warrior, and Diarmuid was the bravest of warriors. How fitting that it was Angus-of-the-Birds who made proud lament over his dead body.

(Enter Fionn.)

FIONN: Diarmuid is dead and buried, yet none of his comrades are of a mind to depart this place.

GRÁINNE: There is a completeness about the death of anyone, not least about the death of a hero. His comrades are as much marking the death of Diarmuid as mourning him. Diarmuid's memory will live on, and your part in his death will sully your memory.

FIONN: I tell you true that each time I poured water on to my palm I had every intention of saving the life of Diarmuid; but then an image of you Gráinne flashed before my mind and as if they had a mind of their own my fingers opened to let the water-of-life fall to the floor.

GRÁINNE: Well, you have plenty of time to regret your actions.

FIONN: And what about you, Gráinne?

GRÁINNE: I recall an occasion when Diarmuid and I met a foreigner on our travels, and this foreigner claimed that he regarded everything in life as but a shadow. Now for me also everything is but a shadow.

FIONN MAC COOL: And would you share the shadows with one such as me who never wavered in his love of you?

GRÁINNE: It's a thought.

(Enter Angus-of-the-Birds, followed by Oisín, Oscar, Dering and Conán Maol. They realise as they enter that they come upon Fionn and Gráinne in intimate conversation.)

ANGUS: Diarmuid is among the spirits of air now, and not a day will go by without I hearing him speak. And as for you, Fionn, women and children will die as a result of you insisting on his death.

FIONN MAC COOL: It was never my wish that Diarmuid should die, only that Gráinne should be my wife.

> I killed a comrade
> Not in battlefield red:
> I have killed a comrade
> Killed him is his own bed.
> All for the love of woman
> Jealousy overtook my head;
> All for the love of woman
> Jealousy overtook my head.

(The company sans Fionn and Gráinne continue:)

> Fionn has troubled mind
> His mind will know no rest
> A woman's love he has won
> A comrade he has betrayed
> Dishonour to the Fianna !
> Dishonour to the Fianna !
> Fionn his dear wife has saved
> But Diarmuid is in his grave

DERING: No one can bring the dead back to life. It's time that we all went about our normal business.

(Without accompaniment Gráinne sings:)

> The world is but a toy
> A woman needs a boy
> I am as happy with Fionn
> As I was with Diarmuid
>
> Fol-del-dil-dil-deroy
> Fol-del-dil-dil-deroy

(Gráinne exits in distracted fashion. She is followed by Fionn.)

OISÍN: Not much good can come of these recent events. Indeed, I foresee a time when not alone honour and chivalry disappear from the world but when also the magic that we take for granted will meet with disbelief. Priest, physician and sage will all laugh at the magic as something only worthy of children.

(Ends)

Like it, or Lump it

A Mope's Memoir

BY JOHN MURPHY

*Follow lowly psychiatric client John Murphy
as he backs the wrong causes in his twenties
but then see how much later he comes to
find friends among the artistically
inclined in his locality...*

"Everybody's hustlin'."

Donovan Leitch

CONTENTS

$\mathcal{I}$NTRODUCTION

I speak of the public house expert who, of course, is no expert at all.

If you are up to the level of a public house expert, you should have no difficulty taking in and understanding this autobiography. The public house expert will have some understanding that both R.D. Laing and the earlier C.J. Jung addressed the topics of mental illness and the supernatural; and it has been my experience that the public house expert is more than certain that these two authorities have said all there is to say concerning mental illness and the supernatural. Fair dues to the public house expert! But I think he's wrong.

The public house expert may also insist that a psychiatric client can never really get anything right. Here, I have to admit that this opinion of the public house expert is accurate if applied to me. In this book I really have to play down the extent to which all my best efforts went awry, even if whenever I believe I can get away with it I do glory in my failures.

You might, of course, wonder have you any worthwhile business with me. And in this regard, I cannot advise you one way or other, only than to say, for boast that I return to again and again, that the more solid citizens of this world are clear in their determination to have nothing to do with me.

John Murphy
2008

1

EARLY DAYS

A NEW SPECIES

I speak of a novel phenomenon. That is the recent phenomenon of almost entirely disengaged psychiatric patients in walkabout in society. With the kind of forensic exactitude that historians love, I can say that this new species first began to appear at bus stops and on high streets in the 1960s with the introduction of Largactil – a drug whose name is derived from the word 'large' in the recognition of the large number of psychiatrists who prescribed it! These very same gatherings of this half liberated people in towns and cities may have prompted some few onlookers of the more sentimental or perhaps wiser kind to momentarily think that there might be a book to come from such gatherings. Here is one such book … and it is scarcely addressed to those others who, when they witness gatherings of the new species, only gather their belongings closer to themselves and all the more wish themselves by their firesides watching detergent commercials, unthreatened.

OLD IRELAND

I just caught the last of old Ireland where horsepower was horse power in the performance of farming tasks. The only possible vice was alcohol. And everybody went to Sunday Mass.

If I never inherited the cunning, thrift and industriousness that was such a feature of those times, I can say that I brought some little commonsense with me from a time that was no more than a generation or so away from the era during which, when people rose in the morning and were desiring of a cup of tea, they first had to set and light a fire.

THE MAGIC IN MY CHILDHOOD

Even if the meanest writer is wont to mine his childhood for magical detail à la Dylan Thomas and Patrick Kavanagh, I can't invent what wasn't there. The few remaining sensual memories of childhood are of food. The very 1950s memory of having gone fasting to Mass on a Sunday morning and returning to a breakfast of sausage and black pudding. The pleasantly sour taste of milk enjoyed from a former whiskey bottle in the schoolyard in warm weather. And the little sachet of sherbet powder and accompanying little lollipop purchased in a village shop, this little treat always tasting a little bitter and so somehow suggestive of the exotic.

But what magic there was in my childhood will only go to bore the reader because it was necessarily of the intellectual kind. Like I walking out of an evening to the little public roadway to meet a farm worker who earlier left the farm by bicycle but who kindly returned to deliver a copy of Tom Sawyer into my impatient hand.

THE OLD CATHOLICISM

Of course, the old medieval Catholicism was all about the countryside in those days. But I have to rely on someone else's recall to note that a green-covered Catechism attempted to warn me when I was no more than seven or eight of the dangers of 'calumny and detraction'. But even I, of the poor recall, cannot fail to remember that in national school I had impressed upon me some bizarre details concerning Christ's torture and death that I failed to find any further mention of in the Gospels or the Apocrypha[1] or *Ireland's Own*[2] – the most macabre of which details was that Jesus wore but the one garment throughout his life and when the Roman soldiers came to strip Jesus his skin and flesh necessarily came away with his clothing.

---

[1] Biblical or related writings not forming part of the accepted canon of Scripture.
[2] Very traditional Irish magazine published weekly.

$\mathcal{A}$MNESIA

At the admission stage of my most recent and most triumphant hospitalisation yet, I was able to hand in a typed letter by my general practitioner. This letter had been composed and typed up by my general practitioner at a speed that shocked this slowcoach writer; and later in a hospital consulting room this letter left the admission doctor in the hospital in little doubt as to two contrary realities: that no great danger was presented by my current illness and the absolute imperative that I be hospitalised. His work done for him, and mindful of a somewhat new mood in psychiatry, the young admission doctor saw fit to query my childhood.

"Amnesia!" I truthfully – and cheerily – made reply to the doctor's facial expression of one ready for the worst; for I knew only too well that, if any accusatory statement in a psychiatric file is ever to have any consequence, the benefit is likely to accrue only to a doctor or lawyer.

But I am certain of two truths: no one surrenders their reason except on foot of much suffering; and those that deny this to be so are hiding something.

$\mathcal{T}$HE BIG LIE NOW PROMOTED AT EVERY LEVEL

But, of course, the denial that experience is character forming is now a large part of the culture. Need I mention the so called science channels on TV that are doing the best they can to ensure that the day mankind perishes mankind will be in considerably greater state of ignorance than many times in its previous history. Sometimes the denial that experience is character-forming is presented as comedy.

Take that web site and book publishing enterprise known as the *Darwin Awards* that supposedly honours 'those who [supposedly] improve our gene pool by removing themselves from it in a spectacularly stupid manner'. There's no reason to suppose that all those whose sorry and silly end is reported in the *Darwin Awards* were the keepers of 'stupid' genes; and the only scientific conclusion I can draw from the *Darwin Awards* is that its creator, molecular biologist Wendy Northcutt, is the sort of graduate that makes my gripes against university culture appear restrained.

MYSTERY GENE

At the age of four I began to pee too frequently. There was talk of I having to see a doctor about this problem. This was my first time learning that doctors held the solution to all of life's problems. No doubt someday scientists will discover the mystery gene that causes four year olds to pee too frequently. It's no secret what scientists can do.

THE MUCH SNEERED AT FIGHTBACK OF THE HAPPIER CLASS OF LOSER

It is a fact that many of those who begin to half-realise that they are not the most likely to succeed turn to art. This process of failure encouraging a substitute activity is given the ignoble name of displacement by some of the more superior authorities. Sigmund Freud even felt compelled to justify at length the apparently to him puzzling phenomenon of the successful artist … What then of the psychiatric client who goes through life turning out little bits and pieces of art that have a way of ending up lost and that rarely if ever make much of an impact? That manner of psychiatric client is no stranger to me, I being that manner of psychiatric client for most of my life. And yet even at the age of fifty-six I don't – I can't – relinquish the hope that I might achieve some little success.

My creative urge has been there from the beginning. At the age of four or five I dressed up as a tramp and insisted that my photograph be taken. And whereas it would be less than sensible for me to itemise here my every subsequent attempt at artistic statement of both the silly and the sensible kind down the years, I must salute the fact that I have devoted an insane amount of time in this effort.

Paul McCartney admitted in recent years that the 'from me to you' quality of the Beatles' early singles was a deliberate sales pitch … so it will be appropriate for me to ask you, the reader, to sit back and enjoy the presence of a man who could do with your company.

$\mathcal{A}$ LAUGHABLE TRAIT THAT HAS NEVER GONE AWAY

I suppose I also was fond of voicing my little learning from very early on. I once told a farm helper as he worked in the meadow that there were stars so distant from us that their light had yet to reach us.

"I supposed that when it does, they'll put an end to the Shannon Scheme," he replied.

The Shannon Scheme was the name for Ireland's first hydroelectric power station, this power station termed 'a white elephant' by one politician at the time and prompting one comedian to say much later in the 1950s that he was shaving himself with a white elephant. The politician was Eamonn de Valera and the comedian was Jimmy O'Dea.

$\mathcal{T}$HE UN-DESIRED HURLEY STICK

One Christmas day morning of a time when I had learnt the truth about Santa Claus, I nevertheless awoke in some excitement to see precisely what toy this particular Christmas had brought. I had hoped for something that would engage my intellect. But there in the disused fireplace in my bedroom – this location meant to banish any doubts that I might have that I was to be the beneficiary of some stranger making entry to the house in unusual manner – I saw a hurley stick and I felt a great disappointment.

I should explain that a hurley stick is an implement used in the Irish national ball game that is revered for its considerable skill and great entertainment value. But this ball game is at its best the strict preserve of mostly athletic men and most definitely robust men. Strictly the preserve of athletic and robust men and officiated over by men of no less resolute character … even if these latter have been described as demagogues in their view that theirs is the only culture that should prevail.

My deep dismay at the sight of this hurley stick a Christmas long ago explains a lot about me. No matter what, I was not one to go forth and engage my fellow man in ersatz[3] mortal combat on the sports field, win a life partner in the thoroughfare of life and together produce copies of ourselves, preferably exact copies at that. Nor was I one to age wisely and to routinely but perceptively observe – and intermittently remark upon – the various stage points in the decline of the health of body and mind reached by all others in the district in their journey to the grave. I am but a ghost in the world, bringing ghostly insights to you.

---

3 (Of a product) made or used as a substitute, typically an inferior one, for something else.

$\mathcal{I}$NHERITANCE

We also owe the better part of ourselves to other people. From my father I believe come whatever little talent I have for analysis. I remember my father once taking three or four pieces of straw in his hand and explaining to my brothers and me that that the four pieces of straw were stronger when held together. I doubt that such artful comment would be uttered in a family that valued remunerative work to the exclusion of everything else.

I trace my small talent for comedy back to my mother. Indeed, the title of this book refers to a frequent saying of my mother's, this saying of hers always uttered as reminder to somebody or other that they had but one option. On the face of it, the saying *Like it, or lump it* might seem like a harsh rebuke; but the saying always came with the explanation that it was supposedly first uttered by a (named) maidservant in a doctor's house to her doctor master in times when no one dared talk back to doctors. All told, the old saying is quite appropriate to present purposes.

$\mathcal{S}$ONG ENTERS MY LIFE

My very first introduction to popular song occurred in the course of two visits to a local cinema with my father and brothers. The soundtracks of the two movies I saw acquainted me briefly with the fact that song could express yearning. But it was a spirited housekeeper who worked from time to time in the farm house who, brought the record player and four records into our house and thereby could be said to sow a love for songs in my soul that would pretty much dictate the course of my life.

One of the records was a ballad as the term is understood in the international pop world and was titled 'Take Good Care Of Her' and once again I was taken by the capacity of song to express yearning. Another of the records featured Dominic Behan singing two songs of his own: a rebel song titled 'The Patriot Game' and a perhaps more interesting song carefully concealed as a B-side and titled 'Love Is Where You'll Find It'. The latter song had to be carefully concealed as it contained lines that at the time would be considered risqué and corrupting and perhaps even blasphemous –

When Adam first met Eve
He kissed a technicolour cheek
And asked her if she minded it
She picked an apple from a tree
Saying love is where you'll find it.

GOING DOWN FOR THE FIRST TIME

I gather that my parents decided that when I was quite young I was not cut out for physical work. But, then, I began to fail in my studies in the local national school. A child who wasn't destined to labour in the fields had to succeed at school; and my parents decided on the drastic measure of sending me to an Irish language boarding school. I suppose I should be thankful to the Irish language boarding school for the fact that, even if I am not now able to converse in Irish, I can more or less understand the Irish language radio or television news. I am more thankful to the Irish language boarding school for the reason that my spending time away from home so early in childhood may have helped me to have the courage eventually to quit university and take to labouring in England.

SNOBBERY AMONG PUPILS IN THE IRISH LANGUAGE COLLEGE

As is amusing to me to report now, there was snobbery in the lives of the children in the Irish language school. The snobbery had its origins in some Dublin children who were in this boarding school because their parents fancied that proficiency in the Irish language stood to advance their children's career prospects in the Irish Republic and their parents felt, as consequence of this, that they need feel no guilt in ridding themselves of burden of these same children for an entire school year. The snobbery that these parents managed to pass on to their children was of the virulent kind and it got to me …

I remember one day while on one of the many walks in the countryside that were compulsory for us children being told by some person in authority that there was a man who wanted to see me. The man in question was a distant relative but a stranger to me; he lived near the school and my mother had prevailed on him to visit me. I was not in any way prepared for this man's visit and I certainly was not prepared for his appearance. Everything about him from his humble bicycle to his ancient overcoat to his simple gift of a packet of biscuits spoke of old Ireland, an old Ireland love of which the boarding school might attempt to foster but which the contingent of Dublin boys would be happy to see die. Every moment I spent in conversation with this man was agony for me, as I feared my snobbish peers would get to observe my visitor's appearance. In the event, they didn't.

COMING-OF-AGE AND GOLD BIBLES

At present I watch a little TV. Hardly a week goes by without the TV listings declaring some movie or other to be a 'coming-of-age drama'. A cliché in these dramas – and perhaps a compelling reason for the very existence – is the sexual awakening of hero or heroine. I suppose the book that best defines this cliché of this awakening in factual memoir is James Joyce's *Portrait of an Artist as a Young Man*. I think the picture Joyce paints in his self-portrait of he watching a very young woman wading in a stream is written from the perspective of one who knows and rather takes for granted that there is to be a Nora Barnacle awaiting him down the road of time. Not everybody is so lucky.

But, then, perhaps my first glimpse of coming-of-age does truly foreshadow how life would turn out for me. The Irish language boarding school was a mixed school and in true courtly love fashion sex reared its head during the course of my first of two years in the school in the shape of a short-lived cult that arose among some of the male pupils and that concerned itself with one female pupil. I remember feeling a little agnostic at the time about the cult of this particular female, she being chocolate box pretty and even then a rather dated representative of the female ideal. That didn't stop the boys sending her notes.

Inevitably, this early expression of libido by the more likely male pupils had to have some tangible consequences. But I fear the more likely male pupils were on a loser if they hoped that the object of their cult – this already self assured female – was about to be the one to make the consequences of the cult tangible as it were. For when it came to public display of affection such as the kissing of a female pupil in full view of a gathering of pupils, the archly feminine pupil was nowhere to be found and it was a more athletic pupil that had the daring to step forward and accept the kiss.

I remember thinking at the time that the athletic girl was more deserving of attention than the self-assured little lady that had been the recipient of so many handwritten notes. But that, then and for most of my life, was the extent of my involvement in the favourite game of interplay between the sexes. I was and have been for the most part a mere observer.

The fact that libidinal expression among the pupils reached the level of kissing came to the notice of the headmaster. He chose to address an assembly of the entire school concerning the matter. While speaking, his features had a look that I have come to describe in my private lexicon as the pissed look. The pissed look is most often seen on the faces of street preachers who become intoxicated before the fact of their presiding belief that what they believe to be the truth in whatever they happen to be saying in oration is self-evidently the truth. The headmaster was equally convinced of the truth in what he was saying and what he did manage to say was that there was a long way to go - the Primary Certificate, the Intermediate Certificate, the Leaving Certificate and mortgage-taking presumably – before anything of the sort that had so animated the pupils in the school in recent weeks could be entertained.

If love was out, war was perhaps a possibility.

One of the buildings in the school was of mere timber construction and it was divided into two dormitories. There was always some rivalry between the boys in the two sections. Suddenly, an imaginary war broke out between the two sections of the building; and the boys from both sections managed to conscript the whole school in this war. Note passing having proved such a successful portion of the school's adventure with courtly love, note passing was also a feature of this war; but in the war the conveying of messages was an undertaking of supposed danger.

The headmaster got to hear of this war before anything remotely untoward happened; and it was a self-assured – even relieved – headmaster who, before another assembly of the pupils, declared the war at an end.

Both the exercise in courtly love and the exercise in war had been rather sensible affairs; and over forty years later I am inclined to suspect that those same worldly wise pupils of Dublin origin were the instigators of both events. But, in the course of my second year in the school, something of less sophisticated and more superstitious nature excited the imagination of the pupils. Simply, a country boy – a country boy wouldn't you know – came up with the notion that there were what he termed gold bibles hidden in a little used outhouse in the school grounds.

Here it might be possible to rhapsodise on either element of the schoolboy's fantasy: the gold or the bibles. But I prefer to dwell on the consequences of his fantasy. Quite simply, as a number of pupils became excited about the prospect of hidden gold bibles, some few pupils attempted to force open the door of the outhouse where the bibles were supposed to be stored. Only a very insecure, rusty nail was keeping the door to the gold bibles from being pushed in. But just when it looked like the door was on the point of yielding to the mob, the pupil who first came up with the notion of gold bibles rushed forward in a very worried and excited state with the aim of stopping the mob from doing something outside the law.

The worry and fear of this pupil that the authorities would take a dim view of the door of an outhouse being needlessly pushed in was apparently sufficient to convince the formerly excited pupils that there were no hidden gold bibles after all. The great fear of the pupils of authority is evident in this story.

FIRST VISIONS OF AN OUTSIDE WORLD

Something was happening to Ireland in the time of my childhood that would, for good or ill, change the culture beyond recognition. One day as I was in my father's motor car returning from the Irish language college and my mother was happy to break the news to me that we now had a TV in the farmhouse. The minute I got in the door I spent half an hour watching a little drama about parachutists called *Ripcord*. *Ripcord* was a TV series that consisted in the main of meaningless aerial shots of parachutists in free fall and so it was destined to never receive a repeat showing even on those nostalgia channels.

The pop radio was what would really fuel my rebellion later on; but television also had its moments. Surely, it was some sort of epiphany for me to watch an episode of *The Man From Uncle* and see amid all the spy antics an actual 'happening' in Greenwich Village, even if the said 'happening' was cleverly explained away in the storyline as the mere misconstruction of the same spy antics by a bunch of credulous patrons of a nightclub. No matter, in a farm house where a trip to a local town was an adventure even adults could not undertake too often for fear their conscience might condemn them as extravagant, a 'happening' in Greenwich Village was there on the screen to be witnessed by me.

THE INEVITABLILITY OF THE NEXT OPPRESIVE INSTITUTION

In my childhood the adults believed in the permanency of things. I remember a priest urging people from the pulpit (from the altar actually) to be careful in choosing a marriage partner for as he maintained they would not just be struck with the same partner for the rest of their natural life but for all eternity. Quite a prospect! Quite a prospect at the time also was what I term the greyhound track vision of life. People were placed in their traps and by that I mean they were contained in the educational system until they began their career which was understood by all to be a most unswerving race to the finishing-line ... or death. What a sad vision this was!

For my second-level education, I was sent to the diocesan college thirty miles away from my farm home. I was rather an ailing greyhound back then and I have to concede – nay insist – nearly forty years later that my thus being placed in the care of priests of questionable mentality was not so much the best option, but entirely the only option.

'CLAM' – THE DRINK OF THE DISPIRITED

Rather by way of substitute for the normal tea, milk and perhaps sugar that is a feature of mealtime in most Irish households, in the diocesian college we students were given for mealtime beverage a concoction that contained all three of the aforementioned ingredients but only in shape of a swill that was prepared some time before it was brought to table. This concoction, this swill, went by the name of *clam* in student slang. There was an advertisement on television at the time for a brand of tea that went 'PG Tips, the great pick-me-up!' and this prompted a student of college into mournful parody as he said 'Clam, the greatest knock-me-down!'.

I must suspect that, all question of miserliness aside, the purpose of clam was indeed to keep the students down. In such context, I can't help remark nothing gives a certain sort of Christian more pleasure than the fact of pleasure denied to others, either as matter of decree or – better still – by reason of incapacity.

REIGN OF TERROR

"I won't let any bums take over my college!" was a line spoken by a president of the diocesan college who came to power a number of years after I had graduated from the place.

The likes of the above comment was never uttered during my time in the college. For the simple reason that there was no reason for the likes of this comment to be uttered in the place in my time. Because, at that time, the authority of the priests that ran this college was beyond question. Dissent of any kind was not yet portion of reality.

The terror began in deliberate manner at the beginning of each term. A sinking feeling couldn't but overtake me every time I deposited my belongings in my dormitory at the start of each term. I knew and everybody knew that the start-of-term roll call was only minutes away. When in accordance with custom the students assembled in the biggest classroom in the college, the college president – who was entitled to wear the purple of the Caesars as portion of his soutane – would stride into the room and read out each name from a ledger. Each and every student knew that he had better be quick in declaring himself present. The purpose of the terror attending this roll call was plain: you were being told that you were now back in detention and you should never forget the fact.

I shall be mercifully brief and oblique in acknowledging the horrors of four years of such detention.

ALTHOUGH DOMINANT, THE BOLD ARE OUTNUMBERED BY THE DAMAGED KIND

And to speak somewhat in connection with death, I have to make one wretched comment. There is an attitude among even hardened journalists – or perhaps especially among hardened journalists – to cast John Fitzgerald Kennedy as a hero. Perhaps he was a hero. Whether he was a hero or not, journalists of a certain kind do admiringly report the fact that John Fitzgerald Kennedy had a keen appreciation of his own mortality from an early age. Perhaps this appreciation of Kennedy's contributed a little to the fact that he had the most expressive smile of greeting ever captured on camera. I am happy in this book to hold up the flag for people who could never command so commanding and perhaps rapacious a smile as that of President Kennedy's.

THAT MOST MAGICAL ESSENCE, 'THE TEN PER CENT'

The diocesian college president more than once told us students how fortunate we were to be in such an institution. He said on one occasion that our presence in the college alone was enough to add ten per cent to our results in the life determining examinations. But, in honesty, I believe the ten per cent advantage I gained from being educated by priests has wider implication than that. The typically fleshy priests couldn't help but imply that the learning they were imparting was a way to power.

Even the dry jokes the priests told went to underline our great good fortune as students. Once, for example, the priest-president told of a predecessor's encounter with a mother of a prospective student of the college. The pushy mother told the president of a former time that her son was burning with brains. "Let us hope, replied the president of old, "that the conflagration doesn't catch on to the college!" We were being told by implication that such things as IQ or even knowledge itself were of no consequence; but that, if we were possessed of certain kind of learning and the arrogance that went with it, all mere functionaries would fall before us.

This *ten per cent* is strong stuff! It can even lead one to dismiss with a word some of the authorities mentioned reverently in the broadcast chatterings of the ruling class!

HAIL, HAIL ROCK 'N' ROLL

I am tone-deaf but I began to pick up on a notion from some of my fellow students in the diocesan college. This notion of theirs was to the effect that popular song was not just the height of fashion but the thing most expressive of life in the second half of the twentieth century. They never put this notion into words beyond singing a few snatches of hit songs of the time; but the notion was someway prevalent and I did pick up on it.

One night, in my isolated farmhouse home, while the rest of the family were watching TV in another room, I turned on the old wood-panelled radio set that was normally only turned on for the news at mealtimes; and I began to turn the dial in search of the hit songs of the day. Suddenly, the names of pop and rock 'n' roll bands were important to me, these being names such as Dave Dee, Dozy, Beaky, Mick and Tich, the Dave Clark Five and the Tremeloes that are nearly forgotten now and the names of other bands whose fame endures to this day. I had found a new and enduring pastime in listening to pop songs.

THE TIMES THEY WERE A-CHANGIN'

Of course, some of songs I was listening to in my unhappy teens were preaching revolution if not of the global kind at least of the personal kind; and that sort of message could not but find a willing listener in me. Dylan's speaking of sons and daughters being beyond their parents' commands made it easier for me to think that I could and should change my circumstances. I was only biding my time.

Of course, my new belief that I could and should jump ship when the time was right didn't come independent of a more painful realisation. I had known for many a long day that I was not one of the blessed, as it were. I knew I was not the most capable of people, I knew I was not the most hip of people. But this knowledge of my own inadequacy, far from persuading me that I should stay on the straight and narrow, had the effect of convincing me that I should do something bold.

Even at this early stage I was one to think that the new era that was dawning would have the capacity to come up with something that would change me into something new.

TOP STUDENT

I emerged the top student of my year in diocesan college. The top student in Christian Doctrine, that is. Through the post I received the congratulations of the college president and a cheque to the value of three pounds. It was the only money I was to earn as a direct consequence of my education.

I may be mad but to this day I have some difficulty in understanding one bright and studious fellow-student who briefly went on for the priesthood but who in his secondary school days apparently followed the utilitarian ways of the majority of students and wilfully decided not to pay much attention to Christian Doctrine.

MATRICULATION BY TRICKERY

Another letter came to the farmhouse that did not contain welcome news. This was the letter announcing that I had only received two honours in the nicely titled Leaving Certificate. To go from seven honours in the Intermediate Certificate to but two honours in my Senior Leaving Certificate is not the sort of detail that would look good on a CV, were I ever to assemble a CV.

To make matters worse, the two honours I received in 1968 were in the subjects of physics and chemistry. Science subjects. I think I can explain how I came to get two honours in science subjects. To this day I have, I admit, an interest in science, provided no mathematics is involved. But my interest in science does not quite explain my honours in physics and chemistry. My honour in chemistry is easily explained. There were a considerable amount of marks going in chemistry for knowledge of the atom; and the layman chemistry teacher produced a ten page photocopied document on the atom. And I who love conceptual novelty had no difficulty in grasping and remembering these ten pages. Physics was a much harder subject. But my physics teacher was the hardest working teacher I ever came across; and by virtue of his persistence I had no choice but learn the subject.

So, I matriculated on the strength of my two honours in science subjects and proceeded to pursue a Batchelor of Arts degree in university! But to actually proceed with this little piece of trickery I had to put up a fight.

At the instigation of my parents, a local farmer with academic credentials called to the family farm to convince me of the folly of I, an apparent scientist, pursuing an Arts degree. A small sized man, and a soberly and tidily dressed one, he spent about two hours trying to convince me that I was making a mistake. I saw off all his arguments. But I don't doubt that, as he observed my progress down the years – or rather lack of progress – he was more than happy to conclude that it was madness on my part that had me turn my back on science.

It's all very academic now. But under no circumstances had I any hope of getting a science degree; and under my actual circumstances – by this time having lost interest in study – I had no chance of getting an Arts degree either.

But, as I pursue the only little trade I was ever capable of, I am happy that I spent a year pursuing a BA and became a little more familiar with such things as Mystery Plays – sometimes called Miracle Plays – and Wordsworth's *Prelude* and even Thomas Hobbes's *Leviathan*.

NOWHERE ELSE TO GO

The poet says death happens when the coffin is the only place for you. Similarly, jail and psychiatric hospital is for people whom society can no longer contain in their natural habitat. There was the inevitability of the corpse going into a coffin, a criminal going into jail and the unduly distressed going into psychiatric hospital of I going to university. In fact I didn't go to university: I was sent.

A DREARY UNIVERSITY

Of course, I hold jaundiced views on university life. I am most unlikely to have been impressed by the undergraduates that distinguished themselves in student politics. I remember one chap going for political office being allowed to speak in advance of a lecture, and he declaring that he would, if elected, exact a tribute of one shilling from each undergraduate for the underdeveloped world. At the end of this candidate's impassioned address, the lecturer – a nun – took the podium and chose to grimace out of simplistic respect for the force and compassion of what she had just heard. The candidate in question was elected but we never again heard of the shilling tribute.

There were many other indications that this university was not much of a university. A few students of the Christian persuasion attempted to organise a Bible study group. But even the humble event of a Bible study group organised by earnest Christians was more than the Roman Catholic chaplain of the university could allow. It is worth my remembrance in my middle age that Bible study was a no-no in University College Cork in the sixties.

Also, one student who stood out from the crowd made a comment in print that has stayed with me down the years. This student was a bit of a poet who chose to describe himself in print in fashionably negative terms. He said that he was a manic-depressive. Perhaps he was. But my suspicion is that he was nothing of the sort. And my further suspicion is that he would run a mile from an actual manic-depressive.

$\mathcal{I}$MPORTED REVOLUTION

The Girl On A Motorcycle [4] is a 1960s movie that seems to take the view that endless shots of Marianne Faithfull in tight leather bike wear is entertaining in itself.

As she motors through the continental countryside, passing through many a town that only seem remarkable for their graveyards, Marianne does ask one interesting question: Why don't they revolt? By 'they' Marianne means the young people. As you know the young people did revolt and as you probably know also John Lennon took the view that this revolt came to nothing as just the same people retained power.

Anyway, there were some revolutionaries in University College Cork in 1968/1969. Alas, these revolutionaries lacked any originality and were more than happy to take their ideology from Chairman Mao. How embarrassing Chairman Mao is now! If ever there was a man who fulfils the rightwing idea of a rock 'n' roll bogeyman that exploits the young for his own ends, it was this Chairman Mao. Reject all aged authority except mine, was Mao's dictum and he got away with it.

Anyway, the Maoists of Cork and their one Stalinist adversary did liven things up just a little in this most staid of universities. I attended one of the Moaist meetings in a college lecture room and I attended one of Maoist movie shows held where else but in the Imperial Hotel. I wasn't about to take it any further than that.

I did, of course, buy and read the Moaist pamphlets that were for sale on campus. I read in particular about one mass meeting of students in Dublin where one speaker got up and said:

"I'm not going to quote Marx, I'm not going to quote Mao, I'm going to quote the Rolling Stones – This could be the last time!"

In the pamphlet that quoted this great line, the speaker of this great line was condemned as an anarchist. My reaction to this condemnation was, however, to condemn the condemners and form the view that both the Rolling Stones and anarchists must have something going for them.

If I am to be perfectly honest, I did in my own idle way of talk begin to describe myself as an anarchist to my friends in the college. But, alas, you won't find me at the barricades. I excuse or at least console myself by saying that anyone who tells the truth about something is not aiding and abetting empire.

---

4 *The Girl on a Motorcycle (La motocyclette)* is a 1968 British-French film starring Alain Delon and Marianne Faithfull and featuring Roger Mutton, Marius Goring and Catherine Jourdan. It was listed to compete at the 1968 Cannes Film Festival but the festival was cancelled due to the May 1968 events in France.

STUDENT LIFE

Ah yes, but surely my two fellow students and I who shared quarters and mealtimes got up to all manner of serious discussion and drunken capers and so on?

Well, as I remember it, the medical student and the technological student and I only arrived at one startling conclusion in the course of the year and it was that Jefferson Airplane had the best name of any rock 'n' roll band. Ever. Indeed, the thing that most animated us in the course of the entire year was a religious programme for teenagers on daytime TV. Every week as the credits on this programme began to roll a thirty-second segment of Bob Dylan's *All Along The Watchtower* emerged from the black and white TV. That was it. That was the highlight of my year in university. The weekly thirty-second dose of Dylan.

I don't wish to pretend that I spent every night during that unhappy year inside in my semi-detached lodgings. For even that was indicative of how I would pursue the entire business of a 'night out' throughout my life, I took my tone-deaf ears on a few occasions to a place called the 06 Club. The 06 Club was a beat club in days when Irish rock 'n' roll bands were termed beat groups. Bands such as Skid Row and The Gentry performed there; and the name Skid Row was more indicative than The Gentry of the status of beat groups in those days.

If I remember correctly, the 06 Club didn't even have a bar licence. The point being that it was only by some kind of miracle that Skid Row and The Gentry had found a venue to play in Cork City at this time. The venue itself looked very like a disused building on the inside. The walls and timberwork were unpainted and the only decoration was some large print graffiti quoting little phrases from rock songs. This graffiti was not of spontaneous origin but was presumably organised by the management by way of improving the décor.

I believe I did see the college student poet and manic-depressive pretender among the crowd one night at the 06 Club. But I made no effort to talk to him or to anybody else in the place. Decades of my life would pass before I was ever to achieve the status of a person attending a gig or concert.

MY LUCK

It may well have been my luck that, when I was staring defeat in university in the face, I took the same approach as the legendary business executive who said: *You can't fire me, I resign!*

HOMILY 1

JOE NASH – THE FOUNTAIN THAT NEVER FAILS

You might just have consumed a meal of fish and chips and some carbonated drink in some junk food joint in some drab provincial town – not daring to enter any beer and spirits tavern half out of your own feelings of self disgust and half out of fear that forced conviviality of such an establishment might weaken your resolve – and with heavy heart take yourself to a bridge below the town and stare lovingly into the swollen water. So far all is going to plan! But you haven't reckoned on the strange serendipity that is Joe Nash, for unseen he is standing right beside you and whispering to you instructions a moment earlier you would not have wished to hear.

Alternatively, you may be one of these new lay preachers who, notwithstanding what is in the circumstances an unfortunate birth name such as Jim Rocks, has managed to worm his way into the favour of Roman Catholic clergymen who, now that things are breaking up on all sides, are more than happy to share their preaching-time with none other than yourself. All is going swimmingly … until the trouble with the secretary of a parish council goes national. You know, of course, that in time you will overcome this trouble … and possibly once more rise to the top as the leading figure in your own self founded evangelical troupe. But right now you question how are you going to survive the next twenty-four hours … as you hear the press and TV people in noisy assembly outside your front door and as you ponder when the police are going to arrive. But, then, the indemonstrable Joe Nash – his countenance and his voice – enters your consciousness (as he always does in times of ultimate trial) and you know with certainty that all your larval adversaries will fail and fail dismally to impact adversely on you. After all, you have Joe Nash on your side …

2

A LONELY DROP OUT

DROPPING OUT

I cannot actually claim to have run away to England. What I did was to go on a working holiday to England. I was to stay with relatives in Birmingham; and I did stay with them for three months. But when the time came to return to Ireland, I concealed my real plans to my relatives in Birmingham but dropped a one line note to my parents back home and took the train to London.

What can I say of the three months I spent in Birmingham? One thing I don't remember is when I received the hardly surprising news that I had failed one of my four subjects in my first year in university. In theory I was to sit another examination in the autumn in the hope of progressing into second year; and in theory I was to spend much of my free time during the summer swotting up for the examination in the autumn. But I hadn't the heart in Birmingham to even as much as glance at a text book. I knew that it was not in my power no matter what I did to actually pass the examination in the autumn. The fact that I didn't even try to study made it a little bit easier to do the bold thing at the end of summer and take the train to London.

But what of Birmingham? My relatives got me a job on a building site. If I can boast that I worked for three months on a building site, I have to admit that this boast is not quite the whole story. My job was that of labourer; but in truth the tasks I was given were far from the hardest on the site.

The first day on the building site I found myself working alongside a man from my own parish. He was almost overcome with emotion when he learnt where I was from. I have to speak of this man as a gentleman. I also have to speak of him as a tragic fellow. He was engaged in labourer's tasks when he was of an age when he should be otherwise engaged. He was also a man that was living in a country that was cold to his socio-ethnic group, when all the while his gentle heart was with the green countryside I now walk nearly every day. As I recall this man's fate, I must acknowledge my good fortune in having a family that never gave up on me. I heard in time that this gentleman I met on a building site finished his days in an Irish nursing home run by the religious. I would like to think that he lived out his last years in dignity.

In the light of this man's tragic life, it seems almost coarse of me to mention that I saw The Who and the Bonzo Dog Doo Dah Band in a Birmingham club with the somewhat nihilistic name of Mothers. But I am forever reaching out for that which is a little beyond my grasp.

$\mathcal{T}$HE TEMPTING POWER OF MIDLANDS' BITTER

On one occasion back in class in the diocesan college, the magisterial priest-president told us students:

"You know if you're working a pneumatic drill all day, you won't feel like reading a book in the evening!"

In helping build the Good Hope Hospital in Birmingham, I never worked a pneumatic drill. I did for a while work that much less wearing a tool known as a Kango. So I was not especially too tired to study in the evening. But, you know, after a day on a dusty building site in summer it proved far more tempting for me to lord over a pint of Ansells bitter than to try to decipher obscure Irish quatrains [5].

OF MY FIRST MOVES IN LONDON, OF MY CRUELTY TO MY FAMILY AND OF THE DISMAY I CAUSED ONE UNDERGRADUATE

The theory of my escape to London was that I should somehow become one of the new phenomenon: *les* hippies. But there was never any question of me allowing theory to come before practicalities. I quickly found lodgings and neither did I waste any time in taking myself to a labour exchange. I gave a false name at the labour exchange. Not an entirely false name … I had just about enough cunning to retain the name John.

That I made no contact with my family back in Ireland at this time, I would feel guilty about to this day were it not that I am mindful of the fact that I had to reach the age of forty years before I found any peace in my life.

I also caused a little surprise among my acquaintances in university by my choosing to drop out. By now the reader should be aware that, if ever there was a dope that was expected to take all that life threw at him without a murmur, it was me at eighteen. One chap in university was so shocked by my decision to leave the cool corridors of learning behind that he wrote a letter to my mother who was a stranger to him. In the letter he waxed eloquent, saying:

Truth is stranger than fiction. The invincible is far from the inevitable.

It is, it is, Sir!

---

[5] A stanza of four lines, especially one having alternate rhymes.

ℱACTORY WORK AND FANTASY

My first job in London was as a sort of tea boy in a neon sign factory. I was going fine until I innocently decided to dump a large portion of the plastic materials the factory was using to make its product. My next job was as a labourer in a factory that recycled automobile fenders. Business wasn't so good in this factory and I was let go after two months. I was next employed in a large engineering works. I gave over a year working there.

At the weekends I went drinking with those I shared a house with. I can even lay claim to the detail that I drank a certain amount of barley wine – a potent drink apparently. My fellow lodgers and the man who was my landlord were all factory workers. I was to discover that, perhaps in common with all factory workers, these fellow lodgers of mine were susceptible to dreaming of another life. We began to hatch this plan to buy a van and import bric-a-brac from India. My landlord was Indian. My co-conspirators in this plan were less than wise. One feature of their plan was to actually smuggle bric-a-brac from India. I considered this a strange idea. One of the conspirators was from Belfast and he was only blinded for a moment by our fantasy plan for a better life; and when his brother heard of our crazy plans and spoke against them that was the end of the matter.

I don't think this plan about buying a van was the only element of fantasy in my own life. Even in my Birmingham days I was a dutiful purchaser and keen reader of the underground press. In London I was no less a slave to the *IT* (the *International Times*), *Oz*, *Gandalf's Garden* and the very commercial *Rolling Stone*. Reading these publications was as close as I got to my ambition of being a hippie.

I did, of course, make it to the Isle of Wight to see the man Joan Baez calls the 'Dada King' – Bob Dylan. Naturally, I don't recall seeing that precise moment when the white-suited Dylan raised his right hand demonstratively in his singing of 'One Too Many Mornings', whereby with said gesture Dylan hoped to get across to his worshipping audience the idea that they could express themselves as well as he could. (Some chance that!) But I did for a while possess a Dylan bootleg with a photocopy photo of that interesting moment in Dylan's Isle of Wight performance by way of the front cover.

On most Saturdays for my three years in London I made my lonely way through the carnival thoroughfare of Portobello Road with its antique-sellers and novelty-item-selling hippies. I was following a dream and perhaps I still am.

_I_NTERREGNUM

In the heavy-duty engineering factory I worked alongside a fellow of tragic circumstances. He was polite and likable fellow of mixed race. I believe that he had only one lung and yet he was working in this less than healthy place. Worse, he was the kind of person people hit on, and one of the people that hit on him was his father who turned up occasionally to disrupt his life.

This unfortunate fellow was a worker in the factory long before I joined the workforce. Yet when the tall, weedy, very proper English foreman was choosing a _protégé_ for elevation within the factory he didn't chose this abused fellow; no, he chose me. Perhaps I should remind myself more often of the gentle and noble and abused chap by way of acknowledging how much light and happiness there is in my life.

Protégé of the foreman I may have been, but one morning I decided not to go to work. And I never did go back to that heavy-duty engineering factory. Instead, for seven to nine weeks I took myself to a local park. I had no money at the time. But, if I remember correctly, my landlord excused me from paying rent at this time. I still had to eat of course. But, as my luck would have it, the unfortunate fellow I mentioned above owed me some money; and every Friday evening I went to a particular tube station to collect a fiver from him. This fiver kept me in curry-flavoured rice for the seven or nine weeks I was out of work.

My sojourn in the local park had to end with another visit to the labour exchange. This time something prompted me to give my real name to the official behind the desk. Declaring my real name had fortunate consequences for me, as it allowed my family back in Ireland to trace me. Letters went back and forth across the Irish Sea and I spend a five week holiday back on the family farm.

SPEAKERS' CORNER, HYDE PARK

Another place to go for a lonely soul in London was Speakers' Corner on a Sunday. The speaker there that most impressed me was a certain Mr Axel. A bearded and large sort of man, Mr Axel remained at ground level as he addressed his audience. He could be witty. On one occasion there were two well-known anarchists in his company. One was known to favour the use of LSD and the other was known to stick to a more political agenda.

"Ladies and gentlemen," said Mr Axel, nodding to each of the two anarchists in turn, "the trip and the journey!"

Mr Axel's main subject seemed to be life itself. I heard him say once that, wherever they separate the sexes, they are up to mischief. Who could deny the truth of that? Certainly I couldn't after my days in the diocesan college. Mr Axel also gave the advice now so commonplace that even radio presenters give the same advice, the advice that you should chose a life-partner who you can talk to.

That last advice I never quite had the opportunity to put into practice.

GOING TO MOSCOW

In Russian literature of a certain era, a quite sharp distinction is drawn between those who went to Moscow and those who stayed at home. Presumably those that went to Moscow earned the right to do so, enjoyed themselves there and returned home in glory. I didn't quite earn the right to go to London, and I didn't enjoy myself in London and when I came home I came home to no more noble a calling than signing social welfare cheques; and yet I am of the solid belief that my life would have been poorer had I not gone to London.

_A_ UNIVERSITY FRIEND TURNS UP IN LONDON

The reader would be rather dense if he or she did not understand by this stage that I am strangely thankful to my time in London. I am also thankful to anything that helped prolong my stay in London; and that which most helped preserve my sanity a little longer in London that might otherwise have been the case was the arrival in London of a fellow who had been little more than a acquaintance in the diocesan college but who, in course of my year in university and my visits to the university during my holiday back home in Ireland, was taking on the character of a friend of mine. Why, he even declared during the course of my visit to the university during my holiday in Ireland that he both envied and admired me for the stand I had taken in leaving university behind.

By the time of this man's arrival in London I had a new job and new living-quarters. The job was in a clean and bright double-glazed window factory where you could converse with your fellow workers during the day. My living-quarters were also clean and bright but of very small dimensions. My living-quarters were in fact a small, one room bedsitter in a building consisting entirely of such apartments. I didn't mind the smallness of the bedsitter, only that in the evenings I had no contact with anybody else in the building and no contact with anybody else in London. The arrival of my university friend to share the bedsitter for two or three months with me was therefore a very welcome event.

My university friend got a job in an Indian souvenir shop. Suddenly, my university friend was on friendly terms with an Indian and a dark-skinned Englishwoman who worked in the shop; and I, too, became acquainted with these two. My university friend and I visited the Indian and his family in their home and the English woman visited us two Irishmen in the bedsitter. The Englishwoman who I shall call Susan may have been just a little bit interested in my university friend; but my university friend had already met the love of his life – an American woman – and was corresponding with her on a daily basis. Besides, Susan, who favoured rich, dark colours that matched a darkness in her soul, was on the look out for a strong, domineering man.

THE WRITINGS OF ONE-TIME ANTHROPOLOGIST CARLOS CASTANEDA BECOME A FIXTURE IN MY THINKING

I mention Susan and give her a name because she brought a book into my bed-sitter that greatly impacted on my thinking. The book was the first report by a South American-born and Los Angeles resident on his amazing adventures south of the border with a troupe of Mexican Indian sorcerers. To put my engagement with the writings of Castaneda in context, I might note that I was never likely at any stage to take an avid interest in books by such as explorers, mountaineers and yachtsmen. The world of your mere man of action could never exercise my imagination. But with Castaneda as somehow knowingly naïve narrator the world of actual North American Indian sorcery proved extremely fascinating for me. Carlos Castaneda was the adventure writer to my extended teenage-hood.

I know that, if this work is published, I will do a minority of my readers a favour by introducing them to Carlos Castaneda. I know also that the fashion for Castaneda's writings is long gone. Certainly, the universities would condemn Castaneda's books to oblivion, what with one academic saying that Castaneda's books were interesting but so was *Gulliver's Travels*. But I go along with a comment made at the time of the height of Castaneda's popularity: read him and you can never view the world in quite same way again.

For the record, I consider *Tales of Power* to be Castaneda's masterpiece and *The Eagle's Gift* to be the only book by Castaneda that is badly put together. Also take note that Carlos Castaneda's contribution does not extend beyond his books and there is absolutely no point in researching him on the internet … for all you will encounter are sceptics giving their unsought opinions and salesmen.

THE NOCTURNAL SADNESS OF 'THE BLACK MAGICIANS'

As will invite dismissive retort from some, I have to report that Castaneda's sub-culture sees itself as different from the rest of humanity and is frequently scathing about the rest of humanity. And even if I must allow that I belong all too plainly to 'the rest the humanity' and not to Castaneda's sub-culture, I nevertheless think that one of the put-downs of ordinary people emanating from Castaneda's sub-culture is too good not to be recorded here. Simply, this put-down observes that ordinary humanity, ordinary people are 'the black magicians'.

At the most dramatic moment in Castaneda's reportage of his adventures with a troupe of sorcerers, the world of ordinary humanity intrudes. Except that this intrusion is not seen as an intrusion, but as something of the final lesson that a kindly Earth would impart to sorcerers about to make their ultimate bid for freedom. The intrusion – if it is an intrusion – takes the form of a dog barking in the distance ... and Castaneda's principal teacher explains that the sound of a tethered dog barking in the distance is the saddest sound on Earth, because as the teacher explains this is not so much the bitter sound of a tethered dog but of the dog's human master howling ventriloquist-like for death to take him and release him from his boredom.

Before my hearing deteriorated to the point of being noticeably bad, I was apt just before I fell asleep of a night in the farmhouse to hear this very sound of tethered dogs barking in the distance, this sound that is portion of the nocturnal sadness of man, that is a portion of nocturnal sadness of the black magicians.

MY ISOLATION GETS TO ME

My university friend returned to Ireland to resume his studies and the people he had introduced me began to fade out of my life. Once again in London, I was left without anybody to talk to apart from the few words I might exchange with my fellow workers in the double-glazed window factory. I began to suffer by my isolation. With no great understanding, I began to search for help here, there and everywhere. There follows an account of some of my adventures as I searched for help in London town.

PEOPLE NOT PSYCHIATRY

As I began to crack up in London, I began to look for an organisation that would somehow provide me with an instant circle of friends. I remember phoning up an organisation with the name *People Not Psychiatry* and enquiring had they some sort of residential place in the country where I could go, where I could go and no doubt take delight in human company. I hadn't the wit to realise at the time that the only organisation that provide residential accommodation in the country for lonely souls like me was the government. I did, however, learn that *People Not Psychiatry* were holding support group meetings in private houses and I decided to go along to one such meeting.

The meeting took place in a very grey flat whose one item of decoration was a print of a pen and ink portrait of Sigmund Freud. One is free, I suppose, to decorate one's walls with any manner of cultural hero; but back then and even now I would be suspicious of any man who would chose a drawing of Sigmund Freud as his one domestic icon.

Before the meeting proper began, I tried to engage the owner of the flat in conversation. "You look depressingly normal," I said.

"I don't know if it's proper to discuss my problem," he replied, pretty much killing off the conversation. The nature of his problems may not be that much of a mystery.

For much of the meeting that followed, I was forced into somewhat private conversation with a middle-aged paranoid. This man lived in fear of attack in the streets. Even the most innocent congregation of young men in the street was sufficient to cause this man great distress. Worse, his entire demeanour in conversation in this depressing flat suggesting that he wasn't the sort of man who would respond to this imaginary threat posed to him by young men in the street in entirely passive manner. Conversing with this manner of man was a long way from finding a new circle of friends. I begged him to call a halt to this one-to-one conversation that I might rejoin the group conversation; and I did rejoin the group conversation but not without causing great and visible offence to the paranoid.

As the night drew to a close, the group verdict on my predicament was that I was quite lucky to be holding down a job; and, if there was an implication here that I wouldn't be holding down a job for much longer, that implication had the virtue of being true. Needless to say, I came away from this meeting in a more depressed state again. But, looking back, I don't wish to be too critical of *People Not Psychiatry*. At a time when psychiatry proper was doing very little of a distinctly positive nature for people that crossed its path, *People Not Psychiatry* were the first non-money-making organisation to see a need and make some attempt at meeting it.

THE 'REAL MAN' WHO SET UP A CHARITY

I also contacted a charity that seemed to offer the prospect of me finding something like companionship. But this charity was very much one wealthy and unqualified man's ego-trip. He made a speciality of diagnosing homosexuals and attempted this diagnosis with me. Alas, his prescription that I should approach a priest in my district with a view to participating in parish business was no more palatable to me.

A GROWTH CENTRE NAMED 'KALEIDOSCOPE'

The things I did during the time of my desperate search for help in London! At one point I even attended an aikido class and even contemplated purchasing an expensive martial arts suit. But, in my innocence, I thought I had struck gold when I came in contact with an organisation called *Kaleidoscope*. Indeed, if I had been methodical in my search for a new identity for myself, I would have presented myself at the door of *Kaleidoscope* long before my mental health began to give in. For the fact of the matter was that the educated people in London who were dissatisfied with their lives were not so foolish as to seek a new identity through the use of drugs but rather sought transformation by means of the various radical therapies on offer at one or other of these preciously termed Growth Centres such as *Kaleidoscope*.

Kaleidoscope was situated in a bay-windowed private house in an upmarket area. As soon as you got into the front room of *Kaleidoscope*, you were afforded the possibility of making a cup of coffee for yourself by means of the coffee and electric kettle provided. The provision of coffee making facilities and the rich carpets on the floor all went to indicate that *Kaleidoscope* was a different sort of institution to a flat with a drab portrait of Sigmund Freud on the wall. But, then, *Kaleidoscope* was a middle class institution and the greater level of comfort it provided was made possible by the fact that it charged money for its services.

I attended one encounter group session and a number of bio-energetic workshops at *Kaleidoscope*. Little need be said about the encounter group session except to say that my long unkempt hair had the effect of identifying me as something of a fool in the eyes of the other participants in the encounter group and these participants were also happy to dismiss me on racial grounds. The so-called bio-energetic workshops deserve a more detailed report because they were more interesting and were of greater consequence.

Bio-energetics as understood in alternative therapy circles is a form of therapy where physical movement is used for the release of (repressed) emotions. I would hate the reader to go away from this book with a negative understanding of bio-energetics. Classic bio-energetics is used in Dutch psychiatric hospitals and should be used selectively everywhere in all such hospitals. I even believe that the slightly more 'probing' therapy I received in *Kaleidoscope* could be of some benefit to certain types of psychiatric client, even if the effect of the therapy on me was only to speed me on my way to mental hospital.

At the first of these sessions in *Kaleidoscope* I was in the company of two female clients of the house. We, minus our shoes, were all to receive instructions in turn from an also shoeless therapist seated on a bar stool. Nothing significant happened for me on this first session; and I was unduly suspicious at the time of the sincerity of the school teacher as she responded most fulsomely to the therapy.

For my own sake, for my own intellectual contentment, I am now very happy that I witnessed the actions of this schoolteacher in therapy. For this schoolteacher was experiencing something in therapy that no human being had experienced earlier than the second half of the twentieth century. She was experiencing something which Arthur Janov terms a conscious coma. A conscious coma is a state of consciousness where the wide awake client enters a dream state and most peculiarly can communicate the broad details of what is happened to her or him in the 'dreamscape' to the therapist. Clearly, a conscious coma bears some relationship to the hypnotic state especially where hypnosis is employed to regress the client back to the days of childhood. Yet, in a world where some schools of psychology deny the reality of the hypnosis, it may be necessary to point out that a conscious coma is a unique state of conscious, a fourth state of consciousness to join the other three that are ordinary wakefulness, dreaming and the hypnotic state.

In the schoolteacher's conscious coma the events and concerns of her week gone by were re-staged with I don't doubt as much reality for the schoolteacher if she were dreaming. In *Kaleidoscope* the therapist didn't chose to do anything radical with the conscious coma of his client; instead, he just allowed her wander around in the imaginary drama for a few minutes; and, on noting that the main concern of the imaginary drama was that the teacher felt somewhat overwhelmed by her need to help people, the therapist rather lamely proceeded to have the teacher repeat the line 'I can help some people but I can't help everyone.'

The very fact that such a thing as a conscious coma can be made happen in therapy is vital to some of the argument in the fifth chapter of this book; but for now I am happy to observe that, whereas I haven't in my time met any famous philosophers or artistes, I can boast that I have witnessed someone in a conscious coma.

Nothing happened for me at my first bio-energetic session at *Kaleidoscope*. Indeed, as I have indicated, I was a little suspicious of the sincerity of my two comrades who were responding better than me to the therapy. My second bio-energetic session at *Kaleidoscope* was a far more consequential day for me. So consequential was that day for me that I insist on speaking of that visit to *Kaleidoscope* not in chronological sequence but in more reverse sequence.

For it just so happened at the end of this second session in *Kaleidoscope*, the same three clients as the week before decided to have a coffee together in the waiting room before we went our separate ways. I have to say that the little chat that ensued was to have enormous and scarcely happy consequence for me. For I was to hear the schoolteacher and the other woman eagerly discuss more or less between themselves news of a new therapy that was apparently the daddy of them all. That therapy was known as Primal Scream Therapy.

If sometimes in later life I wished I'd never heard that piece of conversation, the fact of the matter is that I had not taken the aforementioned real man's advice and cut my hair and presented myself to a priest; but instead I had taken my stodgy and incurably rustic self to one of the most archly hip places in London, *Kaleidoscope*. If I did overhear that Primal Scream Therapy was the ultimate therapy, well I suppose I put myself in the way of overhearing this.

The consequences of my hearing a conversation about Primal Scream Therapy lay in the future; but the actual therapy on the day at *Kaleidoscope* also had enormous consequence for me. On this day, I announced in the therapy room that I didn't feel as apprehensive as on former occasions in *Kaleidoscope*, that I didn't feel as apprehensive by virtue of the fact that I had met everybody in *Kaleidoscope* on this day on a previous occasion. Reading into my character from this announcement of mine, the therapist had me repeat amid certain breathing exercises the following line:

"In a safe situation, I feel free."

On my fifth or sixth time saying this line, I quite suddenly realised with therapeutic as opposed to ordinary conviction that the line was true, that – to spell it out for the reader – it represented an abiding axiom of my life that in a safe situation I felt free.

In surprised voice I informed the therapist of this my first response to the therapy. The therapist was amused at my surprise but pleased that I was responding to his therapy. In theory, this response of mine to the therapy would mean that in a week or two or perhaps more I, too, would be experiencing a conscious coma in *Kaleidoscope*. Alas, that was never to be. I never did return to *Kaleidoscope*. For I left that bay-windowed house that day a changed man. For a few hours I even had my first experience of a therapeutically wrought phantom pain, to wit a not entirely unpleasant headache.

More to the point, the next few days were to prove that the therapy I received in the bay-windowed house had converted me from a depressed fellow who was losing his ability to cope into someone exuberantly manic.

HOMILY 2

More on Joe Nash

I am proud to say that I braved the elements the day they buried the mortal remains of Joe Nash in a local cemetery. A stormy day it was with rain and gusts of wind making it unpleasant for all who stood by as they lowered Joe's coffin decorated with gold-effect crucifix into the ground. I never had that much dealings with Joe while he was alive; but I was not the only one on that inclement day – nor am I the only one in more recent days – who was and is convinced that Joe is still to the good. By that I mean Joe is now in a state of permanent bliss … and we, who remember Joe and who would hope to eventually share in his present good fortune, would do well to remember Joe in as detailed and heartfelt a fashion as possible. Therein lies our hope.

Now, I have heard it said that Joe never achieved much to speak of. They even say Joe was a waster. But a broad smile touched with some little bewilderment overcomes my face when I hear talk of this kind. Do the people who go in for character assassination of the good Joe have any appreciation of what I might term the final balance sheet? And speaking of balance sheets, I don't doubt that many who speak badly of Joe Nash don't have two cents to rub together for the weekend. Even if I instantly concede there are also those who speak ill of Joe who are overburdened with wealth but I draw no distinction between the impecunious and well-to-do critics of Joe Nash. For the biggest impact these degenerates have on my person is to prompt a justly superior smile in me. And I know for a fact that I am not the only one smiling.

3

THAT NATION-STATE OF
AN ENGLISH HOSPITAL

$\mathcal{I}$ GET CARRIED AWAY

The events of my last morning in the window factory are embarrassing to recall. The fact of the matter is that I went berserk … but in a cunning fashion. I went from worker to worker requesting them to bring a crucifix to work on the morrow; and, in accordance with the response I got to this bizarre request, I began to divide the workforce into two camps. I have to say that I enjoyed some success in splitting the workforce … and indeed at one point one of those workers most committed to my cause pointed triumphantly to a mock battle-axe that hung on a steel girder that he had fashioned in an idle moment, this gesture of his by way of declaring his sudden conversion to a belief in magic as opposed to reality. Of course, the police, who don't believe in magic, were called to the factory; and, seeing that no damage had been done to person or property, the police had the sense to humour me away to an obvious destination.

$\mathcal{C}$ANLEY HOSPITAL

The police took me to Canley Hospital in the countryside, where the vast grounds were home to many two-storey red brick buildings termed villas. The villas served as residential quarters for the large patient population. I must say at this point that years later an Irish nurse working in an Irish hospital asked me not to mention the name Canley, for as she put it the name Canley "offended her ears". There need be no doubt about it that, if there ever was a hospital that was of such grandeur and such scale as to distinguish itself in darker days as a place of evil in the world, it was this Canley. Anybody who moved through Canley in the 1960s could easily (especially if they were a little paranoid) catch glimpses of the definite evil that once was.

PSYCHIATRY AS A MILITARY EXERCISE

The male nurses in Canley all wore white coats. Except in the case of the most junior rank of nurse, every white coat had an epaulette attached with the help of safety pins to its shoulders. The colour of the epaulette served to indicate rank. I cannot be certain which was the lowest ranking colour in epaulette but it was either a combination of yellow and green or more likely plain green. The middle ranking colour in epaulette was red. The highest ranking colour in epaulette – the colour sported by charge-nurses – was blue. Anybody who wished to formulate a mystical theory of colours could well begin with this system of colour of epaulette distinguishing rank among psychiatric nurses in England.

I have the distinct memory of seeing one nurse going off duty exchanging an epaulette with a nurse coming on duty. This may have been a one-off occurrence or a regular occurrence. But it did appear to me at the time that there was more attention in this military exchange of epaulette than in any possible interaction with the patients.

The primary colours were also evident in the unbreakable tableware we patients used at meal time. Cups, saucers and plates came with a green, red or blue line that formed a circle about their edge. I seem to recall that once in an Irish hospital that the activities of a nurse in gratuitously waking a patient in the middle of the night were excused on the grounds that it was sometimes necessary to remind patients where they were … presumably the variously coloured epaulettes and variously coloured tableware served a similar purpose in Canley.

I know now of course that psychiatric tableware that gives the appearance of being unbreakable breaks very easily indeed but only into very small, harmless shards.

THE EVIL THAT WAS, AND THE EVIL THAT REMAINS

To their eternal shame, most doctors fail to significantly rise above fashion. The people in Canley whose lives were ruined by the 'lock them up' philosophy of other days were many. This large number of detainees ranged from those who accepted their lot and worked at trade or manual tasks or else wandered the grounds aimlessly; and then there were those who never accepted their life long detention and were conveniently classified as 'incurables'. Even on a summer's day these 'incurables' were obliged to stay within the confines of the small lawn in front of their residential 'villa' and under the watchful eyes of truly indifferent nurses.

One of the 'incurables' spoke to me. I was walking by this group of sad men as they sat outside their villa and he called out to me. I was determined to keep on walking but one of them called out to me, saying:

" You'll never learn anything if you don't listen to people!"

I paused. He continued:

"You'll never get out of here! Look, I was put in here by my landlady."

Regardless of the detail, capricious law and capricious people locked this man away for life; and the worst of it is that nearly all this time in my view he was suffering from no mental illness.

The number of people the doctors lock up may have reduced considerably; but the doctors are still locking up people. And what is a matter of fashion, those so detained long-term are – apart altogether from their detention – the most neglected of all psychiatric clients.

*P*SYCHIATRIC PATIENTS IN CANLEY PROPOSE A COSMOLOGY

I remember well the moment I arrived in Canley. I was in an ambulance with an ambulance attendant and a policeman different to the policemen that took me into custody at the factory. Someone opened the door of the ambulance and I began to step out of the ambulance. But the policeman held out his hand to stop me. Seconds later after this reprimand, I stepped onto the internal roadway and beside a round flowerbed.

Anyway, I arrived in the hospital convinced of the notion that I had been successful in dividing the work force in the factory into two camps and I believed also that my job in the hospital would be much the same in that I would have to divide the patients into two warring factions. I began to canvas the patients towards that end. I also refused medication. But eventually I was held down and injected and that rather put an end to my attempt to divide the patient body into two factions.

But the notion that humanity was in fact esoterically divided into two factions was, if anything, quite prevalent among the patient population of Canley. I confess that this notion of an esoterically divided humanity was to stay with me for quite a number of years; but now I regard this notion in much the same light as those delusional ideas that become *idée fixe* in the minds of some psychiatric clients and so go to disfigure their telling of what may have been some otherwise genuine experience of the supernatural.

I heard one interesting refinement of the idea of a divided world and a divided humanity in my time in Canley. I was out walking on the internal roadway one day when I met up with a party of three patients and the more able fellow of the three drew attention of the Roman-ness of Canley and to the Roman-ness of authority in general in the Western world with the following line of speech:

"Villas … twenty-eight day Section … lunar month!"

This staccato line of conversation has stayed with me. The Roman circus of old was seen as an exercise in justice. This coarse justice of ancient world is now continued and greatly expanded upon by means of television.

A SURPRISE WITNESS FOR THE DEFENCE: THE PARANOID SCHIZOPHRENIC

I consider it advisable to refrain from quoting terms of racial abuse even if only in comparison. But somewhere lower down in terms of infamy than terms of racial abuse lurks the term 'paranoid schizophrenic'. Few mentally ill murderers can go to jail without having this sobriquet thrown at them. And it should be noted that in the case of this infamous term 'paranoid schizophrenic', the epithet is as important – if not more important – than the noun. For, as is indicative of an abiding carelessness in psychiatry, the word 'schizophrenia' is a word of dubious etymology.

In any event, in the lexicon of the well-dressed psychiatrist there can scarcely be a more damning term than that of 'paranoid schizophrenic'. It is therefore something of a choice insult toward these well-dressed doctors for me to assert that the more characteristic delusions of the paranoid schizophrenic are in some ways the least adorned of all delusions and so the most apt to betray their origin in oppressive experience. The more the sub-text of the delusions of a paranoid schizophrenic are concerned with a questioning of the actual privacy of his or her unspoken thoughts or even with his or her attempt at rationalisation of what he or she half understands as violation of such privacy, the more the paranoid schizophrenic is nearer the truth than are his elegant doctor masters.

*R*OBIN HOOD

There was a patient in Canley I chose to call Robin Hood. It was said of Robin Hood that, if a division of the United States cavalry were to ride into Canley, it would cause him no surprise or alarm. Simply, the man lived in the world of childrens' fiction. Robin Hood, Batman and the Three Musketeers and so on were practically the only reality he knew.

Robin Hood must have been about twenty-five at the time I knew him; but he never had much cause to shave. Most times I saw him he had a little grey stubble on his chin. He was always in pyjamas because he was always 'high'. In fact, the only time I knew him not to be high was when he went comatose for three days. I guess he knew no other way of coming down from his 'high'.

In this book I accuse the psychiatrists of pursuing a minimalist form of medicine. But even I have to admit that there was nothing that could be done for Robin Hood, apart from feeding him tablets. The likes of Robin Hood provide the doctors with something of an alibi. Their unstated argument might be stated thus: *We can do little or nothing for our worst patients, so why should we do any more for some of our better patients?*

POSSESSION

There was something of the air of a bucket of rotten apples about Stephen. Tall and thin with a slightly stooped neck and with Buddy Holly glasses, Stephen was the sort of person some people avoided and some few others chose as a companion. He claimed to have 'powers'. Some people believed that he did have 'powers'. I remember on one occasion when the patient I call Robin Hood was angry with me, Robin Hood turned to me and indignantly said:

" You don't believe Stephen has 'powers'!"

Well, as a matter of fact, I did and still do believe that Stephen had 'powers'. There wasn't much education in the man but he was particularly good at coming up with the name of a child – any child – who had just cropped up un-named in conversation. He also claimed that anyone who did him wilful harm was apt to come to grief. I could see where some people would be very tempted to behave cruelly towards Stephen and I could also well believe that these people would suffer for that.

Stephen himself said that his mother was possessed. I wouldn't be one to believe that. But I would be one to believe something else, namely that Stephen himself was possessed. Now, I am quite aware that the advent of psychiatry – in particular the advent of Sigmund Freud – is seen as a triumph over superstition where people formerly thought of as possessed by devils were recognised as being merely mentally ill. But I am sorry to say that, if you hang around psychiatric hospitals long enough, you will come to recognise that possession of a kind is a fact of life in the case of some small number of psychiatric patients. But this does not mean that I would recommend exorcism for one possessed, nor does it mean that I believe in the ancient idea that the supernatural sphere is given over to a contest for souls between God and the angels on one hand and devil and the demons on other.

A HELPFUL NURSE

I would be giving the wrong impression if I were to give the impression that I didn't enjoy myself in Canley. I was 'high' of course; and, because I was in mental hospital, I could do a lot of silly things with impunity. Better still, I was at last in the company of people that were prepared to talk to me.

In the early days of my hospitalisation when I was confined to pyjamas and my movement was therefore greatly restricted, I got great support from an exceptional nurse named Peter. In the great divide between male nurses who are macho-men and male nurses who are that bit more hesitant before the world, Peter not surprisingly fell into the latter category. Bespectacled and just the hint of stoop, he carried himself with some of the self-consciousness of the amateur actor.

Peter wasn't beyond having a little joke at my expense. In my Canley days I was spouting a lot of pseudo-revolutionary nonsense and Peter was one to take notice of this nonsense talk of mine. One day as I was walking the corridor with Peter, possibly just before the two of us went for a walk in the grounds, Peter decided to joke with another nurse who was walking against us and Peter's joke went as follows:

"I'm afraid of a mass break-out by the patients!"

The nurse walking against us laughed. Peter's joke highlighted a fact about psychiatric patients everywhere and that fact was and is the abject dependence of psychiatric patients on the psychiatric authorities. Which fact psychiatry is known to exploit.

_I_NSIDERS – with Richard and Jim

I FIND A FRIEND

Early on in my time in Canley I befriended a second generation Irishman. At the time of our first meeting, he had two books on his person. One was *Alice In Wonderland* and other a book on Zen Buddhism that featured a set of prints on how to catch a bull – this last item obviously intended as spiritual lesson rather than as a set of instructions. I couldn't but be impressed by what these books had to say about my new acquaintance. Again, I have to note the damnably prosaic detail of how so much of my life was decided by the likes of book and songs. Before long, this man by the real name of Patrick and I were constant companions in the hospital.

Patrick was a self-taught but skilled painter. He would spend the rest of his life painting in his spare time; but would never master the very middle-class politics that goes into staging an exhibition. For my part, I had already purchased an Olivetti manual typewriter for what also would be a lifelong effort at artistic endeavour.

We therefore had a common interest in art, especially wayward art.

As we walked the vast grounds in that glorious summer of 1972, we had our little jests. As we walked by the Church of England building, Patrick would ask:

"Does the Church of England have a lightening conductor to protect itself from acts of God?"

Similarly, in repetition of a famous piece of Zen dialogue, I might ask:

"Does a dog have a God-like nature?"

To which Patrick would reply: "Woof woof!"

Nearly all our walks together took us to the Alpha Club, a basement café where for little more than a ration of tobacco elderly patients worked at selling tea and cheap confectionery and Woodbine cigarettes priced in the singular at a penny. There in the Alpha Club, you could see patients in their sixties and seventies seated at metal beach tables as they smoked roll-your-owns and listened to the pop music on cheap pocket transistors.

$\mathcal{T}$AKING STOCK

But, if the experience of the supernatural by the mentally ill is a small concern, so small that the enemies of the mentally ill believe as their right to dismiss all talk of the supernatural by the mentally ill, I don't come to the reader empty handed. For as the obfuscations of C.J. Jung and the romanticism of R.D. Laing will not prepare the reader, I am about to pull a sizable rabbit out of the hat.

Simply, a sizable minority of psychiatric doctors and a sizable minority of psychiatric nurses are in possession of an esoteric body of knowledge that pretty much drives a stake through the vampiric heart of scientific materialism. Because this body of esoteric knowledge concerns matters not of a fleeting or haphazard nature, but of items built into the fabric of life and observably so, I prefer to speak of this body of esoteric knowledge as concerning itself not so much with something supernatural but with something *preternatural*.[6]

The next section reports on my first suspicions concerning the existence of this preternatural lore.

---

[6] Beyond what is normal or natural as against supernatural which is attributed to some force beyond scientific understanding or the laws of nature.

ANTIQUE MYSTERY

I don't think that even in the dying days of the 1960s anybody would be justified in terming Canley a psychiatric hospital. Canley was very much a mental hospital. Indeed, it was in many ways still nothing more than a lunatic asylum. You couldn't reside in Canley without thinking of previous times. That sense of an abiding past was probably most brought to life in the detail that the meadowlands and cornfields about Canley lunatic asylum were still patrolled by a ragged hermit and his pack of six hungry dogs. Old England.

Even Canley village with its two public houses, grocery shop and little pond with two resident swans was not without one architectural feature that spoke of other, perhaps less happy days. I speak of a small, conical prison cell in the centre of the village. This prison cell had a legend as old as itself carved on its wall. The not exactly friendly legend read: DO WELL. FEAR NOT

I often gazed at that legend with a vague feeling of anger. I felt baffled by this legend and my anger sprung from the fact that I half sensed that the solution to my bafflement was well within my grasp. By this time I was already suspicious that language in general held secret message, even if my early attempts at deciphering the message in language only serve to embarrass me now. But in my Canley days I never did get to decipher what it was that so baffled about this stern phrase DO WELL. FEAR NOT. Yet, it is a matter of great pride to me that this mystery of this prison wall legend presented itself to me during my Canley days. And it is a matter of even greater pride to me that I did eventually get to solve the mystery of that legend. For this little matter of the prison cell legend lead me into an area of knowledge of great importance. I refer to the vast subject of the innate pun that I will discuss in detail in segments as the penultimate item at the end of some chapters from here on.

HORACE BATCHELOR

To the Dada-influenced rock 'n' roll outfit the Bonzo Dog Doo Dah Band must go most of the credit for helping ensure that the name Horace Batchelor will live forever. I would also like to contribute my little bit to helping preserve the memory of Horace Batchelor and I ask like-minded writers who come after me to also help out in this most worthy of undertakings. So, who was Horace Batchelor? Who indeed was this fellow whose name should never be allowed slip into oblivion? Again. Who was Horace Batchelor?

Give me a minute to elucidate. In the days before governments took a leaf out of the gangster's book and authorised national lotteries, the only hope an ordinary individual in Great Britain had of coming into extraordinary wealth was to play the football pools. The football pools supposedly called for an element of skill on the punter's part – but only supposedly. A win at the football pools was as random an event as a win in any national lottery.

Yet, according to a frequent advertisement on Radio Luxemburg, the one and only Horace Batchelor and his famous Infra-draw method could help you – help anybody – secure a win in the football pools. Ha Ha. One thing I like about this Horace Batchelor is how he appealed to the scientific instincts of listeners to his advertisement. The great ignorant public that is out there at all times was, at this time in the 1960s, just becoming aware of such esoteric matters as infra-red and ultra-violet. So, how could such a public believe that any system that boasted of an Infra-draw method fail!

I am more than happy to lend the illustrious name of Horace Batchelor to a scientific principle of my own invention, which I proceed to state as follows:

The Horace Batchelor Principle is a fallacious principle whereby that which is most suggestive of the trappings and the cultural history of science is preferred to actual science.

The Horace Batchelor Principle has many among both the uneducated and learned in its grip.

CANLEY IS DISCREET IN ITS USE OF 'ECT'

It was said of one politician and it is probably true of most mainstream politicians that their mere presence is sufficient to reduce a cathedral to the level of a bookmaker's office. Similarly, the use of 'ECT' in a hospital is sufficient to reduce that hospital to the level of a concentration camp.

I have no way of knowing how prevalent the use of 'ECT' was in Canley. Canley was a very large hospital and the authorities could easily keep their use of 'ECT' out of view of the majority of the patients. As it happened, I am only aware of one patient receiving 'ECT' in Canley during my time there. The patient in question was a noble looking Indian who was quite depressed but nevertheless well able to speak. I don't doubt that psychiatry would be more than happy to cite the case of this Indian for whom normal life had ceased as a patient as an example of the type of patient for whom 'ECT' was not alone the best treatment but the only treatment. But I hold the suspicion that this same Indian would in all probability respond well to any number of considerably less violent therapies.

IRRESPONSIBILITY BY THE AUTHORITIES

The psychiatrists in Canley were not at all interested in the part radical therapy played in turning me into someone so extravagantly 'high'. This indifference to the history of my illness was arguably part of a greater culture of irresponsibility that saw me discharged from Canley on double the measure of tablets which – for what, when all expediency demands disclosure, psychiatry admits – can kill.

ONE WISE MAN

Not everybody in authority in Canley remained unaware of the origins of my 'high'. There was a green-suited social worker that I had a few casual conversations with. I told him of some of my experiences in London prior to my committal. In particular, I informed him of the bodily sensations I experienced after my life changing visit to Kaleidoscope. The social worker spoke of these bodily sensations of mine as being consistent with the map of acupuncture meridians in the human body. This was a wise comment. If I had the kind of cunning that some people have, I might have better absorbed this interesting reference to acupuncture and might as a consequence have saved myself a lot of time and bother.

Farewell to Canley

The evenings were getting cooler in Canley. My friend Patrick bought an anorak in preparation for the coming autumn and winter. By this time in the history of the world that item of clothing known as an anorak was associated with paramilitary types across the globe. Whenever Patrick and I set out on one of our walks, particularly at the moment Patrick was emerging from his villa into the open air, Patrick would pretend to discharge a machine gun. We were both apt to laugh at this piece of mimicry.

Inevitably, the time came for me to walk away from Canley. As I did walk away from my villa Patrick urged me to write. I said that I would. We've been corresponding every since.

By this time, I was no longer 'high' and I remembered that when I had been back home on holiday the first thing required of me was that I should get a haircut. I did the sensible thing this time and visited a barber before taking the ship back to Ireland.

THE INNATE PUN:

The more ordinary innate pun

Almost every setting outside the home where people meet at an intimate level has its tradition of the supernatural. For example, theatre people and military people tend to have their stories of the supernatural; and normally theatre people and military can tell their stories of the supernatural with the expectation that they will be listened to. As it happens, people in psychiatric society (that is the people who work in and the people who avail of the psychiatric services) have perhaps the richest tradition of supernatural and preternatural lore of any grouping in society; but people in psychiatric society – be they professionals or clients – are inclined to keep their esoteric knowledge to themselves. This is more than understandable given the particular hostility of official psychiatric literature and the hostility of the modern world in general to talk of the supernatural and the preternatural

In a climate so hostile to talk of the supernatural and preternatural especially by a client of the psychiatric services, I as client of the psychiatric services believe myself well advised – if self advised – to concentrate on a small but worthy portion of preternatural lore that enjoys some currency in psychiatric society. This small body of preternatural lore concerns itself with what I variously term the innate or reductionist or platonic pun. In going into great but by no means exhaustive detail about the small and routine feature of preternatural that is the innate pun, I run the risk of boring the reader or, worse, I run the risk of appearing distracted by the one idea.

But, notwithstanding these real risks, I cannot resist going after the greater prize on offer, that is, I believe, the providing at least a minority of my readers with greater reason to reject scientific materialism.

I should say something about how I came to be acquainted about the existence of a system of innate puns in language.

I recall an African patient in Canley who believed that the forename 'Rod' in the name of the entertainer Rod Stewart could be understood as a term of phallic significance. I now suspect that this African was not going to extend his knowledge of innate puns beyond one or two obvious puns; and in that he would have a lot of comrades. As for myself at the time, I didn't attach any importance to the pun mentioned by the African and I hadn't the wit to connect this pun of his to my own little suspicions concerning language that had their beginnings about this time. Thirty or more years later, I would say that what would go to distinguish someone who is knowledgeable in the ways of the innate pun is that he or she would be not alone aware of the obvious pun on the forename of Rod Stewart.

I returned to Ireland after my time in Canley; and from 1976 onwards I gave many a term in the one Irish psychiatric hospital. In the time leading up to and in the course of my first hospitalisation, I was introduced by others to the notion that there was a large body of puns in the English language and perhaps all language that pre-existed their discovery or use by human beings. In other words, there exists in language a pattern of wordplay that couldn't be of human invention and had to be of preternatural authorship. Down the years I became a little obsessed with identifying and even evaluating those puns that, as part of a grand process, stood to reveal the fact that they were portion of preternatural design.

In this intermittent discussion devoted to puns, I must briefly address the subject of punning-mania. I have read none of the in-depth, technical literature on the subject of punning-mania. For all I know such literature may refer to mental patients who pun compulsively and nonsensically, in which case I can have little problem with such literature and can have little problem with the term punning-mania. But I am not one to pun compulsively and nonsensically and I have never met anyone who did this either … even if I allow that even perhaps the smallest concern with the innate pun is not the most utilitarian of pursuits.

Clearly, the punning-system has implications for our understanding of the supernatural and preternatural. Personally, I am inclined to believe that the preternatural in particular co-exists with the material universe(s) as revealed by science and that this preternatural is every bit as vast and, for the greater part, as indifferent about the career of mankind as is the material universe. I therefore have little time for those who claim to enjoy the favour or know the mind of the ultimate reality in the universe. Which is another way of saying that I am not a particularly religious person. But, that said, I have good reason to believe that there are many people living who have a good understanding of the punning-system but who, nevertheless, retain a religious outlook.

Encouraged by my subject matter, I don't much distinguish between meaningful puns and meaningful rhymes – and I refer to instances of either as puns.

Earlier in the narrative portion of this book I spoke of a small, conical, beehive-like, one-cell antique prison in the centre of the English village of Canley. This prison had a legend as old as itself carved on its stone wall. The not exactly friendly legend read: *DO WELL. FEAR NOT.*

Although greatly intrigued by this legend, I never did get to solve its mystery while a three-month inmate of the large hospital beside the village. Indeed, it was at least four years later that I suddenly realised that the legend on the Canley prison could be translated to *DO WELL. FEAR KNOT*. Such that the legend was in fact issuing cryptic but ever so grim warning of the prospect of the hangman's knot.

You could argue that this reference to the hangman's knot is too local a pun to serve as an overture to this discussion of innate puns. My argument after all is that innate puns are not, in the first instance, of human invention; and I am in no doubt that the authority that instigated the prison legend fully intended its sinister implication. Nevertheless, I feel that this reference to the hangman's knot is not untypical of innate puns in that many a word has the object or concept it names reduced by means of pun to its most physical element, consequence or association. Also, innate puns are at their most discernible when converting some plain or abstract word or phrase into something decidedly negative and sinister ... and things don't get any more sinister than the hangman's knot.

By now the reader is getting the idea that an innate pun is most typically an exercise in *bathos* 7 where a word yields a pun that is someway descriptive or deflating of the thing or concept named by the original word. For more expansive than exact example of this process, I might mention that punning-system is telling us that 'the small guy' (the man of no power and influence) is quite often the fall guy.

Down the years I have developed a technique whereby I could – and the reader now can – unearth a good number of meaningful puns of the plainer kind. The simple technique is to select one monosyllabic word and alter the first letter going from A to Z and then proceed to spot as many direct and poetic connections between the words thus formed. I now illustrate this technique at work in the case of one group of words.

The first word I select is 'back'. The list in this case goes something like: back, black, crack, flack, hack, knack, lack, (Big) Mac, pack, quack, rack, sack, shack, slack, slacks, smack, snack, stack, tack, track, whack. Those on the rack are on their backs and are likely to crack. The punning-system is not politically correct and so it is possible to create some rather racist puns on the word 'black'. To take the flack is to take a whack. A hack perhaps has a knack and nothing more. A Big Mac is at best only a snack. To pack you have to stack. In the old days a quack may have carried a sack and at any time a quack is only a hack. The pessimism of the punning-system is evident in the suggestion that the sack is likely to only contain slack. A smack may amount to a whack. Those

---

7 An anticlimax created by an unintentional lapse in mood from the sublime to the trivial or ridiculous.

on the right tack are on the right track. Poetically, those on the athletic track are on the rack.

The second word to which I apply the one technique is 'bed'. The list in this case goes as follows: bed, dead, fed, head, led, lead, red, read, said, spread, thread, wed. It has long been noted that the wedding leads to the bedding and so 'bed' rhymes meaningfully with 'wed'. The dead are often found in bed. A head is fed. To have lead an army into battle is in a sense to have head an army. A lead pencil requires the use of the head. The punning-system is never more in its element than when converting an abstract word to a physical word, and so to have said something is to have exercised the head on two counts.

By now you will consider the technique I have demonstrated to be either a most enlightening technique or an exercise in absurdity. But the fact of the matter is that, if you read this intermittent treatise to the end without going on to observe innate puns not quoted in this book in your day-to-day life, you will not be able to say you have read this book with any measure of open-mindedness or sympathy.

To spot innate puns in multisyllabic words is a little more difficult. For that reason I shall now mention some general innate puns in multisyllabic words. At the very least a car accident causes a dent. A committee is less likely to partake of alcohol than it is of tea. The same goes even more so for a teetotaller. The anti-mystical ethos of the punning-system is evident in the fact that the fakir is identified as the faker.

The alimentary canal is very much the elementary canal. Conversely, one really taken by the punning-system will have difficulty in hearing the word 'elementary' without thinking of the word *alimentary*.

Far from a voice speaking in loud voice from the clouds that it is well pleased with Jesus, the punning-system is inclined to note that the Beatitudes are platitudes – which they certainly are. The Beatitudes/platitudes pun is the cutting sort of comment that serves to validate the punning-system. There are thousands upon thousands of such extra-meaningful puns in the English language alone.

Incidentally, the *platitude* pun is far from being the only comment the punning-system makes on the Beatitudes. I advise the reader to note all that I have to say later on about references to the bee in language; and then the reader can decide for him or herself if the punning-system has some more complimentary things to say about the Beatitudes … for the Beatitudes are very much the *bee-attitudes*.

Anyone with the slightest knowledge of quantum physics will agree that quantum physics is very much phantom physics.

Frequently the punning-system has a wry take on the world and in present context I might note that 'the clinical' is very much *the cynical* especially in the case of such necessary but neccessarily worldly fellows as the clinical psychologist, the clinical psychiatrist and that near deity; the clinical director.

I could be well accused of giving a false impression by seeming to suggest that knowledge of the innate pun is confined to psychiatric society. For the truth of the matter is that nearly everybody – except the very dull – make the acquaintance from time to time of an innate pun.

That once upon a time favoured denouement of a play or movie known as 'the happy ending' is often from an aesthetic point of view *a crappy ending*. More poetically, 'a happy ending' is very likely to contain the suggestion that it is shortly about to turn into *a nappy ending*. I remind Americans that 'nappy' is the European English term for the diaper.

To refer back to the macabre theme with which I began speaking about the innate pun I might note that the threat of hanging is no longer such a threat in modern democracies where capital punishment is deleted from the statue book; but, then again, as a smoker still hoping to reform I have to point out that lung cancer is very much *hung cancer*.

HOMILY 3

*T*HE LIVING JOE NASH

As his mortal remains lie beneath the verdant sod and as he enjoys eternal bliss elsewhere, Joe Nash remains an example to us all. In such circumstances, it may be a mistake to think that Joe has really departed this world. You may not ordinarily think of yourself as having today met Joe with a lottery ticket in his hand at the one-shut one-open twin-door narrow entrance and exit to the village convenience store as a summer mist dampens down the dust on the street, or you may not believe yourself to having today gone to Joe's dwelling with the intention, as you arranged with him, for you both to go to a forthcoming ball game of some importance. You may not ordinarily believe these things but why not begin to do so now?

As you turn on the tap to shave, the very ordinariness and near universality of the act could well inspire you to think that Joe Nash is there by your side waiting to perform the same humble act he performed thousands of times before that is giving himself a scratch of a blade to better meet the public. Or – and the little scenes I mention are purely by way of illustration – you could be listening to Kris Kristofferson sing 'Me and Bobby McGee' on your transistor and you wouldn't be over-extending yourself to think that a few miles away, thanks in the first instance to the genius of Marconi, no less a man than Joe Nash is lapping up the folk poetry of Kristofferson and relishing it.

Engage thus with good Joe and appreciate the truth of the line in his mortuary card to the effect that Joe has only gone into another room.

4

NO FUN ON THE FARM

ℐ RETURN AS A SMOKER

I returned to the family farm a smoker. In the days leading up to my committal to Canley I bummed a Consulate cigarette from a Nigerian in the double-glazed window factory and I was hooked.

They say that lists are a part of poetry but that lists are not necessarily poetry. Nevertheless, a less than complete list of the cigarette and pipe tobaccos I have smoked includes:

Craven A, Number 6, Consulate, Golden Virginia, Old Holborn, Dunhills, Handy Cut flake, St Bruno flake and ready rubbed, Mick McQuaid plug (named after a maker of rot-gut poteen), Mick McQuaid ready rubbed, Mellow Virginia, Condor plug and ready rubbed, Three Nuns, Digger plug, Clarke's Perfect Plug, Garyowen plug, Golden Nugget Plug, Maltan, Old Road, Four Square half cut, Clan, Erinmore plug, Erinmore ready rubbed, Drum, Duma, Samson, Major, Rothmans, Cutter's Choice, Woodbines, Sweet Afton (manufactured and roll your own), Gold Flake, Hamlet cigars, Café Crème cigars, Half Corona cigars, Benson and Hedges, Benson and Hedges Rolled Gold, Malboro, Superkings, Gold Bond, Carroll's Number One, Player's Navy Cut, Amber Leaf and lately in an effort to commence my reformation, Silk Cut.

Like an alcoholic complaining about the price of tomatoes, I am critical of minimalist psychiatry that, in its minimalism, does nought to counter the great cult of smoking among its clients.

_A_ DROP OUT IS PUNISHED SOONER OR LATER

Now, I have to be honest about both the local community and about myself. I think it would be stretching it to say that somebody home from England and directly out of an English mental hospital would be highly regarded in my local community. But that said, I don't think that I gave the local community much of a chance. Inevitably, at the time of my return I felt a little shame at how things had turned out for me in England.

So for three years after my discharge from Canley, I went to Sunday Mass, I attended my general practitioner to get my tablets and that was about the extent of my outings from the nicely isolated farm. Incidentally, the farm is nicely isolated in that we are two miles from the nearest village and the actual drive way into to the farm – termed a passage – is quite a forbidding hill.

Reasonably happy as I am about this isolated dwelling place now, I do on reflection get quietly angry about the measure of my isolation for those three years after Canley. In particular, I get angry with one Irish consultant psychiatrist whose name and hospital I have long forgotten. Either after getting his name and address from the Canley authorities or else acting purely on my own initiative, I wrote to this consultant explaining that I was a psychiatric patient attending a general practitioner and on such and such a dose of psychiatric drugs. This consultant wrote back to me saying to keep attending the general practitioner and keep taking the tablets and no more. At the very least my extravagant medication regime should have worried him into more positive action than that.

Two GREAT 'MESSIANIC' SONGS

'The Mighty Quinn' - Manfred Mann
'Jumpin' Jack Flash' - The Rolling Stones

Bob Dylan once spoke of 'Tomorrow is a long time' as recorded by Elvis as his favourite cover version of the many cover versions of his songs. That's understandable, I suppose. But Bob was more than impressed – even astonished – when he first heard Manfred Mann's version of 'The Mighty Quinn'. No wonder, as Manfred Mann had a turned a song, which up to then had only existed on demo disc, into a classic.

What to say of 'The Mighty Quinn'? I suppose you could say that Bob, who has had his own dealings with Messiah-hood and his own encounters with Messiahs, has given us not a hymn of faith as such but his own version of *Waiting For Godot*. But, unlike Beckett's play, Dylan's song has just a little optimism. One can't but suppose that 'The Mighty Quinn' will actually appear and fulfil his promise.

The Rolling Stones made their money not by suggesting that there was a party on the way, but by putting across or rather by personifying the idea that the party was in full swing. 'Jumpin' Jack Flash' may have had terrible trials and tribulations, not to mention a portentous birth; but he speaks of himself in the first person and as one very much in your presence.

Many are of the opinion that 'Jumpin' Jack Flash' is the Rolling Stones' best song. No wonder its authorship is in dispute. One commentator went so far as to suggest that the song is autobiographical. Well, I ask you! Many also believe it to be a drug song. But, unless 'flash' be a drug code word that I haven't heard of, the song contains no direct reference to drugs. But only druggies could have written the song!

Songs have so brightened my life at every turn that I am within my rights to celebrate them.

A HOLIDAY IN ENGLAND

Marooned on the farm as I was for three years, I did during this time go on holiday to visit my friend Patrick in London. I fell in with an exploration of Patrick's world, visiting a hostel run by Christian evangelicals where he had spent some time and visiting a commune of sorts in Wales where ex-residents of the hostel had set up home under the watchful eyes of a middle-class couple. I remember that I offered one of the evangelical women in the hostel a roll-your-own cigarette. I didn't have much sense in those days.

In London, Patrick and I had made a little pilgrimage up to see the mere streets of Richmond where the Rolling Stones had started their epical adventure and another little pilgrimage to see the pagoda in Kew Gardens mentioned in one of Michael Moorcock's *Jerry Cornelius* novels.

Otherwise, the holiday was only notable for the fact that I ran out of Wales in a disorientated state.

HOW THE IDEA OF LIFE ALTERING THERAPY FOLLOWED ME FROM LONDON

Down home on the farm with not a friend in the locality, I was easy prey to anybody or anything that offered the prospect of a better life. As fate would have it, that piece of conversation between two women in *Kaleidoscope* that mentioned Primal Therapy stayed in mind. As fate would also have it, second-hand as opposed to purchased copies of the London *Sunday Times* were in the habit of finding their way into the farmhouse on the hill; and one particular issue of this newspaper contained a six-line review of the paperback edition of Arthur Janov's book *The Primal Scream*. This review was very positive. It said that Arthur Janov's Primal Therapy was every bit as revolutionary as was Sigmund Freud's psychoanalysis in its day, only that Janov's Primal Therapy had the potential to do greater good for the world than Freud's psychoanalysis ever did. I wrote to Patrick in London, asking him to send me on a paperback copy of said book.

When it arrived on the farm, my copy of Arthur Janov's book had for a cover a rather lush, even primordial forest scene and not the reproduction of the grim Edvard Munch painting that featured on subsequent editions of the book. I read the book and was convinced of its truth. I never did take on board at the time Arthur Janov's extraordinary admission that neither the purpose nor the effect of Primal Therapy was to confer happiness on the patient. Nor did I quite bring to mind the fact that my one previous adventure with a radical therapy had not exactly ended in glory for me. I wanted this Primal Therapy and I wanted it bad. I became quite a bore in my letters to Patrick in London on how much I desired this Primal Therapy. So much so that in one letter in reply Patrick cynically asked was there money in Primal Therapy. Patrick's question was to the point. There was money in Primal Therapy.

THE INNATE PUN

I recall another conversation with an Irish nurse who was admitting me to hospital. She simply asked me to name my next of kin. For something that is most likely to happen to the disorientated, I was struck by some pun or other in the phrase 'next of kin'.

"There's a pun in that phrase," I said.

"Of course, there is," replied the nurse matter-of-factly but sincerely before moving on with the business in hand.

The most obvious pun on the phrase 'next of kin' is *next of skin*. This pun has the effect of rendering a rather abstract term a physical dimension. But there are many other meaningful puns with this most legalistic yet human of phrases. For example, the word 'next' can turn itself into necks and that, in turn, turns itself into fecks. In combination with any of the foregoing puns, 'of' can become *off* … and it might be worth mentioning also that 'kin' can become *ken*.

I remember a few other occasions when I mention the subject of the punning-system to medical professionals; and their attitude has always been one of matter of fact acknowledgment that there was a significant punning-system in language. I might also mention that at one time I managed to present a consultant psychiatrist who had no professional involvement with me with a computer file of an early draft of this book. I learnt subsequently that consultant had distributed this file among the more learned and enquiring members of the staff in the hospital. This latter response in some contrast to the speed with which psychiatric professionals normally put the more free-associative writings of patients in the rubbish bin.

The ubiquitous pronoun 'it' allows for two crude puns. Nobody need be in any doubt by what is meant when people speak of someone 'putting their foot in it'. The conjunction 'and' rather famously puns with *hand*. The conjunction 'and' is to some extent a happy, positive word connecting different and sometimes disparate concepts within a sentence; and *hand* in the sense of a hand reaching out in handshake respects this positive aspect of the conjunction 'and'. Nobody is in much doubt as to which of the two is the more important party in that famous sixties phrase Simon and Garfunkel and there is every sense in which the phrase meaningfully translates as *Simon hand Garfunkel*. As pun-word *hand* is frequently employed as a transitive verb.

Of course, to say that the suffix '-er' translates as her is only to imply that the other syllables in a word the ends with that suffix go to reveal what precisely is *being done to her*. You might note that the second word in the phrase 'ozone layer' contains the pun *lay her*; but it is the word 'ozone' that presumably yields puns that go to determine the precise punning-statement contained in the phrase. I cannot be quite certain of the likely puns on the word 'ozone'; but in the course of this book I do enable the reader to determine the punning-statement contained in many an obscure word and phrase.

The noun 'ball' seems in the plural at least to be entirely masculine. The punning-system seems to derive particular humour from the anti-working-man stance of the wordplay that has us translate the clothing item known as the overalls to the *overballs*.

In popular usage 'ass' as term for stupid person may involve more a reference to the donkey than to the buttocks. But, anyway, it is worth noting that as a portion of the wry humour of punning-system, the term 'the class-room' translates as the *ass-room*. Also, I might mention that the long-term mentally ill in Ireland (of which I am one) are like royalty entitled to travel free on public transport provided they carry a card sometimes referred to as a travel pass card and sometimes simply as a pass card. I don't doubt that in my minds of some – but let be said not all – bus drivers and ticket collectors the pass card is the *ass card*.

The theatrical genre of farce – which one authority has condemned as comedy without character – is perhaps condemned and perhaps even described by the inevitable pun with *arse*.

The conjunction 'but' normally prefaces a statement objecting to what was just said and so perhaps the no less inevitable pun of butt is quite felicitous.

Pun-references to the knee form quite an important but obscure part of innate wordplay. Be all that as it may, pun-references to the knee would seem to be all bound up with notions of compliance and correctness. There follows a short list of words that either in their pronunciation or spelling contain a reference to the knee (and I leave the reader to decide if these words are the sort of words with which one would associate with the qualities of compliance and correctness): canny, ceremony, crone, drone, funeral, Geneva Convention, genealogy, honey (moon), journey, loony bin, medicine, money, need, ozone layer, prone and vine.

'Toe' meaningfully – and perhaps even injunctively – puns with *blow*. But there is also mention of the toe in words such as preposition *to* and the nouns 'today' and 'tomorrow'. In such puns there is a general reference to the toe as the portion of the anatomy most to the fore in movement.

Incidentally the injunctive pun or, if you prefer, the commanding pun is a definite feature of the system. We are for instance advised to match a patch with the garment of which it is going to become part; and we are most solemnly advised to think before we use ink.

HOMILY 4

THE INFINITE WELCOME OF JOE NASH

I remind myself that you might be one of the many people out there who feel they are unworthy to be part of the fellowship of Joe Nash; and I remind myself urgently that, if you are one of these mistaken people, I should not delay in addressing you.

Believe you me, I can empathise with your thinking that now that Joe is at peace in a climate of endless summer that he, notwithstanding his great good will, just might not be bothered to accompany you as you negotiate your way through your daily frustrations. This feeling of unworthiness may be more apt to strike you – and to strike you hard – if you happen to be one of those people who are accident-prone and for whom nothing goes right. But I am adamant in my advice to you and all those who entertain scruples and misgivings about inviting Joe into their lives. My advice to you all is to forget it! Forget all those feelings that have plagued you from birth that you are not worthy of any honour, least of all the favour and companionship of Joe. Forget, forget and remember you have a definite pal in Joe, who was where you are and is where you are going.

5

HOUSE OF PAIN

CONCERNING MY APPROACH TO THE SUBJECT MATTER IN THIS CHAPTER

Old revolutions – new graffiti.
 – Grace Jones great line turned back to front.

AN ACT OF FOLLY OF THE KIND THAT CALLS FOR AN EXPLANATION

In 1976 I did something that the most powerful man in the world – the President of the United States of America at any time – wouldn't dream of doing.

I turned my back on 'mum and apple pie' and all things that stand between a body and perdition. How I came to be so foolish as to do this requires an explanation. Not too much of an explanation about myself ... it is, after all, reasonably clear that I'm lacking in the sort of cunning that most people take for granted as a portion of their make-up. Rather the required explanation must concern itself with the history of psychotherapy ... and how that history brought me to throw caution and my health to the wind.

THE UNACKNOWLEDGED DEATH OF A TWENTIETH CENTURY IDEA

The fact that human beings – all human beings – are only a shadow of themselves contributed perhaps to the formulation of one great religious myth and one great secular myth. The Biblical myth of the Fall of Mankind and Plato's *Allegory of the Cave* [8] ... are both perhaps born of a vague feeling in the human heart that this world is secondary not to some fairytale existence in the past and not to some fairytale existence in the future but to all that is lost in the troubled development of the individual human being.

Much of the twentieth century thought and experiment concerned itself with restoring that which in the way of health and perception is lost in the troubled journey of the individual to so called maturity. I sadly report that this essentially honourable quest of the twentieth century that sought to allow the individual shake off the burden of his or her past has come to a definite end, to a conclusion, to a death if you like. I also report that there is now an all-out offensive in practically all media, practically all institutions to deny that this quest – and the many quite distinct discoveries that were made in the course of this quest – ever actually happened.

The idea that the individual could be rid of the impact of formative experience of the negative kind began somewhat hesitantly with Sigmund Freud's Psychoanalysis and ended with the brief success and enduring failure of Arthur Janov's Primal Therapy. The latter therapy failed not for any failing of the therapy but simply because the cure the therapy wrought was worse than the disease.

Of course, the Freudian psychoanalytic movement is still a force on the periphery and it is never likely to concede that Arthur Janov worked an unwitting *reductio ad absurdum* as regards all regression therapy. But that the fruit of the tree of knowledge proving too bitter in the case of Janov's Primal Therapy was, in my opinion, sufficient to close the door forever on one particular escape for a troubled human race. This is no cause for celebration.

---

8 The *Allegory of the Cave* can be found in Book VII of Plato's best-known work, *The Republic*, a lengthy dialogue on the nature of justice.

PRIMAL THERAPY COMES CLOSE TO HOME

My life of isolation on the farm continued from 1972 to 1976. Then, my friend Patrick wrote me a letter from London informing me that an organisation had advertised in a British pacifist magazine offering 'Primal Therapy for non-millionaires' and this organisation kept a house within the Irish Republic. The phrase 'Primal Therapy for non-millionaires' was surely a discreet way of saying that this organisation was offering Primal Therapy as described by Arthur Janov on the cheap. To make matters even more tempting for one such as I who might have some worries about travelling to another country this organisation was at least as near to me as the top end of the Irish Republic.

I was told later that most of those who entered therapy in this house called *Avalon* simply contacted the house and a little later turned up at the same house without further ado. I did something different. I entered into correspondence with this house. The house of *Avalon* had its own world-view and normally correspondence from the outside world was read by the members of the household with a considerable amount of shared amusement and contempt for the never very appropriate thinking of all those who were to come to *Avalon*. Even at an objective level my letters to *Avalon* were particularly silly; and so everybody in *Avalon* knew in advance that somebody particularly strange was on his way.

So, one day, with money to pay for my therapy secured from the sale of two cattle gifted to me by my father, in a truck delivering dairy produce whose driver had also been enlisted by my father to take me on this journey of folly, I set off for distant Donegal.

Ghosts I Met on the Road to 'Avalon'

In the writings of Carlos Castaneda there is a beautiful notion about the apprentice-sorcerer who, on reaching a certain level of enlightenment, will as matter of course see the people and towns that figured in his life up to that moment as mere ghosts. I don't wish to pretend for a moment that my trip to *Avalon* had a happy outcome for me … but to me some of the people I met after I alighted from the dairy produce truck and continued on the last thirty miles of my journey to *Avalon* have for me now a very ghostly quality about them.

The first man I met was a taxi driver who I enlisted to take me most of the remaining thirty miles to *Avalon*. If proof were needed that this journey of mine was a journey of folly, there could be no better proof than that my personality and luggage were so unfriendly to road travel that I had to take a taxi part of the way. If I say that the taxi driver was a man just a little obsessed by a local politician, the joke is at my expense. Because, if I yearned to tell this taxi driver that his obsession with a local politician was all Maya [9] and that I, by contrast, was on the journey of a lifetime to partake of a new science that was destined to transform the world, the fact of the matter was that within six weeks I would be returning in a shattered state to my home-place where obsessions with local politicians are quite in order and obsessions with new sciences that do not turn out quite as good as promised are regarded not just as Maya but as the stuff of madness.

I hitchhiked the last few miles of my journey. The first motor car I got into had three young male holiday-makers in it. They were curious about my business. I tried to explain to them all about the new science of Primal Therapy. I explained that breath techniques represented a large part of this therapy. But these young men were only familiar with breath techniques as a controlling device as in Yoga. They found it difficult to understand that people were now using breath techniques to unlock the secrets of the unconscious.

The next and last car I got into also had three young men in it. But these three were locals on the way to the actual fishing village where the *Avalon* commune was situated. They were excited about a pool tournament that was to take place in the village at the weekend. Pool was about to become a big attraction in many a drab pub across Ireland around this time in the 1970s. These three men

---

9 Literally "illusion" or "magic" with multiple meanings in Indian philosophies.

were not so impressed when they learnt that I was on the way to place called *Avalon.*

"Is it physiotherapy that goes on there?" one of them asked in less than enthusiastic voice!

This young man's question helps put *Avalon* in the cultural context of the time. The only therapy understood in Ireland at this time was physiotherapy and even that was probably considered suspect. These, after all, were the days when an acupuncturist, who was treating a client's back injury, had to hide the fact from the same client that he was actually practising acupuncture lest the client become outraged at so being the subject of so bizarre a treatment and run from the healing room in a state of undress.

$\mathcal{D}$EFINING A CULT

In the course of a more recent hospitalisation, I had an interesting conversation with a male nurse whose ultimate career path was to become a nurse for children with special needs. Nurses on that particular career path tend to stand out a little from nurses whose career path is strictly psychiatric. Indeed, when some nurses on the career path to nursing people with special needs come to do a term in a psychiatric ward, they are often shocked by the coarseness of life in such a place.

Anyway, I recently had this chat with a nurse for people with special needs on the subject of 1970s cults. The nurse, who was just a little inclined to pontificate, said that what distinguished a cult was that it involved the surrender of all power by a group of people to a powerful figure seen by the group as heroic, if not divine. According to that definition of a cult, *Avalon* was quite an atypical cult in that everybody that came to *Avalon* were first influenced to do so by a best selling book, *The Primal Scream* by Arthur Janov. I will discuss the quite technical but substantial differences between the therapy practised in the *Avalon* commune and the therapy outlined in Janov's book in a moment; but I should emphasize that I know now that one such as I who has no great tolerance of discomfort – not to speak of pain – had no business pursuing a primal therapy of any colour.

AVALON, THE PRETENCE AND THE REALITY

The most damning feature of *Avalon* was that little phrase they used in advertisement – 'Primal Therapy for non-millionaires'. As I have said, the implication here was that they were offering Janov's Primal Therapy on the cheap.

The first thing you saw when you came to the house called *Avalon* was the unkempt lawn and the garishly illustrated exterior of the house. But, more significantly, the next thing you saw as you stepped in the front door was a notice – a mission statement of sorts – that attempted to be satirical of Arthur Janov and his therapy. Really, I should have taken one look at this mission statement and I should have realised that *Avalon* was engaging in dubious advertising; and then I should have turned on my heels and ran back out the door, back to my lonely station on the farm in County Cork. But I was never good at making instant decisions, never good at thinking on my feet and so I submitted myself to the therapy in *Avalon*.

I was shocked from the word go at the type of therapy the commune had to offer. It was a primal therapy in so far as the client did engage with his or her upbringing; and the client who persisted with the therapy did regress further and further into his or her childhood. There was shouting, there was tears, there was fists banging on cushions ... but at all times the client remained in an adult mode of consciousness. This in sharp contrast to Janovian therapy where the client is frequently reduced to the level of a child or baby. But then nobody in commune was ever ushered into a conscious coma and nobody every uttered a primal scream. (Realise that the so-called primal scream is not a device of Janov's Primal Therapy but an effect of Janov's Primal Therapy.)

For all the shouting and banging of cushions, the therapy in *Avalon* was little more than an aggressive talk therapy. When I – quite pointlessly I can say now – began to point out that the therapy in *Avalon* differed substantially from Janov's therapy, I met with various responses ...

The first response of the bossman in *Avalon* was to run down Janov's therapy. He said that clients that emerged from Janov's therapy lead solitary lives and 'related to nobody'. This serious criticism of Janov's therapy may have been perfectly correct. But this criticism of Janov's therapy did not quite excuse the advertising this therapy commune went in for. Nor did it excuse the many who came to *Avalon* on the strength of Janov's book and who quickly accepted that the commune was, in my view, actually hostile to Janov's methods.

When I persisted with my argument that the therapy in *Avalon* was not the real McCoy, the bossman suggested that I could change the therapy in *Avalon* to my liking. There was absolutely no truth in this suggestion. Quite frequently in the course of group therapy, I would notice that an opportunity arose to take somebody's therapy away from the therapy of anger and towards the therapy of recognising unfulfilled need and the futility of believing such need ever be fulfilled. But such opportunities were never taken up and once or twice when I attempted in hesitant voice to steer somebody's therapy in the Janovian direction I merely sounded silly in the presence of blank, uncomprehending and quite contemptuous faces all around me.

There were quite substantial reasons why the people in *Avalon* made not the smallest effort to engage Janovian methodology in their therapy. If the therapy in *Avalon* challenged everybody in a very painful way, it didn't quite challenge the comfortable, self-righteous politics of everybody involved. The therapy in *Avalon* deliberately shied away from what Arthur Janov has quite correctly described as the nihilism of his particular therapy.

There was a more fundamental reason why people in *Avalon* avoided Janov's methodology. Even as things stood with the one-dimensional regression that was a feature of *Avalon* therapy, the fact was *Avalon* was at all times living dangerously and the possible end of *Avalon*, which came in time, was ever on the cards. Even those seasoned in the therapy frequently found the whole thing too painful and left the commune, sometimes to return, sometimes not. Picture then how any commune or community that attempted to practise Janovian Primal Therapy would fare. Quite frankly I think that a commune or community that attempted to provide as nihilistic a therapy as Janovian Primal Therapy would not have lasted candlelight.

When I persisted further with the argument that *Avalon* therapy was not Primal Therapy, I was told that if my only reason for being in the commune was that I could not afford the substantial fees demanded in Janov's institute, I should leave the commune. Yet, when the time came when I actually decided to leave the commune, my leaving was greatly resisted. People frequently decided to leave the commune and these leave-takings were always greatly resisted. People were also frequently expelled from the commune and these expulsions were also matters of high drama.

One criticism I made of *Avalon* did touch a nerve with the people that ran *Avalon*. The bossman in *Avalon* had lived with the kind of therapy practised in *Avalon* for about fifteen years. The fact that he was a veteran of the kind of therapy practised in the commune meant that he was possessed of some quite formidable characteristics. For one thing, his ability to modulate his voice to suit the occasion exceeded that of the ordinary person. For another thing, he possessed above average levels of energy. His greater energy was a source of pride to him and contributed greatly to his authority in the commune.

There was therefore some of the qualities of air going out of a balloon when I in my unthinking fashion pointed out that this super-energy of the leader of the commune was false. False in the sense that it represented a fundamental deceit in the therapy practised in the commune. After all, the most thorough dismantling of neurotic ambitions occurred with Janov's therapy; and the bossman himself had criticised Janov for turning his clients into listless people who related to nobody. *Avalon* therapy could only hope to turn super-energised people like the bossman because the therapy in *Avalon* built on rather than dismantled the original neurosis.

The falsity of the therapy in *Avalon* carried over into real life. Unlike Janov's therapy where the client surrendered all unconscious hope from the past and where the client accepted his previous history and present melancholic condition, there was in *Avalon* quite a considerable culture of parent hatred. Contrast this great parent hatred with the scene when a vetinerary surgeon called to the commune to put down a dog and the vetinerary surgeon couldn't but be astonished and greatly impressed with the great grief of one bossman.

WHAT WERE THE PEOPLE IN 'AVALON' LIKE?

The people in *Avalon* were very ordinary people. I might even go so far as to say that they were a little too ordinary, a little too straight. As I reflect back on my time in *Avalon*, I am inclined to marvel at the lack of creativity among the people there. I have some small experience of another commune of sorts made up of ex-psychiatric-patients; and nearly everybody in this latter commune had some little pet project going – somebody played the bongos or guitar, somebody did some craft work, somebody sketched. But most of the people in *Avalon* were rather too serious, too sensible to indulge in creative self-expression.

WHAT DID THE PEOPLE IN 'AVALON' DO FOR PASTIMES?

If I mention any other feature of life in the commune, I am not suggesting that these other features of life in the commune were somehow a portion of the therapy. The therapy was something separate and distinct, even if it could not but impact on daily life as lived in the commune.

But presumably even Zen monks take time out for play and the favourite pastime of *Avalon* folk was talking about matters astrological. *Avalon* folk were even in contact with a professional astrologer who compiled profiles of individuals in *Avalon* for a fee. What can I say about astrology? I have to confess to being a little impressed by that which is known as Chinese astrology. But other than that I am inclined to agree with Patrick Moore that astrology only proves one thing – *there's one born every minute.*

MY EXIT FROM 'AVALON'

There was something unreal about my presence in *Avalon*.

Your typical commune person was capable of re-entering the straight world and engaging in some manner of work that would go to fund their time in Avalon. There was a little unacknowledged secret about those people that did re-enter the straight world from *Avalon*; and the secret was that some of those commune persons whose demons had been unleashed in *Avalon* ever only managed to survive in the straight world by resorting to smoking. Smoking was, of course, strictly forbidden in *Avalon*. Nobody who was returning from the straight world to *Avalon* for either short or long stay would be so crass as to show any evidence of the habit that had helped maintain them in the outside world.

My circumstances were a little more desperate than your average commune person. I came to *Avalon* from living a lifestyle where I both depended on tobacco and psychiatric drugs for my existence. Even before I received any therapy in *Avalon*, my mere having to withdraw from tobacco and psychiatric drugs was sufficient to make me prey to quite extravagant bodily sensations. Besides, I had never been the most energetic of people … and indeed the most enduring effect *Avalon* therapy would have on me subsequent to my time there was sadly to only decrease my energy levels further … to the extent that one psychiatrist went so far as to accuse me of sloth.

All this by way of pointing out that the idea that I could imitate my fellows in *Avalon* and re-enter the straight world and take a job was far fetched in the extreme. I began to realise that, if I stayed on in *Avalon*, I would eventually not be able to support myself. Then, as soon as it became apparent that I could not support myself in *Avalon*, the people in the commune would feel the need to kick me out of the commune. But, as it happened, I saved the *Avalon* commune the embarrassment of having to expel me for financial reasons. For I not alone realised that I would not be able to support myself in *Avalon* indefinitely, I also realised that there was no way I could resign myself to a life of suffering without end. So, I went and bought a packet of cigarettes and announced that I was leaving the place.

The meeting in the therapy room concerning my decision to leave had its own share of dramatics. At one point, I made an effort to leave the room and was physically restrained from doing so. One of the men who stopped me was one of the more conventional types in *Avalon*; but then most surprisingly this man having discovered that he had the strength to restrain me began to cry.

Another commune-person – a qualified psychologist – chose to ask me:
"What would Arthur Janov think of your decision to leave?"

This was a most insulting question. Because the presumption behind this question being that my criticisms of the therapy in *Avalon* only went to prove that I was in the grip of some sort of hero worship of Arthur Janov. But let it be said that I never had any hero worship in me for any doctor, be they Doctor Freud, Doctor Janov or even for that matter Doctor Laing.

Eventually the *Avalon* commune decided to let me go. But not without the bossman reminding me that, as someone who had submitted myself to the *Avalon* therapy and who had therefore rendered himself vulnerable to previously unconscious feelings, I would need even more and more tablets to survive and that my very survival was far from certain. What a nice thing to be told as I was about to set out for an uncertain future back home!

THE INNATE PUN:

*R*EDUCTIONISM

I don't think I can complete my examination of the punning system without making some brief mention of the science of reductionism. Most people outside the sciences will take reductionism to refer to Sigmund Freud and his theories of (infantile) sexuality controlling human behaviour. That folklore definition of reductionism is quite useful for the purposes of this book. But I must mention the fact that the idea that low-level events can influence high-events (which happens to be a more general definition of reductionism) is a matter of huge controversy in the sciences. Trouble is there is a significant body of scientists who on their own terms can be said to possess some of the ignorant hubris more readily recognisable in religious fundamentalists; and these scientific fundamentalists delight in taking the idea of reductionism and using it as a stick with which to beat humanity. This wanton use of the reductionist idea has, in turn, led others – notably Arthur Koestler[10] – to go to the other extreme into making the argument that reductionism is of itself erroneous.

The war between the fundamentalist reductionists and the pro-human anti-reductionists is a phoney war. The scientific fundamentalists who use reductionism as a stick to beat humanity are in the wrong; and those who oppose reductionism as an evil in itself are in the wrong. For as the sensible and erudite popular science writer and scientist Paul Davies [11] points out reductionism and its opposite but complementary paradigm holism both have their part to play in well regulated science and I might add in a well regulated philosophy.

Of course, the particular argument of this book is that reductionism as a distinct idea is older than science, is even older than literature. For my particular argument is that, if the idea of reductionism did not quite come to be discussed by human beings until, say, the twentieth century, preternatural design in the world has a longer history of involvement with the reductionist idea. I trust the reader can see the appeal of reductionism to a preternatural

---

10 Arthur Koestler (1905-1983) was a Hungarian-British author and journalist best known for his books *Darkness at Noon* and *The God that Failed*.

11 Paul Charles William Davies, (born 22 April 1946) is an English physicist, writer and broadcaster, a professor at Arizona State University as well as the Director of BEYOND: Center for Fundamental Concepts in Science. He is affiliated with the Institute for Quantum Studies at Chapman University in California.

that wished to make artistic comment on the world. I don't know about you but I am happier that the preternatural should resort to the pun and in particular the reductionist pun than seek to express itself by means of any other more involved and more sectarian code. Indeed, I might credibly boast that Francois Rabelais [12] might just about have understood the punning-system I outline but that it would be very much in his nature to mercilessly mock some recent books supposedly reporting on esoteric codes.

Let me finish this discourse by saying that the pronoun 'I' always translates as eye no matter what the context. As happens with many another word subjected to punning, this translation of the pronoun 'I' has the effect of lending considerable ambiguity to many a statement. For there is a general sense in which 'I' translating as eye can involve a third party, that is (to put it poetically) the person one sees eye-to-eye with or the person who is the apple of one's eye. So sometimes the most bitter and vitriolic statement that includes the first person pronoun can be understood to contain reference to the speaker's beloved.

---

[12] François Rabelais (died 9 April 1553) was a French Renaissance writer, humanist, physician, monk and Greek scholar. He has historically been regarded as a writer of fantasy, satire, the grotesque, bawdy jokes and songs.

HOMILY 5

The Imminent Return of Joe Nash

I don't mind admitting that I have had my bellyful of the back-biters, snakes and rodents and scum-bags and bag-men of every sort who all forego no opportunity – and even go out of their way to create opportunity – to senselessly run down our one hope that is Joe Nash. But I am consoled by the fact that all these presently high-flying critics of Joe Nash are in for the surprise of their lives – and theirs will be a sudden and sharp and not at all a pleasant surprise.

But I must here remind the happy others that never ran down Joe Nash, I must remind all these people of either no great hostility to Joe or of some abiding respect for Joe that your greater discretion or greater devotion towards the one Joe Nash is to be vindicated any day now. And so that you not be distressed by the suddenness of your good fortune, I tell you to henceforth go about your business and your leisure in a state of readiness for the greatest discombobulation of your life …

For you may well be busy filling in a tax-form, worrying just how literal or how figurative you can be in your replies, worrying in particular that you might be on the verge of going over the top in terms of your innocent reliance on 'poetic licence' in the answers you provide, when – on foot of the most violent of audio-visual annunciations – you find that standing by your side and rendering your petty concerns of the moment before and the entire business of filling out a tax questionnaire all entirely of no further concern or consequence – is the same Joe Nash of old. Alternatively, and no less dramatically, you may be wielding a pool cue in your favourite relaxation spot and you might even be on the point of striking the white ball in what you and all in attendance fully understand is a shot that will decide one way or another the fate of the game in progress, when with no less grandeur of fanfare Joe Nash is once again in your presence with all the ease and confidence of one who once gave his treasured hours engaged in the same past time that a moment before was working your brain into the heights of concentration and tension but now is of so little interest.

In anticipation of such transformations, keep a constant look out, I say.

6

THE BAD OLD DAYS

AN IRISH PSYCHIATRIC HOSPITAL

About six miles from the city of Limerick, on quite elevated ground lies Saint Mark's psychiatric hospital. Saint Mark's was formerly a TB hospital. As a TB hospital, Saint Mark's was a place of dread by the citizens of Limerick city and county. Great was the suffering that went on there, apparently. Nevertheless, some of the female nurses out of that hospital were known to marry some of the presumably well-to-do TB patients. To the best of my knowledge no nurse from the hospital married anyone of the later population of psychiatric patients. Car-stickers proclaiming 'NURSES DO IT WITH PATIENCE' may appear on car windows in the grounds of Saint Mark's but only offer testimony to a healthy sense of humour in the place.

Where Canley was mainly functional red-brick, Saint Mark's is completely ghostly white concrete. Ghostly white concrete in shape of flat-roofed box-like buildings with just one round building intended to demonstrate that the architect hadn't fallen asleep entirely. I suspect that those with an eye for architecture would be outraged by the dull, even Soviet-like, 1950s modernism of Saint Mark's; but, for my part, I often found myself quartered in Saint Mark's in the course of the last thirty years and I don't think I ever had the sense of leisure that would have allowed me take exception to the architecture all about me.

Saint Mark's inspires a number of comparisons: a comparison between Saint Mark's and Canley and a comparison between Saint Mark's in the 1970s and Saint Mark's today. Nurses in Saint Mark's seem to compare favourably with nurses in Canley. I couldn't but have the suspicion in Canley that many of the nurses were only working in the hospital in order to escape the noise and fumes of the factory floor. Even in the 1970s the image of a psychiatric nurse in Saint Mark's was changing. Almost gone from the roster were the alcoholic male nurses and harridan spinster nurses that I would imagine typified psychiatric care in Ireland in the 1950s. Instead there was a new breed of professional and sometimes even heroic nurses walking the corridors of Saint Mark's.

Of course, Saint Mark's was a much smaller hospital than Canley in its heyday and Saint Mark's was and is a more restrictive hospital than the Canley I knew as a short-stay patient. Saint Mark's did and continues to suffer from that which most darkens the atmosphere in psychiatric hospitals: the fact that the staff in a psychiatric hospital are ever on the alert for the unknown quantity that is a possible suicide by a patient. The consequences for staff in Canley of a suicide among the patients didn't appear quite as severe as it would be in Saint

Mark's; and as a consequence the patients in short-stay wards in Canley were less herded people than the patients in Saint Mark's.

The big change between Saint Mark's in the 1970s and Saint Mark's now is that in the seventies a large number of patients would congregate around the doors of the short-stay wards in the hope of waylaying one of their doctors in the not very dignified and perhaps not very sensible hope of they the patients hastening the day of their discharge; now in Saint Mark's the reduced number of patients in short-stay wards are more likely to complain that they are being discharged too soon.

One of the things that helped improve matters a little in Saint Mark's was the dedication of a complete building with its own staff to the provision of therapy services. Another thing that has helped a little is the provision of a patient café, even if it is only a vending machine café.

*J*NSIDERS – with Richard and Jim

THE HIP NURSE … AND THE OFTEN SUBTLE RELATIONSHIP BETWEEN GENUINE DELUSION AND THE PRETERNATURAL

He was a tall nurse with lightly cut, very long hair. He managed to wear a suit not as a matter of obligation but as a fashion statement. He helped me a little by quoting from rock and roll song lyrics in a way that implied I would see better days. But one remark of his has stayed with me down the years. He once said to me:

"I once wrote a poem on schizophrenia; but, then, I realised it didn't exist."

I now have to consider that comment by the nurse to be gross over-statement. The supernatural and preternatural are a subtle presence even in the seemingly most irredeemable of delusions; but that is no reason to doubt the reality of mental illness. Those writers who dispute the reality of mental illness outright only present the doctors working in psychiatry with a heresy that they can reject with the greatest of ease. Thus, allowing these same doctors to continue on their merry way with a psychiatry that is sometimes harmful towards the patient and often neglectful of the patient.

By way of illustrating the subtle presence of preternatural in an instance of a delusion that of course remains a delusion, I might perhaps mention the most notorious delusion of them all, this being a delusion of grandeur. I am not, of course, about to vindicate a specific instance of a delusion of grandeur. But I can say that the supernatural and preternatural do not jest with words alone, the supernatural and the preternatural also jest with that seemingly most sacrosanct thing – personal identity. And as further instances of such jests, I might mention such small realities – but realities nevertheless – as the presence of an animal motif in a particular human person and the not infrequent event where without any material reason an everyday object comes to represent a human person.

In a supernatural and preternatural world that this is, notions that are a hundred per cent redundant are not as plentiful as some think.

$\mathscr{A}$ PSYCHIATRIST WITHOUT INSIGHT

I tend for the most part in this book to only mention the better psychiatrists I dealt with.

But I have to say that when a chance of deliverance from some psychiatrists in charge of my case in the 1970s presented itself, I thought this chance of deliverance was too good for me not to take up. The chance came my way thanks to an acquaintance who was both a priest and a psychiatric client. I can say now with the benefit of experience precisely what drove this priest to the high drama of conveying to me through intermediaries his desire to see me. What prompted the priest's urgency happens to psychiatric clients all the time …

Now and then, a doctor decides in effect to tell a patient that he – the patient – is a great fellow and that all his troubles are over. I am well aware that doctor writers of most divergent views have turned out technical tome upon technical tome on the frequent over evaluation by a patient of intervention by a doctor. Transference is, I think, the technical term for this over evaluation. But the fact is some doctors now and again invoke all the gravitas of their profession to tell the patient that they are about to become the subject of a miracle and many patients are sufficiently credulous as to believe this blather.

When I duly visited this priest, he was in the business of frying sausages. I am not much of a cook myself; but to this day there is a part of Roman Catholic Ireland that hasn't advanced beyond the fried sausages forever grimly associated with boarding school. The priest was now greatly enthused by his recent encounter with a psychiatrist outside the locality. The priest had received a morale boosting talk from the same doctor and, like many patients before and after him believed that he was embarking on a new and more pleasant existence. As it happened, the priest was rather mistaken in this belief as he continued to lead a tragic life until he died young of a brain tumour.

But as for the doctor that the priest so fulsomely recommended to me, I had nothing to lose in going to see the same doctor. So, I arranged for a brother of mine to take me quite a distance to the small mental hospital where this doctor worked. When I got to the hospital I found I had to stay overnight in the hospital if I hoped to see the doctor in question. This I did. I met the burly doctor of business-like pomp on the morrow.

The doctor was not long in declaring that he was a great believer in what he called psychotherapy. He told a little story about a nun-matron who took him aside on his first day in another hospital and said to him:

"What we really need here is psychotherapy!"

The doctor's point appeared to be that psychotherapy was not something that a health professional casually added on to an existing conventional therapeutic programme. The doctor told this little story with a wounded expression on his face, thereby casting himself as the hero of the story. Even less convincingly, the doctor towards the end of the interview grouped tablets and ECT and psychotherapy together. I have to point out that your average worldly psychiatrist would not pretend that he was in the business of administering psychotherapy. I have to point out also that your average psychiatrist would be more circumspect in speaking about ECT ... no other psychiatrist of my experience would be so crass as to speak of shock treatment and psychotherapy in the one breath. Some might say that the greater subtly of most psychiatrists in speaking of shock treatment is a mere tribute to their greater cunning ... and so the argument might go that this burly doctor was a plain and earnest man.

The doctor had another story to tell. It concerned a farmer's son who took over the running of the farm from his parents who were still to the good. In time, this farmer's son got married and had a child of his own. All of sudden this son and father became the subject of frequent severe panic attacks. Enter our hero – the narrator doctor – who deduced that his patient's panic attacks were a consequence of he achieving all attributes of adulthood while still remaining a child in eyes of his own parents.

"Of course, I had to sort out his parents," declared the doctor-hero, by way of dramatic conclusion to the story.

Would that it were always that simple!

Eventually I acquainted the doctor with the fact that I had never learnt to drive a motor car. The doctor was not at all accepting of my actual decision not to attempt to learn to drive a motor car. There would have been little point in acquainting the doctor with the fact that a significant number of poets never manage to learn how to drive. (Admittedly, my career as a poet was short-lived; but by way of indicating the enduring nature of that calling, I might mention that G.K. Chesterson [13] said that a bad poet is still a poet). As the doctor continued with his dangerous line of reasoning, I tried to get through to him by telling this joke:

"Did you ever hear about the man with an inferiority complex? A friend of

---

[13] Gilbert Keith Chesterton, (1874-1936) was an English writer, poet, philosopher, dramatist, journalist, orator, lay theologian, biographer, and literary and art critic. Chesterton is often referred to as the 'prince of paradox'.

this man said that the man didn't have an inferiority complex … but that the man really was inferior."

The doctor chuckled uneasily at my joke but continued to insist that I should learn to drive. Years later another doctor remarked that this doctor in this most provincial mental hospital, who insisted that I should learn to drive, was out to have me kill a few people in North Cork! Clearly, this doctor in this little provincial hospital did fancy himself as a fixer to the point of foolishness.

$\mathcal{A}$ GLIMPSE INTO THE PAST

One scene in this provincial hospital helped put my encounter with this fixer doctor in context. The horrible truth was this hospital had only one indoor facility for patients: a square living room. As I entered the room, a charge nurse of saturnine features introduced himself with a commanding handshake. I fancied that this charge nurse spent his most cherished hours in the week in some public house or other. On turning my gaze away from this ogre of a charge nurse, I was no more impressed by the dispirited patients who occupied but one or two of the chairs that lined the four walls of this horrible room. There were prisoners here who could really do with something that they would never receive in their sad lives, namely something one might be tempted to call psychotherapy. Really this room was a living fossil of what psychiatry was and what it meant to be a psychiatric patient in 1950s Ireland.

$\mathcal{A}$ NEW DOCTOR

Fortunately, I lived too far away from this same fixer doctor and his hospital for me to ever become his patient. But, with regret born of the fact that I couldn't really avail of his superior brand of 'psychotherapy', the doctor in the course of our one meeting advised me see a consultant psychiatrist in my medical district of whom he had heard some good things.

This new consultant psychiatrist became a major force in my life for the next fifteen years or so. Those were the days before psychiatry realised that the best thing it could do for generally despised psychiatric clients was to provide them with a context whereby they could socialise with each other. So, as a consequence of the poor psychiatric culture of 1970s and 1980s and my circumstances as a quite isolated rural dweller, this psychiatrist assumed an importance in my life (and in the life of others).

The same doctor was a self-confessed 'townie'. In other words, he was not lacking in cunning and sophistication. I was to slightly subvert and slightly displease this doctor by saying to him that he conformed to what the English satirical magazine *Private Eye* jokingly declared was the modern-day understanding of God as someone who 'liked jazz and tolerated the Beatles'. Nor was he lacking in intellect and learning. Most important of all, he took enjoyment in conversing at length with patients. Many a night I spent an hour or an hour and a half in conversation with this psychiatrist.

They say 'eaten bread is soon forgotten' and now it is very tempting to look back on those conversations with nothing but regret. In particular, I am tempted to compare and contrast these intense yet often silly conversations with this psychiatrist with my present situation where, whenever I like, I can drop into a day-care centre and chat and joke with my fellow psychiatric clients to my heart's content. But those long ago conversations with this urbane doctor did help keep me going through very bad times.

On an even more serious note, I have to acknowledge that this doctor took a stand on my behalf when there was talk about locking me up for good. Taking all circumstances at the time into account, it is hard to see how I could have got through the bad years with any other doctor than this man of whom I speak.

$\mathcal{A}$ FRIGHTENING HOSPITALISATION

I spent much of the 1970s and much of 1980s in a state of constant crisis. At one point early on in our association, the doctor I have just been speaking of suggested that I go into hospital to undergo tests that would allow me try a new medication. Alas, I was scarcely a day in the hospital ward when severe condition of panic overtook me. I even took to hiding from the nurses ... a difficult or rather impossible thing to do.

Every day that followed was worse than the one before. My mental health was in a unique form of rapid decline. I had no real friends in my locality at this time; but a middle-aged tailor I knew from my previous time in this same hospital did pay me a visit. He found me stretched out in bed and almost too demoralised to speak.

"I told you not to go into hospital," he said.

I really thought my decline would be allowed to continue such that I would never get out of the hospital. Indeed, I thought I was in the process of dying in this hospital.

As would be true to say for much of my life, I had at this time but a few fragments of writings of mine back home notwithstanding the fact that I had spent countless hours hammering my little manual typewriter. Thinking that I was in the process of dying, I wrote a pathetic letter home asking that these fragments of writing be handed over to a relative of the family who was a published writer. In my heart of hearts, I knew that these fragments of writing were of no value and that the idea that a writer could turn these fragments into something publishable was merely preposterous. But, thinking that if I was to die, I wanted some little record of me and my time spent writing to survive me.

One day, more in desperation than hope, I asked my psychiatrist could I go home; and he quite casually said I could. Other doctors might not have been so willing to let me go. But this doctor in charge of my case was always very indifferent to what others in the psychiatric service might think and he being exceptionally wise he had no difficulty in seeing that by far the best prescription for me was that I be allowed home to recuperate.

At home, I recovered from the state of absolute terror after a few weeks; but, of course, I continued to live in crisis.

There will be those who will find this melodramatic tale unconvincing in that they will argue that as a voluntary patient I always had the power to leave the hospital. But, to say the least, I have found in my case that rule permitting the voluntary patient to self-discharge is never that easy to put into effect.

THERE IS ALWAYS A MAN GOING DOWN TO JERICHO

Jimmy was a junkie in his mid-twenties. He had some of the innocence of a teenager and some puppy fat to match. He was not addicted to any specific drug, only that he would routinely take anything that provided escape from reality. I phoned him up when we were both out of hospital and he gleefully announced that he had a 'feed of alcohol' on the previous night.

Jimmy knew that he was not going to last. On one occasion, he argued with me that Neil Young in referring to junkies as 'setting suns' was saying that junkies would rise again. A sad outlook for a young man.

The rules in Saint Mark's for junkies were very strict. They were not allowed to leave their ward. The purpose of this policy no doubt was to prevent the junkies from bringing narcotics into the hospital. I never saw Jimmy acquire narcotics in the hospital; but I cannot be certain that Jimmy remained narcotic-free in hospital. All I know is that he quickly got in trouble with the authorities. Worst of all, Jimmy began to verbally challenge the authorities; and, as a member of the most despised caste in the hospital, Jimmy was not alone wasting his time but setting himself up for a fall.

Eventually, the authorities decided to expel Jimmy. Expulsion from a psychiatric hospital is quite different from discharge in that the authorities arrange for the expelled party to be escorted home by the police and there is no compelling reason to believe that the police relish this sort of taxi work. Shortly before his expulsion, Jimmy engaged in a heated argument with a doctor. At the end of this argument the doctor smiled and said to Jimmy: "I hope everything works out for you; but somehow I don't think it will!" This was the easiest thing in the world to say, because regardless of what anybody chose to do Jimmy was very much a condemned man.

But I have a reason to honour Jimmy. In the course of our time in hospital, we were joined in our dormitory by a patient who was dying at the comparatively young age of sixty or so. He was bed-bound but not quite a spent force. As a misfortune for this patient, the two night nurses on duty at the time of his dying were of wicked nature. From the patient's relatives, they learnt that this patient smoked and that he had been violent towards them. Gleefully seized on these details concerning the dying man, the wicked male and female nurse chose to make life difficult for him. They even took to moving him from his bed to the day room, even though this served no purpose except to increase his suffering – at least as I saw it.

This is where Jimmy came in. Seeing what was happening, Jimmy took to talking to the dying man and to bring him water at regular intervals. The dying man's relatives became a little aware of what was happening; and they actually acknowledged Jimmy's good work by presenting him with gifts of soft drinks and sweet food.

THE FOUNTAIN OF KNOWLEDGE NEVER QUITE RUNS DRY AMONG THE DERANGED

I speak next of a patient; she had grown up with an alcoholic father. Even the doctors admitted they could not extract much in the way of personal detail from her. She had a boyfriend in the outside world and there was every indication that that relationship would go all the way to marriage. For that end, she was prepared to silently accept cruel treatment by the doctors in hospital.

Under no circumstances had she the slightest interest in a welfare dependent dreamer like me.

But on at least three occasions she, with a leer of a smile, quoted a portion of W.B. Yeat's epitaph to me, *Horseman, pass by*. On finding that I failed to tumble on each occasion as to what she was trying to put across, she finally gave up, dismissively saying:

"You're very slow!"

$\mathcal{T}$HE NON-SUMMERS OF MY TROUBLED YEARS

I dreaded the coming of summer in those decades. Summer meant the coming of the ultimate tussle with nature when everybody on the farm was expected to give their all. I refer to the saving of the hay – this the fodder snatched in defiance of the elements that would go to nourish the animals through the winter. In those days, I did not just find the long day in the meadow demanding, I found the entire summer a trial. I was of delicate mental health and far from relishing the greater vibrancy and urgency of life in the countryside in the summer I practically recoiled from it. Indeed, I almost felt physically shaken by the convoys of large agriculture vehicles that thundered around the roads and farmlands at harvest time.

So much did I dread the hay-time that every year when the last bale of hay was loaded in the last meadow to be emptied I ritually recalled my brief involvement with the martial arts in London; I did this by cradling my head in my right arm and hitting the ground more or less head first and rolling my body in a ball, stretching my right hand outwards and emitting a war cry as I came to my feet. All working beside me were amused to witness this strange salute not to summer's beginning but to summer's end.

THE INNATE PUN:

Punning on Myself

I shouldn't neglect entirely that I have been the victim of a little punning myself from time to time. In the good days when I was given to performing comic material of mine before pub and theatre audiences, one of my themes concerned a mythical parish by the name of Ballydull. This prompted one MC introducing my act to say that the problems of Ballydull could only be addressed by the use of Prozac. To this little too severe a jest, I responded with the most savage of counterattacks.

Enough said …

HOMILY 6

JOE NASH ... AND LIFE ON OTHER PLANETS

I intend to deal with the above vexatious subject with the greatest of brevity. And vexatious indeed are the people who have a fondness for bringing up this subject in conversation, debate and dispute.

Suppose these vexatious people say that there are alien civilisations on other planets ... are these civilisations not very likely to have heroes of their own similar – but yet quite dissimilar – to the one Joe Nash? And where then lies all your discourse about this same Joe Nash who as a matter of fact never really merited all the attention you now pay him? Needless to say, this last question is addressed to yours truly in the expectation that this question will leave me floored and as tongue-tied as the politician caught on still camera with an open suitcase of legal tender which the accompanying newspaper report makes plain was not raised by the boy scouts and was not earmarked for the homeless.

Enough! I'll address the topic of Joe Nash and life on other planets when and only when we encounter such life ... when it may well prove to be the case that so different is this alien civilisation to ours that it does not pose even the smallest difficulty for the homely regard in which we of pure heart hold Joe Nash and will continue to hold in high regard by reason of the completely irrelevancy of any reports of lower or higher life forms in other worlds that may or may not emerge.

And I will expand on this commonsense attitude of mine to say, that instead of vexing our minds with the entirely hypothetical, we might be better employed to extend our understanding of Joe by reference to this our own planet and its features that we all know so well. In line with this present train of thought of mine, I would welcome books with truly honest titles such as ARIZONA – WITH JOE NASH or even since the topic of outer space has been mooted SPACE COLONISATION – THE JOE NASH ANGLE.

7

SOME LIGHT AMID
THE DARKNESS

ᴛHE EVER-PRESENT JESTS OF THE PRETERNATURAL

In the bad days when I was without a friend in my locality, I corresponded with two people who were in effect pen friends. Both of my pen friends were given to using the name 'Bernard'. I believe this double use of the name 'Bernard' amounts to a small jest of the preternatural. For you will be aware Saint Bernard dogs derive their name from a pass in the Alps, in which location they were once employed by Monks of the Hospice to rescue stranded travellers. If cartoons – quite popular in the 1960s – are anything to go by, these same monks used dogs to rescue and revive the stranded travellers with the help of a small keg of brandy suspended from the dogs' necks. Whatever about the brandy, I surely was in need of revival in those bad decades.

Everybody's life – no matter how prosaic – is subject to a good number of poetic jests pertinent to themselves alone as a portion of preternatural design. You might in elevated moment be tempted to make much of such jests, but in more rational moments you may come to observe that the most striking element of such jests is their mockery.

ᴡHY ELECTROCONVULSIVE THERAPY OR 'ECT' IS SHOCK TREATMENT

The public – not the doctors – have got it right. 'ECT' is shock treatment, and the acronym itself is a huge misnomer. The idea that an aftereffect of the shock is of greater consequence than shock is not a sensible idea. Even the perceived benefits of 'ECT' – and these 'benefits' are mostly perceived by doctors – are to be attributed in the main to the violence of the shock and not to the convulsions that follow.

You might not have come to spot the *Horace Batchelor Principle* at work in the sorry business of 'ECT'; but that is because the term 'ECT' is one of the most notorious examples of 'argument by nomenclature' – and 'argument by nomenclature' is the most difficult of all falsehoods to refute. The *Horace Batchelor Principle* is hard at work within the actual term 'ECT'.

_A_ CONTINIUM OF EVIL

According to the Concise Oxford Dictionary a continuum to be a continuum must be 'not discrete'. So perhaps I should have indulged in oxymoron and titled this section THE DISCRETE CONTINUUM OF EVIL. For the fact of the matter is that, whereas the following people may be in almost total ignorance of each other, I regard a certain type of academic or scientist who insists on a very strict materialistic view of existence, a certain type of politician who may, for instance, excuse delay in reform of psychiatric services by referring to the great neglect of the mentally ill in former times (almost as if he was nostalgic for such times) and the entirely mindless vigilante who opposes with menace the arrival of a community of psychiatric clients in his or her area as all being part of a continuum.

_I_NSIDERS – with Richard and Jim

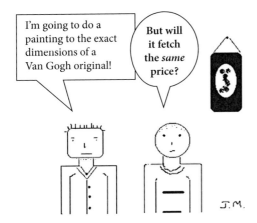

THE PROFESSION OF PSYCHIATRIC CLIENT

These days, I somewhat richly describe myself as a 'professional psychiatric client'. These days, there are quite a number of people throughout Ireland to whom the same sad description could be applied. But to people of my father's generation it did not seem plausible back in the 1970s and 1980s that anyone leading the life of a professional psychiatric client could continue to do so indefinitely. My father knew of a time when, presumably for a pittance of a wage, a middle-aged woman drew heaps of stones by donkey and cart to help make a roadway through that portion of our farm that was bog land, this roadway of continuing benefit to those who work the farm today. To my father, it did not seem possible that the world would continue to support one as idle as me.

"Borrowed time!" my father said to me on more than one occasion, meaning of course that I was living on borrowed time. These comments rattled me a little at the time of their utterance. But even in those times there were straws in the wind that indicated that, far from deserting an unlucky fellow like me, the psychiatric services were destined to prove even more helpful to me.

For instance, one day I received a letter in the post containing a card entitling me to free travel on public transport in the Irish Republic. At first I thought it was a case of the authorities mistaking me for a senior citizen. But there was no mistake. Rather like royalty, unemployed psychiatric clients were now permitted to travel free on public service buses and trains in the Irish Republic. It wouldn't happen in America!

THOSE SADLY BLINDED BY LIFELONG WATCHING OF THE TAM RATINGS

Not everybody is impressed with professional psychiatric clients travelling free on public transport. On one particular TV chat show the presenter was in the habit of extolling some product or service only to declare that each member of the studio audience on the night would receive a sample of the goods or service. This great bountifulness always announced with the catch phrase: 'There is one for everyone in the audience'. On one episode of the show, the presenter by way of a promotion for the national bus service offered everyone in the audience free travel for a week on the same bus service. Just then an unseen studio hand threw a soft toy representation of a red setter dog – a representation of a red setter dog was from of the bus company's logo – into the waiting arms of the presenter and the presenter smiled at the audience and into the all important camera and said:

"You're all mad!"

We must have comedy …

LITTLE THINGS CAN HELP ONE SURVIVE

A novel by J.P. Donleavy features a character who, though he be a brash and 'on the make' type, derived pleasure and comfort from reading magazines that delved into the lives of movie stars. I was of a generation who felt that we could do better than this character with a vicarious interest in movie stars. Rightly or wrongly, we felt that the fashion of the day for cultural heroes who were famous musicians or composers threw up a more enquiring, more engaging and more spiritual pantheon of heroes than the more subservient heroes of previous times.

This is a prologue to my admitting that I broke the monotony of my more isolated days on the farm by receiving though the post a copy of *Rolling Stone* magazine once a fortnight. From the perspective of a farming brother, it is now merely the stuff of a joke that my father took to hiding each copy of *Rolling Stone* until nightfall in the hope that I might do a little extra farm work in the daylight hours without distraction from the very serious – if not pretentious – journalists of *Rolling Stone*.

I now regard *Rolling Stone* in the same poor light as I regard the many other magazines of empire that litter the shelves in newsagents and supermarkets and that are strangely regarded as the leading journals in their various fields. The standard magazine retail rack is now an affront to human dignity and an attack on human liberty.

$\mathcal{A}$MATEUR DRAMA AND DRAMATICS

In 2005 in the pleasant back garden of a daycare centre, I was chatting with a fellow psychiatric client when he happened to observe that we both had served time in a psychiatric hospital within the last year.

"Not good for our record," I commented.

"Not good for our CVs," my companion agreed.

The trouble with being a psychiatric client is that even events that should bring good fortune have a way of turning sour. In the youth of a writer, however mean, there can surely be nothing more rewarding than to engage with an amateur drama society. The chance to observe stage craft first-hand and the chance perhaps to bluff one's way into the company of even more exalted practitioners of the dramatic arts are just some of the benefits that should befall a pilgrim writer who would engage with the amateur stage. Alas and alack, I look back on my involvement with amateur drama with more embarrassment than a sense of achievement.

Anyway, a postcard came to the farm house on the hill inviting me to a meeting in the parish hall concerning the formation of a drama group. I attended this. Now, it is probably true to say that the most damning thing you can say about any project – and that about which a project will most ensure its failure – is for any such project to be commenced for questionable motives. But it was announced at the first meeting of this drama group that the chief motive for initiating this drama group was to provide a way for young people in the parish to socialise without necessarily involving a public house.

On the third or fourth night in the parish hall we got down to the practical business of choosing a play we might come to perform. Our eventual choice was interesting, in that we opted for a period drama from a neglected Kerry playwright of old – George Fitzmaurice. The same Fitzmaurice was better in his day at capturing the dialect and the concerns of rural folk than anybody else. So much so that one play of his performed by the Abbey players was praised above a play by W.B. Yeats on the same bill; and that proved disastrous for George. Because the Abbey was the only outlet for Irish drama at the time and two of the founders of the Abbey – Lady Gregory and the same W.B. Yeats – fancied themselves as dramatist reporters on the peasantry and any rival to them in such enterprise was not going to get a second chance on the Abbey stage.

Our rehearsals of our fifty minute play progressed but slowly. There was one actor in our company who was taken with the notion that our small group should engage in simultaneous rehearsal of different sections of the play in different rooms in the parish hall. But given that I had been chosen to direct rehearsals of the play and that it represented an almost physical challenge for me to maintain order over the one rehearsal, I had to be emphatic in refusing to go along with this novel suggestion that our little troupe engage in bi-located rehearsal.

The matter of choosing a name for our group took up a lot of time in our leisurely progress towards staging a play. My identification with Prince Hamlet still a little too much to the fore, I persuaded the group to take the name 'The Strolling Players'. This prompted the father of one of our actresses to remark with a laugh on the occasion of some small but typical failure on the part of our decidedly amateur organisation that The Strolling Players was not an organisation about which punctuality might be expected.

A night was selected for our first performance of our play in the parish hall and all of a sudden the night for this performance drew nigh. With two nights to go to the big night, I was standing in the forecourt of the parish hall when I heard my name called out with tremulous urgency by a man with some responsibility for running of same parish hall. Strangely, this man of standing in the parish was calling for my attention in tones more often associated by subordinate who is about to impart bad news to the boss. I felt momentarily empowered by this manner of servile address – the first time and indeed the only time so far I have ever been respectfully spoken to by anybody.

My innocence! For, of course, I was only so respectfully spoken to because the speaker had some guilt tinged news to impart to me, namely that the parish hall would not be fitted with the twentieth century conveniences of lighting and heat in time to allow our performance proceed on the chosen night.

Quite a crisis! One solution proposed – a prize instance of lateral thinking – was for us to stage the play in the hall of a neighbouring village on the appointed night and to hire a fleet of buses to ferry the locals. But seeing as the neighbouring village was a bitter rival on the sports field to our own village, the prospect of bussing theatre-going locals from our village to the rival was a complete nonstarter. All seemed lost.

But the gods who sought to so discomfort us hadn't quite reckoned on the fact that The Strolling Players had in the background discreet movers and shakers. For when I turned up at the parish hall on the eve of our cancelled performance, I was quite dumbfounded to learn that the performance was not cancelled but was to go ahead on the appointed night.

Indeed, when I entered the parish hall on this eve of the night of destiny, I could scarcely believe the accredited industry that was afoot. Even though the hours of darkness had long since set in, a team of electricians were working flat out to – you might say – electrify the hall. I spoke to one bemused electrician who wondered what great art merited this extraordinary urgency.

But did we – The Strolling Players – deserve such military intervention by an elite unit of electricians from a local capital town? Just about. But I must admit to two failings – among a multitude of failings – of the production on the night.

One was the lighting. Ah, the lighting! It transpired than our only hope of lighting the fifty minute traffic on stage took to the form of beaming a strong search light from the back of the hall. But this decidedly minimalist approach to lighting presented difficulties of its own, in that in order to avail of this search light, all other electrical facilities in the hall – such as for heating and possible subdued lighting in the auditorium – had to be entirely disconnected. With the result that our little drama on match-making in Kerry long ago took on a lot of the character of a World War Two prisoners-of-war escape movie.

But in the end this production before a partisan audience yielded enough laughs to be judged a success on this night. And if the production had a multitude of failings, I was very much to blame.

$\mathcal{J}$HE STRANGE STORY OF THE SPOTTY WIMPELS

They say that anybody who claims – or, perhaps worse, who manages – to make a statement without any cogitation whatsoever is definitely mad. If that is true, I must have been definitely mad in the 1980s.

One night, like many a night before and many a night since, I was listening to the pop radio in my fortress that is the farm house on the hill, when I heard the disc jockey speak of Spotty Wimpels on the precise understanding that Spotty Wimpels could be anything you cared to imagine provided your definition of same contained some wit. The instant I was acquainted with this most trivial of invitations to define Spotty Wimpels, I was arrested by something that was more a feeling than a thought that I had a worthwhile definition of Spotty Wimpels within my grasp; and without any further thought on my part – if there was any thought at all to begin with – I typed out the following statement on a nearby manual typewriter:

Spotty Wimpels are small burning candles that march four-aside in columns of twelve behind a taller burning candle known as the Sergeant Major. When the Spotty Wimpels have all burnt out, a new Sergeant Major leads out a column of eleven and the old Sergeant Major – now reduced in height – falls in to make the twelve. The reason why Spotty Wimpels are so named is because they can spot a Wimpel a mile off.

I sent off this statement to the disc jockey in question; and the disc jockey read out the statement on air. Modestly, I am inclined to relate this humorous statement to claims from antiquity of inspired statement. I believe that the supernatural and preternatural realms are at least as populated and as various as the material universe and that forces and entities from these realms do from time to time inspire human statement; but the notion that inspired statements from antiquity can be attributed to someone who has black holes, supernovas and gamma ray bursts in 'his care', I take with a grain of salt.

MY FIRST REAL CONTACT IN MY LOCALITY

To my little creativity – and indeed you could argue to the smallness of my creativity – I owe the better portion of my social life. One day in the farm house on the hill I happened to draw a snail on a piece of paper. Thus began a wishful project – to wit, a cartoon series titled *Snail~Trail* – that never got anywhere and never could have got anywhere. Yes, for a good while I sought out possible illustrators for this cartoon series to the point of even advertising in newspapers and I even engaged in silly correspondence with interested illustrators – occasionally even managing to insult such interested parties. But the fact of the matter was that, whereas all the gags I devised for *Snail~Trail* possessed a little delicate wit, the entire concept was just a little too delicate and could only have ever succeeded were I *myself* possessed of a talent for sketching up to Art College standard – which clearly I am not.

Nevertheless, in the very early days of this doomed project, I went about finding some artist in the locality who might instruct me in the art of drawing. Thus I made the acquaintance of an art teacher and artist who – for purposes of identification – I name as the Publican.

At the time we first met, the same man's mother owned and ran a public house, which the same man would inherit in time. Even though the traditional public house in question was not a venue for traditional Irish music sessions as such, the same house was nevertheless sufficiently revered in music and art circles that anybody passing through the town with slightest culture in them would make this public house a port of call. I was therefore privileged to occasionally sit in this public house and once heard someone break a house rule of sorts and sing a song of a fabled lodging-house where –

You'll get a feather bed and an old pig's head
But don't forget to pay before you leave.

I am confident that I imply no insult in identifying my friend as the Publican. For I recall a conversation – one of the many occasional conversations I have had with this same friend down the years – where the topic of the annihilation of the human race came up. But my friend ventured the hopeful opinion that as far as he was concerned there would always be a Celt – an Irishman – in the world. I don't doubt that, if pressed, my friend would also insist that that there would also always be in the world a genuine Irish public house with open fire, where a man or woman could slake their thirst and listen to a song or tune whereby – although the song might well speak of death and although it might be winter out of doors – the listening man or woman might feel that life was worthy and that death and desolation were somehow secondary.

As people with our toes in waters of the great ocean of artistic expression, the Publican and I would I suppose be that bit more alert than would say provincial or national journalists to the presence of *Flash Harrys* in the world of art and literature. There would be those who would laugh at such provincials as the Publican and I outraged by some shaper getting newspaper coverage that he or she didn't deserve – and I don't deny that such querulous discourse is as old and eternal as one tradesman speaking ill of another – but I would value and even revere and see great merit in such provincial chat that would forge its own critique away from the corridors and centres of power.

But all this is to miss the point, the point that in my first meeting up with the Publican on rather false pretences as I have explained was for me an entrance to an Araby. In plainer terms, my making the acquaintance of the Publican was to lead me into the company of many others of one age with myself and with an interest in the arts. I was not alone in the world any more … something of special importance in the life on one who routinely has to stand his ground in routine interviews by doctors. The Publican had opened a door and I am extremely grateful for his act of kindness in this regard.

THIS JOHN MURPHY

I am just a little unforgivably embarrassed by the fact that there is a John Murphy behind every whitethorn bush in Ireland and just to distinguish myself from the crowd I am inclined to boast that I am the only John Murphy who has heard of Lord Buckley – and the beauty of this boast is that it serves to exclude both the uneducated and the learned with equal force.

More of Lord Buckley anon.

MY ONE CONTRIBUTION TO THE THEORY OF ART

My meeting up with people who were not ashamed to discuss abstract ideas inspired me somewhat. For instance, I hadn't long made the acquaintance of the Publican when I formulated my little theory of the three modes of art, these being the court, the folk and the outlaw. The terms folk art and outlaw art are reasonably self-explanatory; and court art could be defined as that which enjoys the favour of establishment-types. I thought at the time that I had made a great discovery with this triple classification of art; but more modestly I would now say that this triple classification is revealing as to my character and outlook.

I have to note that in the realm of contemporary Irish court art there is at least one if not two literary novels that treat mental illness but only as a criminal pursuit. Yes, like Brendan Behan who pointed that in the opinion of a number of society people his name should never be seen in print except perhaps in the *Policeman's Gazette*, I know there is a culture out there that believe the likes of me should be at best a minor character in a book and not the author of a book.

Accordingly, even if – as I age – I gravitate more towards classic literature of a certain kind, I can never afford to abandon entirely my interest in folk and especially outlaw art. I am grateful to the Beat writers of old for celebrating the lives of those who would be different and for insisting that the official version of anything was likely as not to be wrong. I am grateful for the continuation of that idea in such as comic book art that will, for example, wittily confuse the identities of Sherlock Holmes and Sigmund Freud with a broad stroke insinuation that these two may not be quite savoury characters.

THE INNATE PUN:

THE SCATOLOGICAL PUN

I am sincerely of the belief that there is a sense in which, at the first level of punning-system, words and syllables logically and inevitably translate to scatological puns for no greater purpose than a rather mindless joking. Of course, I would not get away with this belief of mine if I did not proceed to argue that there are many other levels to the punning-system where the felicity of particular puns serves to validate the entire system, including the first level of which I have just spoken.

If truth be told, I am less than impressed by some of the modern comedians who seem inclined to compensate for a lack of wit with frequent use of offensive terms. I could here be accused of double standards. On my own terms, I don't accept from some comedians what I am inclined to accept from the preternatural design. But I have to say that is the way it is. On one hand I have a problem with comedians who resort to vulgar language but otherwise fail to entertain; and on the other hand I accept at a philosophical level that words and syllables inevitably suffer reduction to vulgar puns and rhymes and that there is some comedy in this alone.

For example, the noun 'word' translates as *turd*; and there is comedy in that translation as it stands. But there is more subtle statement in the 'words'/turds pun that revolves around the fact that ignorant preacher, the grubby politician, the slick TV presenter, the corporate spokesperson and many another frequently use words in order to tell lies. The 'words'/*turds* pun is just another indication that the punning-system is fiercely anti-conceit of any kind, even anti-abstraction of any kind.

The fact that the phrase 'caught napping' translates as *caught crapping* and that the translation is a stronger statement than what might be termed the original statement is sufficient proof of the meaningfulness of this piece of the punning-system. In somewhat similar vein few would argue that the hit-man is well defined as the *shit-man*.

So far we have observed the punning-system's predictable use of the scatological pun to signify contempt, worthlessness and negation; but the punning-system can use the scatological pun to convey a more subtle message …

As Jim Hightower [14] has said: "The only things in the middle of the road are yellow lines and dead armadillos." By which we may gather the phrase 'the middle of the road' is not a complimentary one. Even I, who is tone-deaf, have some appreciation of the vacuity that lies at the heart of some middle of the road music. The punning-system most fulsomely salutes the sense of low standards conveyed by this phrase 'middle of the road' in that the phrase very meaningfully and very darkly translates as *piddle of the rode*. To fully appreciate this latter pun you should have some appreciation of the psychological causation of poor bladder function and perhaps also be mindful that those two healthy specimens of manhood Stephen Dedalus and Leopold Bloom took to comparing the volume of output of their respective bladders in Joyce's *Ulysses*.

The punning-system is capable of even greater subtlety with the scatological pun. But to appreciate this subtlety you have to understand that the punning-system is not merely content to record and comment on life but that at times it engages in entirely imaginative and creative poeticisms of its own. These creative poeticisms I describe and name as conventions of the punning system.

I once set about attempting to extract a piece of esoteric knowledge from a most informed psychiatrist. What I wanted to know was what he considered to be the most important letter in the alphabet. Eventually the psychiatrist grew tired of my questioning and said:

"I should have thought that 'P' was the most important letter in the alphabet."

He said this in definite manner of one in authority and in a way that indicated the subject was closed.

Now I have to say that, whereas there is a vast body of significance in the letters of the alphabet, the judging of individual letters of the alphabet as regards their relative importance is not the most sensible of exercises. Nevertheless, proof of the great importance the punning-system lends to pee and peeing is that the whole idea is actually enshrined in one letter of the alphabet. 'P'.

I refer now to the suffix '-ist' in such words as philanthropist, psychiatrist, psychologist and so on. For, of course, the suffix '-ist' always translates as pist. Now, I am well aware that the terms 'pist' or 'pissed' are used to refer to alcoholic intoxication; and I have to say that any esoteric significance I am about to attribute to these terms applies with even greater force in those parts of the world where alcohol is a lawful and even venerated portion of the culture.

---

14 Jim Hightower US-based National radio commentator, writer, public speaker, and *New York Times* best-selling author who has spent four decades battling the Powers That Be on behalf of the Powers That Ought To Be – consumers, working families, environmentalists, small businesses, and just-plain-folks.

HOMILY 7

JOE NASH IN YOUR LIFE

You may be tiring of all this talk of Joe Nash who by all accounts leads the life of a wastrel and whose present existence is one of happiness beyond measure. Without harping on the latter point, I advise you to resist the urge to give up on Joe.

Resist, resist, resist this urge even if you are a twenty-first century man or twenty-first century woman for whom there are not enough hours in the day. When your day is constantly juggling the demands on your time … time at the work-place, time with your family in front of the TV, time at the gym and no time at all to pursue your uncultivated interest in astronomy. Under these circumstances, you may feel that there is no time in your day for Joe Nash. But I have given my advice in this regard and I don't intend repeating myself.

But think again, think of the double benefits of involving Joe in all the videoed highlights of your career: the degrees and diplomas you will win by hard graft, the hononary degree that will be no less hard won, your wedding day, the various celebrations as you climb up the ladder and your public acceptance of all the glittering prizes as they are commonly referred to and then the furtherance of all this with the church ceremonies concerning the birth and growth of your children and their similarly successful careers. The possibility for you to confer honour on Joe Nash is truly endless … and then as sure as an Aborigine's boomerang the return of all these Joe Nash blessed honours to your faithful self.

This is why I insist perhaps against your own preference that, as you step up to the podium to receive yet another glittering prize, you should look into the cameras and heartily thank Joe Nash for all he has done for you. Disregard from your mind entirely that all these recorded acknowledgements of the beneficence of Joe Nash will only go to puzzle your contemporary audience and posterity itself and possibly call your sanity into continual question. Rest assured you and Joe Nash will have the last laugh.

8

MY LUCKY BREAKDOWN

THE HANDOVER OF AN INJURED COMBATANT

I still see the man I call the Publican from time to time. I imagine that I will always be held in some regard by the Publican, even if I have tested his respect for me by my somewhat public exhibitions of madness. But something altogether fortuitous happened in days of my regular meetings with the Publican.

Sitting one day in a public house, we were joined by a friend of the Publican – a tall and powerful man who shared in the Publican's love of traditional music and of the more artistic pursuits in life. At the end of our three-way conversation, this tall and powerful man who I call the Kerryman invited me to his home. The Kerryman is, in fact, a native of my own county of Cork; but so strong is his inheritance from his Kerry ancestors that sometimes in conversation with this man on the phone I am struck by the thought that – not alone in terms of his language but also in terms of his thought process – his is an alien intelligence to mine.

I am obliged, however, to offer the reader some sort of gloss on what all this Kerry-ness entails. I think I can do this best by referring to the comment of an Irish immigrant from an Irish language-speaking district in Ireland to America at the beginning of the twentieth century. Perhaps it was a fellow immigrant who posed the question to this same Irishman: *What about education?* "There is no more education in the world," replied the first Irishman, "only education in how to rob people worse off than yourself!" How much more true is that comment today! The man who made that comment was not from Kerry but he clearly was a man who sprung from a culture – a culture indeed – that had a tap root in a tradition of learning that preceded the English conquest of Ireland. Kerry would be one county where that culture survived longer than elsewhere … and my friend taps into that culture.

More plainly, the Kerryman is a blacksmith of whom it could well be said that he came to great knowledge without going to college … and I very much doubt that contemporary culture is continuing to turn out cultured working men … now the new role-models are a-cultural and a-political characters in American soaps that no one should regard as comedies.

Not long after I first met the Kerryman I visited him in his home and met his wife and children. Things have developed down the years that I attended this family's events and funerals. But apparently in my first few visits to the home of this family, I engaged in rapid and constant contradiction of everything the Kerryman said … all this contradiction very much the action of a very isolated, mentally ill person. Fortunately, the Kerryman was moved towards pity rather towards taking offence before my senseless contradiction. I had found a haven.

The Kerryman has been a rock in my life; more than he and his family might ever know.

It is perhaps measure of how advantageous was this haven and so vulnerable was I back then that I have a picture in my mind's eye of my first meeting up with the Kerryman in the company of the Publican, where it seemed to me that the Publican was somehow handing my clearly fragile self to the custody of the Kerryman.

OF A DUBIOUS HONOUR

How quick are commentators to honour those of magisterial station in life by describing them as wits. The same honour never seems to fall on such as house painters, public house proprietors and psychiatric clients.

THE MISERABLE, MISERLY MIND SET OF THE MATERIALIST WHO ORGANISES FAKE TRIALS

Strange to say, Sigmund Freud is quite an effective touchstone whereby we can establish that some particular authority is a scientific fundamentalist. The simple fact of the matter is that, for all his disdain, Freud, in painting far too human a picture of the frailties that beset the one civilised species we know, was ever likely to excite the enmity of always combative materialists.

Ever so often these scientific fundamentalists conduct experiments to prove Freud wrong. As you might have come to expect, these fundamentalists set up these experiments with little respect for logic, with in fact no respect for what in another sphere would be termed 'due process'. I have heard in passing of one such experiment where subjects were deprived of food for a short period of time in the belief that their failure to dream of food in the course of subsequent sleep would stand to prove that dreams did not have a wishful quality. Some experiment that was!

WHAT TOOK OVER FROM THE RADICAL THERAPIES OF THE 1960s

Except for a small few devotees among the well-to-do, the radical therapies of the 1960s have as good as vanished from the scene. The rest of us with a little money who want – or badly need – therapy with a little more punch than mere talk now flock to what I call the body-to-mind therapies. The body-to-mind therapies I so name because they in some way manipulate the body with a view to improving the state of mind of the patient.

These therapies that I term body-to-mind therapies are now as numerous as the stars. But I cannot pretend that all these body-to-mind therapies are of equal merit ... and if I do allow that some pointedly less powerful therapies of this kind can by virtue of their innocuousness suit certain people with certain problems ... I still have to insist that I for one was so thoroughly broken as I was in 1986 the only way to safe but difficult recovery was traditional acupuncture administered by a properly qualified acupuncture practitioner

MY COMPLETE BREAKDOWN

The question might be asked of me why didn't I in the bad decades seek help from outside the psychiatric system. The answer is simple: I was so demoralised by my misadventures with alternative therapies, I didn't even consider the possibility of submitting to any other alternative therapy.

But, then, in 1986 I had the most severe breakdown of my life. To the point that I largely lost the will/ability to walk. At this time I could – it is true – move in dispirited manner from room to room within the old farm house, but only like someone in that stage of multiple sclerosis just a little before they lose all ability to walk upright and unaided.

But, at this my time of greatest crisis, I was afforded a lucky and dramatic 'break' – as lucky and as dramatic as any fugitive escaping from murderous pursuers. As I lay on my bed in a state of nauseous despair – the daylight streaming in the window – a brother of mine took time off from farming to make a suggestion to me and the suggestion was that I go for acupuncture treatment. His thinking at the time was that, if acupuncture could help heroin-addicts, surely it might help me. Lucky, lucky, lucky me.

Lucky because if I had to enter mental hospital at this time when I could scarcely walk, I am confident my complete destruction would have been set in train. As things turned out, it was my recovery that was set in train. Lucky also that I had brothers to accompany me on my journeys to my acupuncture-practitioner, something that I could not have accomplished on my own at that time.

THE EARLY SUCCESS OF MY ACUPUNCTURE TREATMENT

I had further luck in the fact that my psychiatrist at the time who, motivated out of a desire that I should not pay over the odds for acupuncture treatment, happened to recommend a genuine acupuncture practitioner in Cork. My luck was in big time in that I was to attend one of the fairest and judicious not to say cautious acupuncture practitioners about.

Nevertheless, I went as sceptic to this acupuncturist. My first acupuncture session wasn't long in progress when I experienced a few moments of peace. But I was still a sceptic and, when at home after my first session, I experienced a sensation in my foot that was not the foot that had received the acupuncture needle, I – as I am amused to recall – panicked a little. That instance of panic amuses me now, because not alone do I now know that the acupuncture map of the body is bilateral I can also recall far more painful and far more bizarre bodily sensations in the course of my long engagement with acupuncture.

ANY USEFUL THERAPY OUTSIDE PRESENTLY MINIMALIST PSYCHIATRY IS SURE TO BE DISRUPTIVE

Not only did acupuncture instantly restore power to my feet – and what a retreat back from the abyss that was – it also ensured I would pursue acupuncture therapy for as long as it stood to benefit me.

I termed my engagement with acupuncture therapy 'my adventure in health'. The same engagement was very much an adventure. Because, let it be well understood, that acupuncture has as its only resource the body's own pharmacy and that, when acupuncture is brought to the assistance of one as seriously ill as I was, acupuncture will of itself cause disruption. Now, my acupuncture treatment is something that happened over a long period of time and is something that I am now thankful for on an almost daily basis; but I have to acknowledge that my acupuncture treatment did cause me to be more frequently hospitalised than might otherwise be the case … against which all I have to say is that acupuncture set me free.

But there would come a time when I had to decide that the law of diminishing returns began to apply to my acupuncture treatment in that, if I was to continue with acupuncture treatment, I stood to make no more significant gains but would continue to suffer the disruption that acupuncture causes. With the greatest of gratitude to my acupuncture practitioner, after many years I not unreasonably quit acupuncture treatment.

SOD'S SECOND LAW

A bureaucrat faced with a choice between empowering a section of the disabled population and creating a position for another bureaucrat will always go with the latter option.

THE FORSIGHT OF THE DERANGED

The anecdote I am about to relate happens not to be the most spectacular instance on what might be called manic foresight in my lifetime, but I tell this anecdote because it is one instance in which manic foresight yielded a distinctly beneficial result for me.

However convenient hospital may be to safely let a manic episode pass by (or how convenient a hospital may be to let time mend broken fences on the outside), the fact is at another level my health always declines in hospital. I am quick to feel the 'institutionalisation' of hospital. Accordingly, when in hospital I do everything in my power to get discharged or, failing that, win two or three days leave from the hospital. Unfortunately, getting short leave from hospital is not always as easily arranged at it could be.

On one morning I asked for weekend leave from a non-consultant doctor. She turned me down. I wasn't giving up that easily; so I asked her could I have a second opinion. She agreed that I could. But two hours later my consultant turned down my request in the corridor. That would seem to be the end of the matter.

But, before lunchtime, I set out on a search mission with the distinct belief that I would find something that might overturn that most emphatic judgment of the morning. My search took me to an overgrown pathway about a justly notorious locked ward. At back of this building I came across what I was looking for. That being a two or three foot metal bar that had once been portion of a window and that which could be used by any person of violent intent to kill another person with little difficulty. I could I suppose have taken the potential murder weapon back to my ward; but I wasn't about to throw away an ace as readily as that.

Instead I soberly returned a little late for my dinner in my ward. After which, I took myself to the administration building, enquired the phone number of the hospital complaints officer from the switchboard operator and went to a nearby phone to speak to the former. But when I picked up the phone I found that I had already been put through by the switchboard to the complaints officer; but I was not about to avail of a free phone call and the first thing the complaints officer heard was the sound of my coins dropping into the phone-box before she heard the quite embarrassing news that a lethal weapon had been most carelessly left rather invitingly on the hospital grounds.

I returned to my ward and forgot about the morning's events. But an hour or two later in a psychiatric hospital that, like most psychiatric hospitals, might be described as a sentient being in its own right, it fell not to a doctor but to a nurse to tell me that I could go on weekend leave after all.

*I*NSIDERS – with Richard and Jim

The Real IRA and MI5 and a Chinese Triad are after me!

You're lucky the doctors aren't after you, Jim.

J.M.

THE INNATE PUN:

THE ANIMAL SPECIES IN PUN ... AND THE PUNNING-SYSTEM AS REALITY IN ITS OWN RIGHT

Perhaps humanity has always treated animals in a bad fashion; but in former times humanity did have a spiritual vision of itself as being part of a community of animal, vegetation and geological feature. What is left of that great spiritual vision of humanity. Not much. Not much apart from Walt Disney's Mickey.

As if to remind us that we share this planet with many an animal species, the punning-system in the English language makes much mention of some animal species. A friend of mine, who has some small acquaintance with my ideas concerning the punning-system, failed at first attempt to see how puns to do with animals could be all of a significant, logical and an inevitable portion of the punning-system.

That said, the punning-system tends to invoke all aspects of the animal species it mentions. The real mating habits and other habits of animal species and the folklore and fiction concerning these animal species all serve in some measure to inform the significance of pun-mention of animal species.

I suppose the first species I ought to discuss is that species that has the starring role in English language punning: the bee. By any standards, the bee is a remarkable event in life, so much so that many have come to regard the beehive not as a collection of individual organisms but as a super-organism in its own right or indeed an animal in itself.

Hamlet's 'To be or not to be' and the grammatical term the verb 'to be' serve to highlight the importance the English-language pun places on the bee species. If I am to attempt to define the exact significance pun-reference to the bee, I can only make some rather obvious observations. But such things as the fact that the bee produces much-prized honey and the fact that beehive can serve as an image of female power in the world and the fact that the beehive itself is a society all tend to fuse into one grand idea where the bee is a symbol of life in all its beauty and servitude.

But it cannot be denied that the letter 'B' – perhaps like all letters of the alphabet – has both a positive and a negative significance; and nobody need be in any doubt that phrases such as 'the B-class' and 'a B-movie' translate as the *bum-class*.

Yet, it is both the affirmative qualities of both the bee and the letter 'B' that I would hope would enter readers minds when I quote (without bothering to translate) the very majestic words 'become' and 'becoming'. The power of the inevitable puns on these two words inspire to say that I may not have the full story on the significance of pun-mention of the bee and that I may not have the full story on any other conventions of the punning-system I discuss. What is more, I am perfectly confident that there are many other conventions of the punning-system that I know nothing at all about. Study of the punning-system is like the study of science or the study of life – a subject without end.

I should also say that I don't believe that what I might term preternatural wordplay is an isolated phenomenon. I have some reason to believe that there is much other supernatural comment and cross-reference on life by the preternatural awaiting discovery. Belligerently, I would add that neither parapsychologists nor mystics will be first with the news of phenomena in relation to preternatural wordplay.

Anything I might say about the definite pun-reference to the bee in the English word 'Buddhism' would be speculative; so I prefer to only note that reference and pass on.

After the bee, I turn to another social insect the ant. The ant has quite a formidable presence in the English language; but I am unsure of the significance of the ant in pun. Perhaps, the ant stands in apposition to the bee, with the bee as symbol of bounty and the ant as symbol of more utilitarian models of society. Certainly, I believe our image of the ant as a worker informs its mention in the word 'Protestant'.

Speaking of religion, I guess the next animal I should discuss is the cat. For its part the cat is also portion of a competing twosome. I refer to the fact that the cat as a domestic animal has a rival in the shape of the dog. Again, both the cat and the dog have a formidable presence in the English language, especially as prefixes of a sort. I cannot help but think that, in the case of this image of this famous twosome, the cat is seen as the free animal and the dog as an animal frequently tethered. That in any event is my attempt at an explanation for the fact that the cat enjoys a better reputation than the dog in English language punning.

What then are we to make of the term 'Roman Catholic'? I am aware of a certain viewpoint that sees the guilt-ridden Roman Catholic being somehow that little bit more capable of enjoying life than the entirely strait-laced Protestant. James Joyce seemed to subscribe to this idea to some extent and one modern Irish poet has treated this idea as a given.

There are other words such as 'cattle' and 'bovine' that contain a reference to a quite separate species to the species the words refer to; but while I am prepared for the possibility that this rather confused mention of animal species may hold meaning, I don't have any knowledge of it.

TV is not the most reliable sources of information; but I heard it on a TV documentary that the reason why we have an Easter bunny is that the animal once more associated with Easter – the hare – was considered too pagan. Shakespeare was one to pun 'hare' with hair. The speed and elusiveness of the hare probably go to inform the 'poetry' of the 'hair'- *hare* pun.

Because some animal species figure so prominently in the English language, I must presume that the adverb 'now' meaningfully puns with cow and that the verb 'pull' and the adjective 'full' meaningfully puns with bull. The only thing else I have to say about animal punning in the English language is a small observation to the effect that the not very meaningful phrase 'a cock and bull story' acquires more meaning.

I suspect that a polyglot could make much of the fact that each language within his or her grasp chooses to highlight a different set of animals in what might be termed its obligatory puns.

A book reviewer of a certain kind, whose intention is to be clever rather than informative, may come to say that all I have done in this book is to attempt to lend Freudian reductionism a preternatural dimension. I have to allow that it must be something of a homecoming for some of the more Freudian doctors when they discover the punning-system; but, for my own part, I have to say that I stand a distance away from Sigmund Freud.

I salute Freud as a pioneer, as a thinker who effectively discovered psychic determinism or the idea that it was possible to establish in precise detail that *the child is father to the man*. But I happen to be more impressed with those thinkers who came after Freud and who differed with Freud in that they argued that general vicissitude and general trauma were responsible for character formation and mental illness. I bitterly note that some of those thinkers were never quite accepted as contributing something to the debate about the nature of character formation and mental illness by the universities. I am even more appalled that there is now a conspiracy to write the entire idea of psychic determinism out of the record.

Anyway, I return with a vengeance to the subject of the punning-system. It is important to emphasize that the punning-system is art rather than science and as such it is not a homogenous system. Each pun tends to come with its own nuance; and the nuance of a particular pun will go to decide whether we regard that pun as straightforward comedy and sometimes amoral comedy or as containing some little polemical statement.

Some will say that I lost them in this book when I began to speak of puns on individual letters of the alphabet. But I think that punning on individual letters of the alphabet go to lend respectability to the entire punning-system. It is because that there are so many layers to the punning-system – including the layer of what might be termed letter-punning – that the punning-system *cannot* be explained away as a matter of selection/invention/faith. I deeply regret that I am near but yet ever so far away from knowing more about letter-punning.

In any event, I am convinced that every letter in the alphabet has its own reductionist personality. But I wouldn't claim to be an expert on the significance of individual letters of the alphabet. 'B', 'I' and 'P' I know a little about and have already discussed at some length. 'C' is another letter whose esoteric significance is reasonably plain.

'Phi' is the twenty-first letter of the Greek alphabet and is, I imagine, the basis of most instances of the combination 'ph' in the English language. I hand it over to my readers to decide if they can come up with a rationale for the presence of 'ph' in such words as: Aphrodite, asphyxia, orphan, philanthropy, philosophy, philately, schizophrenia, telephone and so on. If I appear to some to have delegated a silly task to my readers, I can only say that the idea that frequently used phrase of the cosmetic industry 'the pH balance' is subject to the kind of humorous punning I have outlined in the previous paragraph is not something I consider farfetched but quite indisputable.

A question arises about reductionist punning in languages other than English. Well, I am in no doubt that reductionist punning is a feature of all language. Alas, the only language besides English that I learnt anything much of in my schooldays is the Irish language and I have forgotten most of what I did learn of Irish. But from my little knowledge of Irish I am aware of a few meaningful puns internal to Irish. For instance, in Irish the word for 'year' rhymes with the word for 'sun' and that represents a meaningful pun.[15]

I must consider punning internal to a language to carry more force than any inter-language punning; but it is arguable that a detailed study of inter-language punning would reveal one culture commenting on another with the help of the preternatural. Alas, I know but a few Irish-English reductionist puns and here I am only going to quote but one such pun.

I once questioned the value of Irish with an Irish language enthusiast. She explained that Irish held particular value because words in the Irish language tend to have a more literal significance than, say, words in the English language. For instance the English word 'town' is of itself at this point in time an abstract word; whereas the equivalent term in Irish 'baile mór' has more literal value in that 'baile' simply means 'home' and 'mór' simply means big. Even I have to agree that it is pleasing and even evocative poeticism of the Irish language that says a town is only a larger version of the domestic home.

Of course, the Irish word 'mór' is actually long converted into English as the four-letter word 'more' and as such frequently crops up in place names such as 'Kilmore'.

As this book is winding to a close, I am conscious of the fact that I have done great injustice to the brevity of the innate pun. For pertinent and ever so terse witticisms are no longer witticisms when explained. You could write a long essay on the evils of nationalism; but, for its part, the punning considers it sufficient to note that the flag is only a rag.

---

15 The Irish for year is *bhliain* and the Irish for sun is *ghrian*.

HOMILY 8

A PAUSE PERHAPS IN YOUR CONTEMPLATION OF JOE NASH

You may perhaps be one to weary of things, especially familiar things. You may for instance be weary of the current prime minister: you may see him every evening on the television news and you may grow so tired of this that you may utter between clenched teeth: "Wouldn't you think he'd give it a rest!"

Although you may be less prepared to admit it, although you may be greatly ashamed of the fact, you may nevertheless come to feel – if only momentarily – that too much is made of Joe Nash. This Joe Nash morning, noon and night may be proving too much for you.

My advice in these circumstances is not to deny your great shame but to stay with the feeling that prompts this great shame. My advice in fact is to take your anger out on Joe Nash. And yet I would be the first to understand that this very approach that would help clear the air and bring you back tens times more adherently than before to the contemplation of Joe Nash but this may be more than you are capable of doing. It may not be in you to take your temper out on Joe.

My advice to you in these precise circumstances that are a credit to you is not to abuse Joe but to take your anger out on something associated with Joe. For example, you may be aware that Joe in the course of his mortal existence kept a notebook detailing the form of racehorses. You may also be aware that, after Joe died, this notebook became disparagingly known as NASH'S BOOK OF DEAD CERTS and that this notebook became the object of some curiosity and little fame before it mysteriously disappeared. You, however, faithful but disconsolate soul that you are, may imagine that you have this notebook in your possession – I never went with its popular name – and you may further imagine yourself jumping vehemently on the same notebook. I advise that you actually jump while engaging in this mental exercise.

And after a few 'jumps' you will – I assure you – feel thoroughly refreshed and ready once again to resume in your undivided pondering of Joe, that is of Joe Nash.

9

THE GOOD LIFE
BECOMES MORE
THE NORM

CURIOUS

Pity Arnold Toynbee [16] the grandiose English historian. In his *A Study Of History* he condemned all belief-systems that either urged a return to a golden age that never was or that promised an Utopia or paradise to come, managing only to make a curious exception for the belief-system he first heard of in the nursery.

SOME CONFUSION OF MINE

If acupuncture almost instantly put me back on my feet, my lengthy engagement with acupuncture brought its own troubles.

I wasn't long going for acupuncture when I turned very gloomy in outlook and decided that I needed hospitalisation. My psychiatrist at the time decided for the best of reasons to refuse me hospitalisation. But so determined was I that I should be institutionalised, I elected to commit myself to a religious institution devoted to the drying out of alcoholics. To say the least of it, I am not an alcoholic and my decision to enter that institution was quite a mistake. I shall report on my time in the religious institution in a little while; but now all you need to know is that I emerged from the religious institution in a more distressed state again and that I changed psychiatrists and was again admitted to the hospital on the hill, Saint Mark's.

There I was diagnosed as being in quite a bad state and I was put on an injection. This, I would say now, was quite a backward step. But back then I didn't have the wit to realise that my troubles at the time had a lot to do with the fact that I was receiving acupuncture treatment; and back then and presently and perhaps for a long time to come psychiatry was, is and will be incapable or recognising that a patient is on a healing path.

One of the regrettable consequences of me being put on injection was that I had to interrupt my acupuncture treatment by stopping going for acupuncture for as long as I was on the injection. Anybody who goes for acupuncture treatment while on a psychiatric injection is only going to do so once; for more or less immediately after such treatment in such circumstances the patient's mind and body is an arena for a kind of civil war.

After about nine unpleasant months on the injection, I returned to my old psychiatrist and he reluctantly took me off the injection and I enthusiastically resumed my acupuncture therapy.

---

[16] Arnold Joseph Toynbee (1889-1975) was a British historian, philosopher of history, research professor of International History at the London School of Economics and the University of London and author of numerous books.

_A_ STRANGE INSTITUTION

Priests and nuns are for the most part in retreat from wielding authority in education and medicine. But, about the time that bugle first blew for this retreat, the religious began to take an interest in providing services for the addicted to alcohol and other substances. Strange this, for most of the religious engaged in this particular crusade would never have tasted as much as a cigarette or a pint of beer.

In a setting that typified all the petty little grandeur of olden times and so must be described as parlour, I underwent my induction to this strange institution for alcoholics. With all the vanity of old-time petty grandeur, I was treated to a little feast of tea and tasty sandwiches brought in on a tray by an underling. There was some small gothic comedy in that detail, because before long I was suffering from hunger pangs on a daily basis in this strange institution. For this same wicked institution only believed in serving anything like adequate meals on Roman Catholic feast days.

In the course of the induction, the subject of my mother came up and the nun-inquisitor encouragingly asked:

"Was she possessive?"

This question might be considered remarkable for its antique psychology. But I fear the question is another instance of gothic comedy, because – as perhaps could only surprise those as innocent as myself – the way of treating alcoholics and others in this strange institution eschewed even the smallest concession to psychology. Effectively, the inmates of the strange institution were told that their compulsions were sinful and that they should employ self-discipline to rid themselves of these compulsions; and nothing more than that was offered by way of help to the addicted and the troubled.

OUTSIDE THE TEMPLE GATES AT QILNOQUARI

Inside the temple, personalities were praying to a personality-less God.

Outside the temple gates that eternal secondary statement was in progress, to wit a street entertainer with his set of mechanical dolls. His was a retro act. A toy rock band named the Rolling Stonz apparently modelled on a band from the much fantasised upon twentieth century. As the dolls mimed the singing of vocals and playing of instruments, a holographic video highlighted the achievements of the band. Such as the cultural and political revolutions they inspired, much of these references probably fantasy also. Besides, the variant spelling of the name of the toy rock band was ample clue that, notwithstanding the claim that this street entertainment was homage to twentieth century events, this same street entertainment owed much to the so-called reincarnated bands of the twenty-third century. Worse, the only recognisable twentieth century song the mechanical band members were seen to mime to was the only just recognisable 'Day Tripper'.

Forgetfulness is not the worst failing of time.

MY LIFE BEGINNING AT FORTY

I hesitate to personify my change of fortune in my forties. I hesitate to describe my change of fortune in terms of one man. I hesitate because the man who entered my life at the time when I was returning to some health was and is no shrinking violet, this being the man I term the Musicman. At the age of seventeen, this same Musicman sang 'Maids When You're Young Never Wed An Old Man' to his own guitar accompaniment at some talent contest or other.

Maids when you're young never wed an old man [...]
For he's lost his filurum, he's got no ding-durum [...]
Maids when you're young never wed and old man.

We are not told how the Musicman fared in singing these lines in terms of the contest; but we are told that on hearing this singer and this song a seventy year old curmudgeon in the audience – who hadn't smiled for thirty years – burst into loud laughter. The Musicman hasn't looked back since.

I am tempted to describe the Musicman as an Irish Mr Pickwick. The Musicman is a somewhat portly figure; and, if he doesn't quite invent scientific notions, he does quote existing precepts rather as if they were his own invention; and, most to the point, he has a large number of clients with which he can amuse himself. But this surely is one of the glories of the Musicman … in a world that is racing to the conformity of the professional double-income family that takes three foreign holidays in the year, the Musicman is willing to entertain a continuous circus of a flotsam and jetsam of society about himself. I am indebted to the Musicman who has brought much joy to my life over the years.

It was the man I term the Kerryman who introduced me to the Musicman. I half recall the first meeting of the triumvirate when we pub crawled around a local town and a feature of my discourse at the time that is no longer a feature of my day to day discourse – the famous business of the pun – was a hit with the Musicman. So much so, that the Kerryman reported to me later that he himself had gone up in the estimation of the Musicman for having conjuror-like produced another genuine oddity out of nothing – me! Now, I wouldn't wish to pretend that my entry into the life and circle of the Musicman was not a most common place event in the life of the Musicman, this common place event being the discovery of someone different whereby the Musicman's programme of life as entertainment wouldn't come to a halt. But, as commonplace as these discoveries in the life of the Musicman are, each one is a victory and cause for more celebration.

The Musicman took my fame to another part of the county; and a sorrowful eyed woman, who wore workingman's boots not for butch-type statement but with more of a nod to Bob Dylan who once sported the same footwear, after hearing the Musicman's tales of his locating a Magus [17] in me, felt most compelled to travel to see me. All of sudden, I began to believe that my life of failure was to be the subject of glorious vindication.

Notwithstanding the usual reversals that life throws up, the celebration is on-going. As troubadour, the Musicman has been all over the world; and as impresario, the Musicman has much to his credit brought classical concerts and one-man dramatisations and more into rural public houses. This book is but my contribution to the celebration of the Musicman.

---

[17] A member of a priestly caste of ancient Persia.

_A_ GOOD DEVOLPMENT IN PSYCHIATRY

Nobody telephones somebody else with a view to holding a tranquilliser or anti-depressant party. What is more, should some person newly out of psychiatric hospital enters a public house, the first advice – and very bad advice it is – he or she will receive is to throw the tablets away and drink a few beers for him or herself. At a purely inter-personal level, psychiatric drugs have a certain anti-social quality about them.

So, it was indeed a wise move when the Irish psychiatric authorities at least in some parts of the country decided in the 1980s that the most helpful thing it could do for psychiatric clients was to provide them with day care centres where they could socialise among themselves. I understand that a similar effort took place in British psychiatry about a decade or so earlier only that British day-care centres have a more industrial character. But the beauty of day-care centres lies in the fact that the wounded people can and do help each other by merely socialising with each other.

The fist day care centre I attended was situated in a building in the grounds of St Mark's Hospital. This building was not quite a ward of the hospital; and I perhaps paid it the ultimate compliment by describing it as a little republic within the hospital. This centre to this day caters for out-patients and for in-patients who have been passed fit to attend it.

Indeed once this centre opened, I spent most of my day when an in-patient in the hospital in this centre. From the rug material mural on the corridor wall to the somewhat subversive noticeboard to the fact that some of the clients here were only day visitors, there was so much to prefer about this building – known as Block 7 – to the claustrophobic medical wards.

Talk therapy was the main event in this centre and talk therapy may not be the worst way to spend a morning or afternoon in hospital. Especially helpful I imagine were those times in group session when one patient dominated the session to make personal complaint at length. But the pedantic argument of this book remains that, as the only addition to the two-trick psychiatry of _drug and shock_, talk therapy is not enough.

*M*ISSING PAGES FROM THIS BOOK

There a few subjects I mostly exclude from this book but which my conscience requires me to mention. I don't detail the petty delusions that were such a constant feature of my life up to recently. I can't find any comedy in such delusions, only great embarrassment. And I scarcely need to warn anyone that would genuinely investigate supernatural and preternatural lore in psychiatric society that delusion is present in such society as a right and insight only as a novelty.

I might allude to the fact that my life did involve one relationship across the gender divide; but concerning this relationship I am not willing to say any more.

I must also mention a group of Japanese doctors who passed like tourists through the Irish hospital of my experience and the very strange interview they conducted with me – in which *they* made extraordinary assertions about *my* life. I can't really report on this particular meeting except to say that the details of the meeting were recorded in a small stand-alone file and that this file doubtless contains mention of a joke that the Japanese doctors raised in course of the meeting purely and only I believe as device to distract from the gravity and extravagance of what *they* said.

Readers go away from this book rather empty-handed, if they go away still thinking that the patients in a mental hospital are the only ones in such a setting who hold with seemingly bizarre ideas.

*I*NSIDERS – with Richard and Jim

ᛊHE DEATH OF MY FATHER

So far death came closest to me with the death of my father. He was a long time dying. He died at home. But I wasn't directly involved with his care. Nevertheless, I was there to hear some of the more frivolous things he might not be of a mind to say to other members of the family. For instance, he often quoted the line of a song to me that went 'Take my boots off when I die'. Once he explained to me that the said song was a military song.

I guess of the two sides to my father one side was vaguely legal, vaguely military. For instance, when herding cattle he would speak of 'arresting the cattle'.

But all throughout his life but especially in the two decades before his death, he attempted to reach out to me. I remember once I pretended that I was unable to rise from my armchair and he pretended to assist me to stand on my feet. I guess that was the nearest we ever came to embracing.

The night before my father died he told me he was lonely. However exactly arose my response to his confession of loneliness to me I can't exactly say; but I did end up reading a portion of 'Ode To A Skylark' to him.

When I had concluded reading Shelley to my father, I said 'Goodnight' to him and he said 'Goodnight' in grateful, if not slightly happier, voice.

Looking back some few months before he died in a brief moment when he experienced a little joy he told me that he enjoyed me.

SECRET ART

Not everything that I learnt in my mad years is retained in full. For instance, I was one day playing about with the alphabet and with numbers when I came up with a little formula that yielded the following graphic:

Alas, I have lost the little formula that yielded this graphic; but I am adamant that this graphic arose as the result of a mathematical formula. I am in no doubt that the above graphic makes mention of the camel species; and I must in the circumstances suspect that there are other mathematical formula that make mention of other animal species. Which is to say that I believe that half poetic, half reductionist statement by the preternatural is not confined to either the realm of wordplay or implicit statement in nature and artefact, but even extends to 'original' visual jokes and for all I know may even at a stretch extend to music.

What some are very happy to describe as the platonic sphere, I believe to a be a very crowded sphere. But even if I use the word platonic elsewhere in my discourse on the innate pun, I have to confess to misgivings about this term *platonic*. Plato seems to argue that the human drama is a badly realised version of an ideal enjoying some existence elsewhere. But I am more inclined to think of the human drama as taking place in a hall of mirrors. In other words, in case you have not grasped the point, I am unashamedly insisting that the preternatural is not reluctantly but rather fulsomely inclined to acknowledge the human world, if not quite on those terms the religious in particular might wish for.

The fact that preternatural shows such a fondness for animal motif will not surprise those who will not be shocked to learn that the preternatural in its statement on the human world shows more of the sensibility of a poet than of a moralist.

FOUND ART

Picasso said of himself: "I do not seek, I find."

This quote inspired me to coin the term *found art* to describe something I have encountered on a number of occasions in recent years. By *found art* I mean those haphazard images that appear in artefacts – images born of such as peeling off some paintwork or the accidental daub of a paint brush and so on – and I believe these same instances of found art frequently make some representational statement.

But trust the tabloid journalist – no less than the excitable religious – to miss the real story. For you as know, tabloid journalists frequently serve up for our amusement stories of instances of group mania concerning some religious image that appears suddenly in some material or other and all the greater the intended comedy be if that material is something entirely perishable such a food-stuff such as toast. Ha ha.

But to the reader who will want to make use of such a term and who will perhaps come to notice events of the sort the term alludes to, I proffer the term *found art*. Now, I have most fortunately but only recently become aware that the term *found object* is a respectable term in art circles; but that latter term I am convinced only goes to damn with faint praise what is you might say a vast art form.

THE GOLD – AS DISTINCT FROM THE BRASS – IN THE LIFE OF A PSYCHIATRIC CLIENT

There is a certain sort of psychiatric doctor for whom mental illness can ever only be a tragedy. What devotion such a doctor has to him or herself we can only begin to imagine. To such a doctor the only reward of mental illness is the crude lesson it dispenses on the fragility of the human mind. So confident is this type of doctor of his argument that he is prepared to rope in the 1960s drug-culture as another instance of something whose only value was in a demonstration of the fragility of the human mind ...

My earnest advice to any young person is not to attempt to replicate the 1960s ... but if I am happy to regard the 60s as a train station that we passed along the way ... I nevertheless have to mention such things as The Who's early singles, the Beatles' *Revolver* album and their *Strawberry Fields/Penny Lane* single and the Rolling Stones *Exile On Main St* as demonstrating something more majestic than the mere fragility of the human mind.

The contempt of a doctor capable of overlooking such richness as I have just listed is, as William Blake [18] might say, a kingly title.

And do not, dear reader, entirely despise the value of lessons as to the fragility of the human mind. It can – I realise – be argued that the psychiatric clients come to over-value the humbling nature of mental illness; but, against that, you may not have lived – and there are certainly many people out there in media land who have not lived – because they have not stood alone by a window in a psychiatric ward – itself a slightly unusual occurrence – and have not seen the motorised traffic on a roadway in the distance and have not understood that same traffic to be part of another, entirely different world.

---

[18] William Blake (1757-1827) was an English poet, painter, and printmaker. Largely unrecognised during his lifetime, Blake is now considered a seminal figure in the history of the poetry and visual arts of the Romantic Age.

PSYCHIATRY GOES ONE BETTER

The weekly journey to and return from the day-centre in St Mark's Hospital was a exacting one, involving two car and four bus journeys. But then the psychiatric authorities opened a psychiatric day care centre in a local capital town that was a mere thirteen miles from my home on the hill. This day care centre resembling nothing so much as a town dwelling-house for your average middle-class family, which is probably precisely what it was prior to its purchase and conversion to a day-centre for psychiatric clients not ashamed to attend it.

A most valuable portion of my routine is the day I travel to a local capital town and partake of society in the psychiatric day centre. As it turns out I can make small report on the little jests that make life pleasurable in this day centre. And it is perhaps a fatal failing of psychiatric clients that too many of their jests make mention of doctors. For instance a client of a day centre – a woman normally given to very up-beat statements – reported as follows:

"Doctor _____ asked me how did I rate myself?"

The answer the woman gave to the doctor's question, she then repeated for the benefit of her mostly smoking audience beneath a perspex-roofed annex facing the back lawn in the day centre, saying:

"'Above average,' I said!"

This woman's report of the answer she gave a doctor would have brought forth smiles and perhaps a little laughter from her listeners. For everybody among this woman's listeners would be just a little aware that in the view of important people out there in the locality every client who attends this day centre is below average.

But the up-beat woman is correct. We who attend the day centre are above average.

FOR THE RECORD

A psychiatric diagnosis/classification can attach to your name forever. So I should point out that the doctors have reduced the charge against me. Worried a little by a certain jollity in my social life and endeavours and attitude, they no longer label me a schizophrenic nor manic depressive but say I am suffering from something of a more convoluted name of even greater obscurity.

$\mathcal{I}$, HUMANOID

There is a wonderful science fiction short story titled 'Halfjack' by Roger Zelazny.[19] A halfjack the story explains is a slang term for somebody who is half-man and half-machine. The twist in this story occurs when the hero of the story explains to the surprise of another character that he is a halfjack not as a consequence of an accident but as a matter of choice.

I only have a small knowledge of science fiction; but I understand the term 'humanoid' is some times used in science fiction for a human being who has gone a little of the way of being a machine. I suppose I am something of a humanoid. I wear that most character-revealing accessory that is spectacles; but I doubt that spectacles reveal anything about my genetic history. Also, I am happy to take one psychiatric tablet in the day and that vital tablet adds to the extent to which I am a humanoid.

But the notion that scientists hope to replace by stealth a diseased human race with a race of humanoids is now quite a respectable idea. The idea has made the crossover from the one-shelf repository of a teenager's book collection and into the glass panelled libraries of the smug literati. This ambition of scientists to replace the human race with a race of humanoids is not at all hindered by – and to some extent may be the real begetter – of the great falsity in much of the thinking and research pursued in the life-sciences.

$\mathcal{E}$ATING AWAY AT OUR WORLD

When globalisation has at once entirely misrepresented by simulation and has uprooted and destroyed all indigenous cultures, globalisation will of that very moment inanely announce its bankruptcy.

This scenario is not without some sort of precedent in nature. For there is the sort of parasite that is only known to come to stand-alone maturity at the precise moment it has killed off the host body.

---

19 Roger Joseph Zelazny (1937-1995) was an American poet and writer of fantasy and science fiction short stories and novels, best known for *The Chronicles of Amber*.

SOME PEOPLE WE CAN AFFORD TO LOSE

Those scientists who would trace the causation of schizophrenia back to a virus in cats and those journalists who credulously report on such scientists should all be dispatched (and quickly dispatched) to the Himalayas to search for the Abominable Snowman or, perhaps, better still, they should be dispatched with no less urgency to the moon to see if it really is made of green cheese.

THE CASE OF THE REAL ROLLING STONE

I may be regarded as a interloper when it comes to discussing music … but if I am going to expend energy on putting a CD in a music machine I am most likely to pick a CD by some of the classic rock 'n' roll bands of the 1960s and 1970s: The Rolling Stones, The Doors, the Band and Led Zeppelin. The Rolling Stones are my particular favourite in that to my tone-deaf years they bring the most variety of texture to rock band song that can have its origin traced back to Chuck Berry and Bo Diddley.

In the days when the Rolling Stones were dangerous and much later days when they were not, rock journalists instituted a long-running discussion/conceit as to who was the real Stone. Brian Jones was a candidate for a while but then attention switched to Keith Richard … but such was the earnestness of this search for the 'real Rolling Stone' that you might be forgiven that there was some as yet unknown figure in the Rolling Stones circle who better personified stylish disregard than any actual Rolling Stone.

Anyway, it amuses me to recall that not so long ago in an effort to upstage me the man I term the Musicman informed me the very minute I stepped into his motor car that he had just recently heard on the radio that –

"The only real Stones were the Flintstones !"

That's me and my pals. Teenagers – and argumentatively so – up to and perhaps including grim old age.

THE INNATE PUN:

PROPER NAMES ... AND SOME PUNS TO DO WITH RELIGION

Most classic love songs in the pop idiom might leave you thinking that the singer was undergoing torture. One such classic recording is 'When A Man Loves A Woman' as sung by Lou Rawls. A typically snide disc jockey announcing the details of this recording proceeded to laugh and say: "I'm not going to get into names!"

Given their respective music and respective characters, Lou Rawls and Cliff Richard would have to be living in a more meaningless universe for Lou Rawls to be known as Cliff Richard or for, more laughably, Cliff Richard to be known as Lou Rawls. So, I come to the subject of reductionist punning on proper names. I have to say that I can only discuss this subject in the light of my limited knowledge of the punning-system.

One perhaps novel detail of punning on names that I might mention is that the word 'name' itself comes with a pun that pretty much defines the entire business of punning on proper names. For – as will hold some incidental resonance for those conscious of the history of psychoanalytic literature – the word 'name' contains a very meaningful pun with the word *aim*, this mention of aim having nothing to do with an ambition to win a seat in parliament or a golf tournament but, as you might have guessed, having all to do with the ambition or potential of the person or item that bears a particular name.

But I must utter an immediate word of warning: sometimes the pun-content of a name can have literal value but quite often it will have only mostly figurative value. I will discuss the figurative value of puns on proper names shortly.

For now I want to note that I cannot really discuss punning on the names of friends and acquaintances or even punning on local place-names. For me to reduce the names of friends and acquaintances to vulgar concerns would be bad enough in itself but for me to actually attempt to connect the personalities in question to these vulgar concerns would not be a wise undertaking.

Whether you are an agnostic about or a fan of the Beatles, you shouldn't really fail to see that the band that woke up the twentieth century makes a passing reference to the life-affirming bee in its name.

I have to concede that, if the earlier mentioned idea of a fundamentally *esoterically* divided humanity has any merit at all, it should very much come to the fore in respect of punning on proper names. But I am not really sure about this idea of an esoterically divided humanity. I can say however, that, when it comes to punning on proper names, there is quite a wide spectrum that goes from names that suggest compliance to names that suggest apostasy.

There is a temptation to think that a famous name involve some reference to the perceived persona and indeed the work of the famous one. One poet has chosen to place the music hall star Marie Lloyd and Sigmund Freud the father of psychoanalysis in the one poem. But, as may be more damning of the scientist than the entertainer here, there can be no doubt that Marie's and Sigmund's surnames quite unavoidably involve a pun.

There might not seem to be much sense in looking for meaningful puns in the name of a country. The names of countries last as a rule for long periods of time and the countries themselves go through various phases of liberality and repression while bearing particular names. Yet I am tempted to remark that for the moment it still seems appropriate that 'Poland' translates as *po-hand*. In similar vein, I might remark that one translation of 'Ireland' is *wire-hand*.

In the days of the cold war, there was a sense in which a statement from the Kremlin meant a statement from the *gremlin*. And indeed there was also a sense in which such a statement was likely to promote a *grim-line*.

I can, I suppose, look on the American empire from a philosophical perspective. Strong beehives will raid a weak beehive for its honey; and it should not come as much of surprise to me or anybody else that near global empire of America is the guarantor of an unjust world where near half the human population endure at best a subsistence living. Some people, of course, don't see it that way; and for this sort of people the White House is the *lighthouse* – a beacon of liberty in a dark world.

But I am more inclined to regard the whitehouse/*lighthouse* pun as possibly more a reference to the likely colour of an actual lighthouse; and, as one who knows that the punning-system ever targets human grandeur, I am in no doubt that the preternatural is saying that the house that commands the greatest military force in human history, the Whitehouse is the *shite-house*.

Needless to say, there are many vulgar puns attending religious terms and religious figures. But sometimes a particular vulgar pun concerning a religious figure would appear to be not so much derisory as character-revealing. I have thought better of detailing any of these derisory or possibly character-revealing puns to do with religious figures; but that is not to stop my readers from identifying and evaluating such puns.

I confess I have never really made much of a study of anagrams; but I pretty much take it for granted that, like meaningful puns, meaningful anagrams occur in greater number than can be easily explained away. One rather Christian anagram would have us believe that 'vine' and *vein* are one.

Satirists working in the Irish context have until recently shied away from using Jesus Christ as a character, presumably because so many people are of the belief that they have a personal relationship with Jesus. But these same satirists feel free to make use of the more abstract character that is God. Anyway, I can proceed to discuss puns on the name 'God' with a little more liberty.

I must refer to some teenager in a local town who most likely I never met. But this teenager was probably the cause and perhaps the victim of some little tension in his home and he also probably was not the greatest of communicators in that likely as not he spoke mostly in grunts. For as I went on my way in the same local town, I was able to read a piece of graffiti composed by this teenager; and this same piece of eloquent graffiti declared:

GOD IS [A] COD.

Indeed, there can be little doubt that the angry paternal God that figures in the imagination of many is a cod.

Of course, the more seriously committed religious people will, if they allow themselves give any credence to the punning-system, be tempted to argue that punning-system is the work of demonic forces. But I think the boot may be on the other foot. For I think the punning-system is a statement of the preternatural at its most unchallengeable; and it may well be the major religions of the world have their beginnings with more petty supernatural forces. This is not exactly the most modest paragraph a writer ever composed; but, in the light of the huge intolerance with which religion is conceived and presented, this paragraph might be excused as an attempt to restore some balance.

Those more thoroughly opposed to religion than I am will be inclined to say that religion has frequently sought to exploit people's fear of the grave by telling them fairytales of Heaven, Paradise, Nirvana or reincarnation. I don't like having to say it, but it does rather appear to me that neither the actual material universe nor the actual preternatural can inspire much belief in such things as Heaven, Paradise, Nirvana or reincarnation. In this book I am reporting on the punning-system and I have to say that punning-system would appear to represent bad news for anybody who thinks there is some home awaiting us beyond the grave.

My final observation on this most instructive example of twinned words is that, unlike 'scatology', 'eschatology' contains a mention of the word 'hat' – and *hat* in this context is probably a mocking reference to human vanity. My readers should be in no doubt that I consider the twinning of these same two sombre words to be a remarkably positive statement by the preternatural.

It is difficult not to conclude that religion has overstated the bounty that the preternatural is prepared to confer upon us. But the fact that there is a preternatural at all renders it likely that life is eternal … and that is a small but significant consolation. With some repetition of pattern, life will always have some perhaps sadder, perhaps happier, perhaps lesser, perhaps more extravagant presence somewhere.

We may well wish for more than that; but I think it fair to say that we haven't been offered much of a proof that there is more than this.

Maybe?

$\mathcal{E}$NVOI

The Irish Social Welfare department has for logo a dove departing in flight from a pair of open hands. I see this logo frequently for it is present on the cover of what has long been the most important book in my life – my social welfare cheque book. I suspect also that the same logo carries the hope that whoever has to avail of the services and support of this same welfare department might magically fly away and so no longer deplete state coffers.

But even if I can never hope to fly the coop, it might help if you were to say that I haven't laboured entirely in vain at the qwerty keyboard.

And we'll take a cup o' kindness yet
For auld lang syne.

$\mathcal{E}$ULOGY

Delivered by Niamh Murphy in Churchtown
on Friday 28th February 2014

My uncle John was born in 1951 to my grandparents Jack and Nora. He was their eldest child and he was called after both his grandfathers – John Murphy and John Hickey.

John was born in Cardiff to where his parents had emigrated. His sister Margaret – who died as a baby – was also born in Wales and Gerry, Pat and Michael were born here in Churchtown.

John returned to Churchtown as a two year old when Jack and Nora returned to Ireland as a consequence of Jack's elder brother Bill being badly injured in a farm accident.

To his family and friends John was a student of human behaviour. He held the view that the poets and writers of literature and song led the major changes in society. He felt people like Bob Dylan and Pete Seeger carried the mantle in his time similar to the writings of Mark Twain and Charles Dickens who helped to stir the human consciousness of ordinary people in the nineteenth century.

John was an artist – a writer – by choice and an intelligent person but sadly he had difficulties with his mental health all his adult life which hindered him from making significant progress with his writings; but despite his troubles John had many poems and booklets published over the years.

John grew up on the family farm at The Leap and went to Churchtown National School, Ring College and St Colman's College in Fermoy. He also attended UCC but left for England before completing his degree. He returned to the farm at The Leap in 1972 where he remained for the last forty-two years. For all of his life he worked daily on his creative writings. He was his own worst critic and on many occasions destroyed months of work in the fireplace. Luckily quite a body of John's work is preserved.

John was always supported at home by his brothers Pat and Michael who looked out for him unfailingly over the years. My father, Gerry, was John's publishing agent from afar – a job Gerry took on with enthusiasm but without much success as in the end John was rarely satisfied with his own creativity.

John's best friends over the years were Mick Culloty and John Nyhan. He was lucky to have such dedicated supporters in his life. John always said that Mick Culloty and John Nyhan and himself lived by the redeeming power of story, poem, song and tune.

In his autobiography John speaks poignantly of his father, Jack, when he wrote: '*The night before my father died I read to him a portion of Ode To A Skylark by Shelley. When I had concluded reading Shelley to my father, I said 'Goodnight' to him and he said 'Goodnight' in grateful, if not slightly happier voice.*"

John traced his talent for comedy back to his mother. Indeed, the title of his autobiography *Like it, or Lump it* he credits to his mother Nora who usually uttered it as a reminder to somebody or other that they had but one option.

Some years ago John wrote a short poem about 'remembrance' which seems appropriate as we bid him farewell. It reads as follows:

*When your day is at an end
and you feel you need a friend.
When your dream was not so good
and nothing's as it should.
Remember me, I'm very near
think of me, and I'll be here.*

Our family do not believe in long eulogies and so I will finish by saying that John is now *At Peace* with his father Jack and his mother Nora who did all they could to protect and nurture him over all the years. It is doubly sad that it is only a few weeks since his mother Nora died. Perhaps ... Nora has just taken the boy she loved so dearly to be with herself and Jack in a better place.

May John enjoy his eternal reward and may he, Jack and Nora now All Rest in Peace.

Go dtuga Dia suáimhneas síoraí dó. Thank you.

CARRY ON

by John Murphy

One day when the brigands have quit the scene
Gone back to war or for a beer
Carry on grandfather
Carry on grandmother
Carry on the other
Carry on the innocent and the old
Carry on governor
Carry on servant
Carry on the feeble, young and old
Carry on the kind hearted
Carry on all

Carry on son
Carry on father
Carry on mother
Carry on sister, so strong
Carry on small
Carry on brother
Carry on tall

Thank you all

'Carry on' was John Murphy's final creative output written three days before he died.

Ballygrace
Churchtown
June 2017

I first remember John as a small boy going to primary school in Churchtown. I was older than him but my sister, Patricia, who is now living in Bury St Edmunds would have remembered him better and has a lot of recollections of school times.

I got to know John on a personal level from meeting him at McCarthy's Irish Nights in Buttevant. John was a contributor with his own original material which was very important to him. John's association with Mick Culloty and John Nyhan was also very important as they gave him time and space to perform.

I liked to attend the Cork Yarnspinners at An Spailpín Fánach in Cork. I mentioned this to John one day and he said he would like to accompany me. An Spailpín Fánach suited him and he was a regular contributor. John got on well with Bob Jennings, Pat Speight, Charlie Conway and Jerry O'Neill, who also wrote his own material. Students from UCC often attended and would question John's complicated material. John was at his best in these interchanges explaining his opinions.

In *Anthology* John's writings are now preserved as part of the heritage of our community. I am delighted that this is the case and that the proceeds from *Anthology* will be for the benefit of the Churchtown Heritage Society which is an organisation founded by Gerry Murphy, Denis Hickey and myself.

Noel Linehan

Other Publications / Associated Publications

1994

The Xtra Magnificent Yeti; a booklet of poems by John Murphy.
Published by Noah's Ark Press (now Bruhenny Press), Churchtown.
Softcover ISBN 0-9524931-5-2. 20pp.

2003

**The Boss Murphy Musical Legacy: Irish Music from the
Churchtown area of North Cork by Dr Colette Moloney**.
Published by Noah's Ark Press (now Bruhenny Press), Churchtown
and the Churchtown Village Renewal Trust. ISBN 0-952-4931-2-8.
186pp.

2004

Images from BLOOM; a book of illustrations from the storyboards
and quotes from a feature film based on James Joyce's epic novel
Ulysses. Published by Odyssey Pictures Limited.
Sponsored by Bruhenny. Softcover ISBN 10-0954735919.
Hardcover ISBN 13-978- 0954735920. 128pp.

2005

The Annals of Churchtown; published by Churchtown Village
Renewal Trust. Compiled by Denis J. Hickey. Other contributors:
Caroline Hennessy, Colette Moloney, Jim McCarthy, Noel Linehan,
Albert Daly, Gerry Murphy, Bill O'Flynn, Anne Murphy, Brigid
(Manning) O'Sullivan and Denis Pat Costelloe. ISBN 0-9524931-3-6.
767pp.

2016

William Murphy (1816-1902); The Weight Thrower;
published by Churchtown Heritage Society and Liscarroll
Community Council. 44pp.

Bruhenny Press (formerly Noah's Ark Press)